# MURDER IN MONT SAINT-MICHEL

BOOK 19 OF THE MAGGIE NEWBERRY MYSTERIES

SUSAN KIERNAN-LEWIS

SAN MARCO PRESS

Copyright © 2021 by Susan Kiernan-Lewis. All rights reserved.

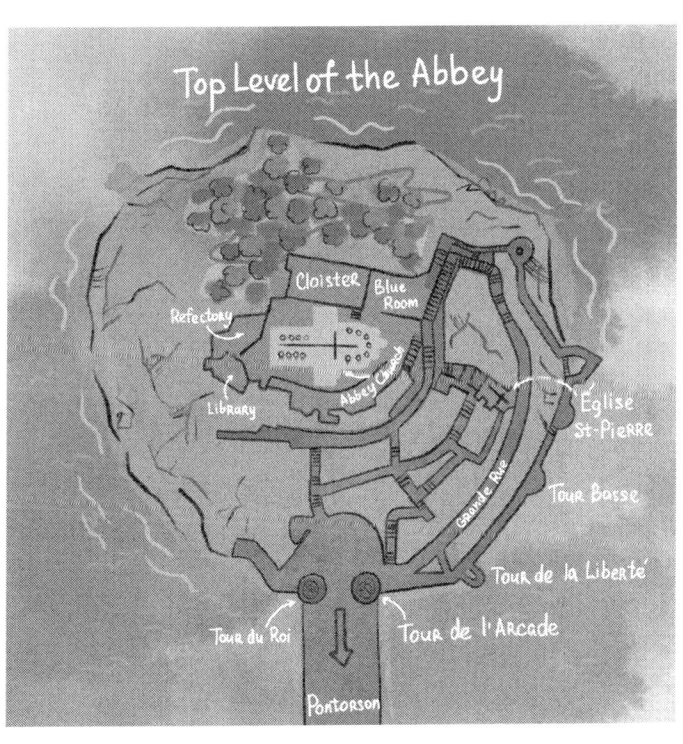

# 1

There was something about Paris in the rain that always made Maggie wistful.

She was sure it was the unique combination of emotions unimaginable in any other city in the world.

Unfortunately, tonight that balance was undeniably and painfully skewed toward the negative.

As she and her husband Laurent walked to the trendy little *brasserie* in the Latin Quarter where they were to meet Zouzou, Maggie felt the fog on her skin as it rolled in off the Seine, cold and damp and smelling of fish and garbage.

The *brasserie* was located down a quaint little alley not far from the famous St-Michel fountain, but obscure enough that Maggie didn't think it would be easily discovered by the average tourist. It had been twenty years since Laurent had lived in Paris, and Maggie found herself wondering how he knew of the *brasserie*.

The décor inside was typical of the kind of homespun Parisian *brasseries* that Maggie knew her husband preferred. Silver candelabras perched on white starched tablecloths while patrons sat nearly elbow to elbow at long dining tables.

Laurent was leaning back in his chair, appearing more interested in the pedestrians huddling in their winter coats outside the huge Palladian window than he was their dinner companions, the young couple seated opposite them. Maggie picked at her Chicken Basquaise although it was one of her favorite dishes

The knot in Maggie's stomach had grown steadily since they'd arrived in Paris last night. And tonight it felt big enough to swallow her whole.

She'd been wrong about Paris and that was a worry. She'd thought it would be the first step to getting back to where she and Laurent had always been—on an even keel, on the same page, reading out of the same playbook. But that mutual playbook reading was nowhere in sight.

"Uncle Laurent has known me since I was a baby," Zouzou said as she reached over to clasp her boyfriend's hand.

Maggie saw Laurent's eyes flicker at the movement and she wondered if Zouzou really knew her Uncle Laurent at all. If she did, she'd know that he did not approve of her choice of male companions.

Maggie glanced at her husband. Even in the dim lighting of the *brasserie*, he stood out. A ruggedly handsome man, with a wide mouth and full lips, he was taller than the average Frenchman and sat with the erect bearing of someone who'd served in the military. Maggie knew for a fact that he had not. Not at all.

Maggie and Laurent had indeed known Zouzou Van Sant since she was a baby—in fact, even before she was born, Maggie mused. The second and youngest child of Maggie's best friend Grace Van Sant, Zouzou had lived the last eight of her eighteen years in France helping her mother run the Provençal bed and breakfast that Laurent owned.

Maggie and Laurent had come up to Paris from their *mas* in Provence where they lived on a vineyard that Laurent had inherited a year before he and Maggie married—twenty years ago now.

Zouzou was living in Paris while she apprenticed with Alice Van Dubron, France's current premier master *pâtisserie* chef. Zouzou was living her dream, Maggie thought as she smiled fondly at the girl. She was training to do what she'd dreamed of doing ever since she was small—becoming the finest American *pâtisserie* chef in all of France.

Maggie smiled at Zouzou's boyfriend Anzar, a slim, shaggy-haired young man with sharp eyes and a thin cruel mouth.

Of course Grace probably didn't expect Zouzou to live celibate while she was in Paris, Maggie reasoned. But then, being the mother of a young girl herself, it was very possible she absolutely did.

Worse, there was every indication from things Anzar and Zouzou had said that the two weren't just dating but actually *living* together.

That, as Maggie well knew, was a whole different kettle of *poissons*.

"What part of the country are you from?" Laurent asked Anzar, his voice low and deceptively smooth.

Maggie glanced at Anzar to see if he had any indication that Laurent meant more than what he appeared to be asking. The boy's face broke open into a smirk and he shrugged before answering, which told Maggie that he had no clue that Laurent's question was anything but innocent.

"I consider myself a citizen of the world," Anzar said, preening. "Here a little, there a little."

Zouzou giggled, equally unaware that Laurent was anything but enjoying her boyfriend.

"How did you two meet?" Maggie said quickly, hoping to delay the inevitable moment when everyone became all too aware that Laurent was not a fan.

Zouzou giggled again.

"You tell the story, Anzar," she said, her eyes going to her boyfriend as she let out an appreciative sigh.

"Okay," he said hesitantly, reaching for his wine.

Maggie felt her stomach clench in disappointment at his reaction. Clearly their meeting had been written in the stars as far as Zouzou was concerned. But Anzar hadn't been paying attention. And now he was stalling for time.

He sipped his wine, smacking his lips and then turned to Zouzou.

"Why don't you tell it, *chérie*? You tell it better than I."

Maggie thought she could detect the slightest hint of a wobble in Zouzou's up-to-now consistently adoring gaze but it was quickly erased by the girl's obvious desire to tell the joyous beginning of their story. In fact Maggie saw the exact moment when Zouzou decided to ignore the obvious fact that Anzar had no recollection at all of their first meeting.

"I was making a delivery in the Latin Quarter," Zouzou said, turning to Maggie and Laurent. "My bike hit a stone and I went flying. I was carrying a flat box of two dozen chocolate mousse and they went everywhere!"

She laughed and glanced again at Anzar as if hoping he might pick up the tale from this point, but he only buried his face once more in his wineglass.

Laurent snapped his fingers at the waiter but otherwise gave no clue that he wasn't listening to Zouzou's story. Still, the gesture bothered Maggie. She turned to Zouzou and affected an intensely interested mien of concentration to make up for Laurent's clear lack of attention.

"So Anzar was standing right there," Zouzou said, looking once more to Anzar. "With a big dollop of mousse on his boot!"

"It is a wonder he wasn't able to recall such a memorable moment," Laurent said, turning his hooded gaze at Anzar.

Now Anzar was starting to get a clearer view of the full picture. He cleared his throat and pulled his collar from his neck in a quickly developing look of extreme discomfort.

The waiter came into view and Laurent indicated he wanted the bill.

"Well, Anzar has an incredibly demanding job," Zouzou said, now looking from Laurent to Maggie as if finally twigging that everyone was not in love with her boyfriend.

"What is it you said you did?" Laurent asked Anzar.

"I write a blog for a very popular night club in Le Marais," Anzar said stiffly, his eyes going to Zouzou as if for support. She squeezed his arm.

"You didn't tell me you were doing that!" she said.

"It just happened."

*Sure it did*, Maggie thought.

A part of her didn't blame Laurent for his cynicism about this young man. Anzar was clearly treating Zouzou as an afterthought and had likely only showed up tonight for a free meal. She hated seeing Zouzou with someone like this, but until she knew more about him beyond the fact that he appeared louche and ill-mannered, she wasn't going to worry Grace with a bad report.

*Unless they really were living together?*

The waiter came with the check and Laurent handed his

credit card to him. The waiter processed the bill at the table, gave a short bow and departed.

"Thank you so much, Oncle Laurent," Zouzou said. "I was so glad you and Aunt Maggie were able to come and meet Anzar. How long will you be in Paris?"

Maggie smoothed out the creases in her napkin.

"We're actually going to spend the weekend on Mont St-Michel," she said. "Have you been?"

"Mom and Dad took us there once, I think," Zouzou said. "When Taylor and I were little. But I don't remember much." She turned to Anzar. "It would make a fun day trip. We should go sometime."

"Sure," he said, draining his wine and scooting his chair back.

"Well, I haven't been in years either," Maggie said. "But this time we're there as part of a retreat."

"Oh, cool," Zouzou said shrugging into her wool bomber jacket from the back of her chair.

The part about the retreat was true as far as it went, Maggie thought. They *were* going to the island as part of an arranged group retreat. But what Maggie hadn't revealed even to Grace was the fact that this particular retreat was one designed to address marital discord.

She glanced at Laurent who had said no more than a dozen words during the whole dinner. His face, normally unreadable, seemed to loudly broadcast his irritation in a radius that encompassed the whole restaurant.

Maggie had thought, since Laurent was so fond of Zouzou, that he'd be different in Paris. But the steely resistance and shuttered eyes she'd endured for the last week had stayed firmly in place. After two months of a slowly burgeoning bewilderment as to what could possibly be troubling him, Laurent's affect had taken a dramatic turn for the worse a week ago.

At first Maggie thought his sour mood had to do with the fact that their foster son Luc had decided to remain in the States another year after finishing his studies instead of coming home to work the vineyard alongside Laurent.

Maggie knew Laurent was disappointed but when she tried to draw him out about it, he shut down.

A year ago she would've thought nothing of it since at that time their daughter Mila had been behaving like a true *enfant terrible*, turning on any and all at the slightest provocation. But in the past six months Mila and done a head-spinning turnaround. She'd not only reversed course to become the epitome of sweetness and light as she had once been, but to everyone's astonishment she'd actually become passionate about—of all things—wine. Her dream now was to become a *sommelier*.

Normally this unexpected change would have delighted Laurent beyond measure. It was his greatest hope that his children would share his life's work in the vineyard. But even Mila's metamorphosis had only nominally affected the glowering disposition of the man Maggie had lived with for the past three months.

A man who, frankly, had become a stranger to her.

# 2

After saying goodnight to Zouzou and her young man Laurent and Maggie walked back to their hotel on rue de Seine. Maggie slipped her hand into his as they walked but she could tell his mind was elsewhere.

"I wonder if Grace knows about Zouzou's living situation," she said, hoping to prod him out of his dour thoughts.

"You will not tell her," he said.

Maggie hesitated. On the one hand she felt it was a good sign that Laurent was pulling out of his funk long enough to have an opinion about Zouzou's situation. On the other hand, it was frustrating that he seemed to have so much trouble with the concept of *talking things over* as a couple. His usual my-way-or-the-highway edicts had once been almost charming—especially since Maggie could usually tease him out of his position or ignore them altogether. But lately they had become less amusing as he became more intractable and contrary.

"*I* would want to know if it was Mila," Maggie said.

"Mila would never do something like this."

Maggie nearly laughed out loud until she saw that Laurent was not joking. A year ago there was virtually nothing that either of them would have put past Mila as far as bad behavior went. She'd been a snarling, sullen source of exasperation for the entire family.

"Well, as outrageous as that notion is," Maggie said dryly, "I would still want my best friend to tell me if my eighteen-year-old daughter was living with someone."

"*La crapule*," Laurent said, using a colorful and very unflattering reference for Zouzou's young man. "She can do better."

"I agree," Maggie said as they stopped at a cross walk. "And she probably will in time."

"It will do no good to tell Grace," Laurent continued. "It will only anger Zouzou and make her latch on to this *salaud* all the harder."

Maggie admitted that Laurent might have a point, but in itself that was not an argument against telling Grace. It was simply an argument in favor of telling her and then advising her on how to handle the situation. But Maggie held her tongue. She could tell Laurent wasn't in the mood to debate the point.

They walked along the Seine, past the forest-green *bouquinistes'* sheds, each locked for the night, the fog thick on the water, the *Bateaux-Mouches* visible only as ghostly floating hulks in the dim light.

The rain had stopped for now but the air was cold and felt ominous and troubling—as if something was coming.

"It's nice to be back in Paris, isn't it?" she asked.

Laurent only snorted.

Maggie knew that Laurent was a Parisian born and

raised. She also knew he had no love or fascination for the magical town. And even after all these years together she wasn't sure why.

The remainder of the walk back to the hotel was a quiet one. Maggie was left feeling even worse than before they'd come to Paris about the state of her marriage. But she reminded herself that that was largely because she'd stupidly had an expectation that seeing Zouzou might jolt Laurent out of his malaise.

She glanced at him as he collected their room key from the hotel night desk. As usual his face gave nothing away. He'd received a few mysterious phone calls on the train trip up from Aix-en-Provence that he'd left their train compartment to take in private. When she'd asked about them, he said they were just business.

For reasons she couldn't put her finger on she knew the phone calls had nothing to do with business. With anyone else, she might be tempted to imagine his estranged behavior, combined with lying about the phone calls, was because there was another woman.

Maggie felt a squeeze of pain in her stomach. Who was she kidding? Just because it had always been inconceivable before didn't mean it wasn't conceivable.

Then this evening, before they left for dinner, Laurent had a brief conversation with Luc. Luc's request to stay longer in the States hadn't been a total shock. He'd been hinting at it all year. But it hadn't made the reality of it any less disappointing.

Jemmy would start the fall semester at Georgia Tech in Atlanta and had spent the summer with Luc working the *Salvador* vineyard with him in Napa. At the time that Laurent had green-lighted that trip, he thought it might instill an interest in Jemmy for the wine business. Up to now, he'd shown little interest in Domaine St-Buvard, the family vineyard.

Maggie knew Luc's request to stay longer in California troubled Laurent—although he insisted that it didn't. Had Luc said something else in his latest phone call to upset Laurent?

Maggie loved Luc dearly and knew what an unhappy start he'd had in life. But as much as Luc adored Laurent and worked so hard to fit into the family, she couldn't help but think there was an artificiality or awkwardness that seemed to hold him back from truly belonging.

"Are the boys enjoying their time in Atlanta?" she asked as they walked up the stairs to their room.

Mila was visiting Maggie's mother for a few weeks. Luc and Jemmy had recently flown to Atlanta to see Mila, their grandmother, and their cousin Nicole.

"They are fine," Laurent said. "Jemmy said he'll call us later."

"I think we're supposed to be incommunicado on this retreat," Maggie said, frowning. "Hopefully he'll call before they take our phones away."

Laurent didn't answer.

"Did Luc say anything more about his plans for next year?"

"You know what I know," Laurent said.

"I got a text from Nicole today. She has a whole week of activities planned for them. The Coca-Cola museum, the aquarium, Stone Mountain."

Nicole was Maggie's niece, raised by Maggie's parents after Maggie's sister Elise had died under mysterious circumstances in the South of France eighteen years ago.

Nicole, who now went by Nikki, lived in Atlanta and worked as a social media manager for a marketing company.

It was essentially because of Nicole that Maggie and Laurent had met.

As they walked Maggie couldn't but notice that Laurent seemed to trudge, his shoulders rounded as if carrying a heavy weight. Laurent was usually indefatigable. The things —both emotional and physical—that might fell a normal man had little effect on him. She'd seen him working for hours in the fields with the pickers in their two-hundred-hectare vineyard until well after dark, then come in and put together a meal for the family that would impress an accomplished chef.

*Not to mention have plenty of energy later for extracurricular activities with his wife.*

Tonight she watched him as he dropped his keys and cellphone on the hotel room dresser and stepped into the bathroom to turn on the shower. When he came out, she stopped in front of him and slipped into his arms.

"I can't believe we're back in Paris after so long," she said softly, standing on tip toe to kiss him.

"Maggie, *non*," Laurent said, easing out of her embrace. "It has been a long day and I am tired."

Maggie released him, her arms falling to her sides.

"Sure," she said as she watched him pull his shirt off over his head and turn back to the bathroom and the sounds of the streaming shower. "We should get a good night's sleep for tomorrow."

After he shut the door between them, Maggie sat on the bed and slowly took off her earrings and watch.

It was cool for October, or perhaps she had just forgotten how much further north Paris was from her home in Provence. They had to shut the windows in their hotel room but the night sounds came through even so. The sounds of Paris at night, she thought wistfully.

As she slipped out of her dress and reached for her night gown, it occurred to her that this was the first time in their whole married life that Laurent had been too tired to make love.

## 3

The strong scent of rosemary, woodsmoke and lavender filled the air in the back garden of the bed-and-breakfast and wafted over to where Grace stood at the open kitchen window. She could hear her grandson's laughter coming from the pool area although it was much too cold for swimming.

She turned to refill her mug of morning coffee and her eye fell on the plate of *palmiers* on the counter which Danielle had made the day before. They'd gotten in the habit of giving their guests fresh pastries and holding the day-old ones for family.

Grace smiled when her eyes went to the mudroom hooks, barely visible from the kitchen, where Danielle's garden shears and flower basket normally hung. Just seeing their empty hooks meant that Danielle was out in the garden and gave Grace a burst of pleasure, reminding her once again that life would be so much harder without Danielle.

After her husband died, Danielle, then seventy-four years old, had moved in with Grace to help run the bed and breakfast and raise Zouzou and Philippe. Now that Zouzou had absconded from the nest, Grace was surprised that there was still so much work for the two of them to keep *Dormir* humming.

Once a fine *mas* rising tall on the horizon in a field of vineyards, *Dormir* had been the stately home for generations of *vignerons* that today only a few in St-Buvard remembered.

When Laurent bought the property a few years ago, he renovated it to include three smaller mini-cottages on the property, updated plumbing and a new kitchen in the main house where Grace and Danielle lived, along with a small swimming pool under the plane trees. And of course the garden which Laurent personally installed.

Danielle had lived in this house, now called *Dormir,* with her first husband until their divorce—when Eduard went to prison. The place had remained vacant after Danielle moved into her second husband Jean-Luc's house. When Jean-Luc died, Laurent bought the property from Danielle —mostly for its surrounding vineyards. And then Danielle, Grace and Zouzou moved in.

*Which changed everything.*

Grace smiled as she remembered the day Laurent made the offer to her: *Come back to France and work the gîte.*

She had literally lost everything at that point. Her marriage, her children and her friends—even Maggie. If it hadn't been for Laurent, she might never have come up for air again, never dared to believe in herself long enough for a second act.

Laurent would own the place, he'd said, but she would run it. It would allow her to support herself and Zouzou and remain in the country where she'd discovered she was happiest.

It was the saving of her. No doubt about it.

As she sat now at the kitchen table and heard the happy chatter of her grandson Philippe as he played outside in the garden, her thoughts warm with her gratitude for the life she now had, her eye fell on the flowers Gregor had given her last night.

She tilted her head and rubbed the back of her neck as she felt a headache coming on. Gregor was a handsome, stubbornly sexist—in a good way—Frenchman who had made it clear he was mad about her. She enjoyed his company and his romantic attentions. It was nice being told she was beautiful. She'd lost count of how long it had been before Gregor since she'd had a real date. He was easy on the eyes and she found she was comfortable with him.

On the other hand, at sixty-two, he was eighteen years her senior and did tend to complain about his arthritis from time to time.

*Not that that's a deal breaker*, she thought as she got up to put the *palmiers* away. Not at all. She would hope she wasn't that shallow. Anymore.

Maggie and Danielle both felt she was with Gregor because she was lonely, to which Grace responded, *well, duh!*

But as she well knew—and certainly didn't need it pointed out to her as relentlessly as her friends tended to—there was a big difference between enjoying someone's company and *settling*—which was what both Maggie and Danielle thought she was doing.

She wasn't!

Was she?

She grimaced and resisted the urge to jump up and clean something. Instead she cupped her coffee mug in her hands and felt the warmth radiate up into her hands as she stood to look out the window again.

Last week over lunch with Maggie, Grace had cut her off when Maggie started in with her "you can do better" line. Grace felt a sliver of annoyance. She'd told Maggie, "Well, we can't all have Laurent." That had shut her up. But the problem was, it was true.

Years ago, Grace had believed that her own version of Laurent—tall, handsome, loyal and sexy as hell—would come along. But that was a long time ago and a lot of bad decisions and disastrous repercussions ago.

These days she knew there wasn't a Laurent for everyone. That was just the reality of life. And she had missed her chance. She felt a sour taste in her mouth and felt heat form behind her eyelids as she forced back tears of self-pity.

The buzz from her phone on the counter interrupted the gloomy trajectory of her thoughts and she shook herself out of them and reached for it. A picture of Maggie appeared on the screen, making her smile.

"Bonjour, darling!" Grace said, wiping away a tear that had escaped down her cheek. "Oh, I envy you to be in Paris! Have you done any shopping yet?"

"No," Maggie said. "This is really just a pitstop on our way to Mont Saint-Michel."

"Did you see Zouzou?"

"Yes, she looks wonderful. Rocking a new pixy haircut. Very French."

"She sent me a snapshot of it," Grace said. "Honestly I like her hair longer but it'll grow. Any news?"

"I imagine you know more about the details of her life in Paris than I do. But tell me about your night. You went out with Gregor, right?"

Grace caught a glimpse of movement out the kitchen window and leaned forward to see Philippe. He appeared to be helping their handyman Gabriel do something with the climbing rose bush. Then again, at seven, Philippe's version of *helping* probably involved trapping a lizard or turtle as opposed to any real gardening. She hoped Gabriel was being mindful of the thorns with him.

"I did," Grace said with a sigh. "I really like him so much. It was so pleasant."

"Pleasant," Maggie murmured as if the word were damning.

"I know how you feel about him," Grace said, definitely feeling that headache forming now. "Let's don't get into it again."

"Look, if you like him, Grace, that's all that matters."

That was a new tack, Grace thought. Was Maggie really relenting or was this another ploy to get Grace to ease away from Gregor? Or was Maggie giving up on her?

"Enough about me and my nonexistent love life," Grace said lightly. "Are you excited about your upcoming visit to Mont St-Michel?"

"I *would* be if we were going for a romantic weekend. Now that we're actually doing this couples counseling thing, I'm a little nervous."

Grace frowned. While Maggie had shared with her that the trip was more of a structured tour she thought it was a sort of spa trip to deepen her engagement with Laurent. She hadn't been aware that it was actually a couples counseling retreat.

*Were Maggie and Laurent having problems?*

"Well, I'm sure there's nothing to be nervous about," Grace said. "Mont St-Michel is known for its mystical beauty and restorative powers."

"What if it makes things worse?"

So there *was* something going on with Maggie and Laurent.

Grace felt a splinter of unease. Why hadn't Maggie shared this before?

But she knew why. She'd been there herself. Maggie hadn't shared that there might be a problem because that made it real.

"Darling," Grace said reassuringly, "I'm sure it will be a wonderful getaway that will allow both you and Laurent to step away from your routines and responsibilities and rediscover each other."

"I'm sure you're right," Maggie said. "Laurent is really looking forward to it."

Grace nearly laughed out loud. Like most Frenchmen, Laurent was taciturn and chronically autonomous. The very idea that darling Laurent would be looking forward to any kind of structured group tour—especially where he might be asked to reveal or talk about a personal issue—was just not believable.

And Grace was pretty sure even Maggie didn't believe it.

"At the very least," Maggie said, "I might get some ideas for a book, you know?"

"Oh, I'm delighted to hear you're thinking about writing again. You used to love writing. I don't know why you ever stopped."

"Raising kids and juggling the busy life of a vintner's wife is why," Maggie said with a laugh. "Oh, Laurent is downstairs with the taxi. I need to go. I'll call you when we're on our way home. I told you they're not letting us have our cellphones, didn't I? I'm expecting a call from Jemmy or Mila. If I miss it, they might call you."

"No worries, darling. I'm sure everything will be fine. If it isn't, you can probably manage two days without knowing about it."

"I'm a little worried about Luc," Maggie said. "I don't

think he feels like he's part of the family. Jem mentioned on the phone yesterday that he's so polite with my mother, he doesn't really treat her as a grandmother."

"I'm sure he sees respect and politeness as a way to honor your mother."

"And that's fine. But I want him to act like he knows that Nicole and my mom are his family too."

"I'm sure he does."

"Okay. Now I really have to go!" Maggie said. "Give my love to Philippe and Danielle!"

After disconnecting, Grace stood up and rinsed out her coffee mug. Through the window she saw Philippe was now sitting on the ground playing with something. Gabriel was nowhere visible but he was very good with the boy and Grace knew Philippe was fine. Just as she thought that, Gabriel appeared and walked over to Philippe. who jumped to his feet to follow the handy man deeper into the garden.

As she watched her grandson trot after the older man, a flush of love filtered through Grace that was gently tweaked by a sudden splash of anxiety. Gregor was a grandfather himself, but he tended to joke about how pleasant it was not to live in the same village with his grandchildren.

Could she imagine Gregor living here at *Dormir*?

The sound of Danielle's voice came to her from somewhere in the garden as the older woman called to Philippe telling him to be mindful of the thorns.

*It takes a village*, Grace thought, feeling a comforting warmth spread into her chest.

But as she listened to the cheerful babble of her grandson in the garden, Grace felt a ripple of anxiety grow and throb in a knot right below her heart.

# 4

The rain pounded the train all the way from Paris. Flashes of lightning lit up the clouds in the surrounding countryside and the old slate rooftops of the villages that they passed were shiny with the downpour. Maggie imagined that, had the train windows been open, they would have heard thunder rumbling in the distance.

Maggie sat in their compartment, a cup of cocoa in her hands and a copy of *Vogue* magazine on the table in front of her. Laurent had stayed buried in his newspaper the entire four-and-a-half-hour trip, looking up only briefly to comment on the weather as if it mattered to what they would be doing this weekend.

Maggie strained to catch a peek of the famous island from her seat, but she could see nothing yet. From what she'd read, she knew that when the tide came in, it flooded the road and walkway, making the island essentially inaccessible.

Maggie glanced over at Laurent. She felt torn between

the desire to engage with him and respect his obvious desire not to converse.

She had tried to make it clear what this weekend was all about so that he wasn't going in blind. And yet, he seemed oblivious to what they were about to do. But every time she tried to talk to him, he shut down. Her only hope was that the experience on the island would shake something loose.

She glanced at him from the corner of her eye. Was he going to try?

If he didn't even want to talk to her, what hope did she have that he would open up in a group counseling session?

When the train pulled into the Mont Saint-Michel tourism outpost in Pontorson, Laurent gathered up their luggage and followed Maggie to the stage platform.

Maggie knew from watching YouTube videos that the thirty-minute walk to the island was an easy one with the enchanting view of the flat marshes and the currently waterless bay all around them. But it was still raining and she didn't want to arrive soaked, or exhaust Laurent's patience for the encounter before they even arrived. She called for a taxi to take them and their luggage to their final destination.

The taxi arrived quickly, for which Maggie was grateful. The rain continued to come down as Laurent and the taxi driver transferred luggage to the car trunk. Maggie reminded herself that Laurent tended not to talk very much in any event. Perhaps lately he was a little less communicative than usual. Or maybe she'd exaggerated some of it. She well knew she had that tendency.

As they settled into the taxi for the ten-minute ride to the island, Maggie found her nervousness heightened by her anticipation.

She tried to imagine how he was going to behave in a group session with other couples.

Would he play along? Would he answer the questions that the counselor—a Dr. Antoine Anders—put to him? Would he agree to engage in the exercises and joint interview sessions?

When Maggie had registered them for the weekend a month ago, he'd seemed agreeable or at least not emphatically against the idea. But had he really given much thought to what he was in for?

Regardless of the fact that Laurent was only forty-seven, he came from a decidedly different mindset when it came to how men and women behaved with each other. That different mindset, Maggie thought, tended to include his opinion on psychologists in general and marriage counselors specifically. In fact, in many ways, Maggie thought it had been her contrivance—her ruse really—to reframe this weekend as more of a retreat so he would agree to come.

She hated thinking she had misrepresented the weekend.

But in the end, it would be very clear exactly what it was.

There was no doubt that the differences between her and Laurent were partly a cultural thing—or more specifically a French thing—but a lot of the width of the chasm between them had to do with the way Laurent was hardwired. He was old-fashioned, patriarchal, even chauvinistic, and while Maggie knew that that was tempered by his love for her—and his respect for women in general—it was still hardly a twenty-first century attitude. And there had definitely been times when it was a problem.

*So how is this going to work?* Maggie wondered as she surreptitiously studied him in the taxi. With a sinking heart she realized that there really was no universe in which she could imagine Laurent faking involvement this weekend or participating in the group activities.

She sank back into the taxi seat. The dark clouds roiling overhead had succeeded in blotting out the light from the setting sun. While the fog was thinner now, having evolved into wispy strands that hovered just above the cobblestone pavement, the temperature seemed to have fallen rapidly.

"Bad weather's coming," the taxi driver said, more to himself than to them, Maggie thought.

Laurent merely grunted, which as far as Maggie was concerned was a good fifty percent of how he communicated with his friends and acquaintances back home in Domaine St-Buvard. The taxi driver must have correctly interpreted the noise because he twisted around in his seat with one hand on the wheel as he drove.

"We have the St-Michel bridge now," he said. "Built just a few years ago. Before that, if the tide came in? Pftt!"

Maggie assumed *Pftt* meant that before the bridge when the tide came in, everyone on the island was trapped.

"The first year it was built?" the driver went on, "the bridge was completely submerged by the highest sea level. It was like the weather—or the gods—were saying 'You foolish men are trying to change what I have created?' You know what I am saying?" Then he laughed.

"At the rate this storm is coming," he continued, "it looks like it may happen again!"

Maggie stole a look at Laurent to see if the driver's words were disconcerting to him in any way. As was typical with Laurent, she couldn't interpret his expression.

She watched him pull out his newspaper from his bag and pat his pockets for his phone and wallet. All the while she tried to tamp down a growing feeling that this whole weekend was going to be an unmitigated disaster.

She turned away and watched the swirl of mist and fog

huddled over the ground, obscuring the walkway and roadway except for the few meters directly in front of them.

Just as she was about to tell the driver to turn around and take them back to the train station, the mist cleared and Maggie gasped as she beheld the Abbey of Mont Saint-Michel.

## 5

Majestic, magical, mysterious. Maggie stared up at the eighty towering meters of solid granite—topped by the famous abbey and its statue of Saint Michael. She felt her skin tingle at the sight.

Mont St-Michel appeared like a floating mirage on the horizon, rising up in a heart-stopping manifestation of what the ancient monks had hoped to create—an abbey as close to heaven as possible.

The base of the village loomed before them in a wall of broken rock that supported the lichen-covered eleventh-century Benedictine abbey. Maggie had done her homework on the island. But nothing had prepared her for the sheer enchantment of seeing it like this. Yes, she'd visited years ago. But she must have had blinders on at the time because she felt as if she were seeing it for the first time.

"It's magnificent," Maggie said breathlessly.

As far as hopeful beginnings went, just the sight of this breathtaking fortress was everything she could have dreamed of. Immediately she pushed away her doubts and thoughts of returning to the train station.

A flood of tourists on foot streamed past them as their taxi edged to the front of the village base. The sightseers poured out of the village into a series of five tourist buses parked in the lot outside the base.

"You are spending the night?" the driver asked dubiously, as they watched the horde move into the parking lots.

Except for private events, most tourists to Mont St-Michel were required to leave the island at night. Dr. Anders had indicated in his welcome email that their staying the night would allow Maggie and the participants in her counseling group an opportunity to experience the magical healing properties of the island in a more intimate setting.

"We're a part of a group staying tonight and tomorrow," Maggie said.

"Ah," the driver said as he drove past a squat gray tower flying a French Tricoloure.

"*La Tour du Roi,*" he said pointing to it. *The King's Tower.*

Maggie knew the tower had been built in the fifteenth century to protect the entrance to the abbey. Mont Saint-Michel had stood as a stronghold during the Hundred Year's war against the English when the French had suffered everything the English had thrown at them—and prevailed.

*It's a place for survivors,* Maggie told herself. It was the perfect place to pick up the raveling threads of whatever was coming apart with her and Laurent.

By the time the taxi stopped at the front gate, the heavens were pouring, the rain pounding on the ancient stones, runnels of rainwater gushing down the center of the narrow village streets. Ancient soot-stained brick buildings loomed over them, their shutters shaking against the wind that was now battering the island.

Laurent and the driver pulled the luggage out of the trunk and stacked them on the stone curb of the village street under a timeworn and shaky overhang made of loose shingles.

After paying the driver, Laurent collected both suitcases and hunched his shoulders in his jacket to bear the brunt of the onslaught of rain that pummeled them as they hurried up the steep, winding stone steps that led to the abbey. The narrow village street was hemmed in tight on both sides by closing souvenir shops featuring plaster gargoyles, Tricoloure flags, brass-bottomed omelet pans, as well as restaurants and snack bars.

As Maggie hurried along behind Laurent, careful not to slip on the slick cobblestones, she passed alleys that were so narrow she was sure her hips would graze the sides if she passed through. Houses made of timber and wattle perched atop the roughly mortared stone walls, their dark shutters closed against the weather.

Halfway up the Grande Rue Maggie spotted a statue of Joan of Arc poised at the doorway to a small chapel with a plain wooden door. The plaque over the door read *Église St-Pierre*.

The small stone chapel looked modest and diminutive compared with the drama of the abbey towering directly above it.

Maggie turned to Laurent. She wanted to say to him, "Isn't it beautiful?" but between his fast pace, the relentless pounding of rain, and the occasional crack of thunder, any conversation was impossible.

There were still a few stragglers hurrying to leave the village before closing time, but otherwise Maggie and Laurent were alone on the street.

The temperature had dropped even since they'd left the

train station and Maggie found herself shivering as she splashed through puddles behind Laurent. Her shoes were already wet through and she felt the dampness through her coat.

She had no idea of the level of sleeping accommodations they would find tonight. If it was anything like she was seeing—an actual medieval stone castle—they'd be lucky to have a straw mattress and a wool blanket.

She forced her misgivings away. For the price they'd paid for this weekend—if they didn't have six-hundred thread count sheets, they would at least have proper beds. Wouldn't they?

The winding labyrinth of road finally stopped at a mammoth arch of crumbling stone that looked about to tumble down any minute—or last forever, depending on your mindset, Maggie thought.

Laurent stopped at the entrance. Maggie blinked the rain out of her eyes and stared up at the looming structure. She was still shivering but not sure the rain and cold were the reasons why.

As she stepped into the slick tiled vestibule of the Mont St-Michel tourist office and its respite from the deluge, she shook the rain from her jacket. A registration desk was straight ahead with signs directing tourists to the gift shop.

The vestibule felt very modern, especially after the climb through antiquity that they'd just made from the entrance gate of the island.

A man stood inside the tiled foyer, a broad smile on his face. He had close-cropped auburn hair framing a sharp-boned face and full lips with gentle brown eyes.

Behind him, lights blinked off in the large atrium one by one along the registration and ticket counters that normally greeted hundreds of eager tourists seeking entrance into the foyer of one of the world's most popular tourist attractions.

"Maggie and Laurent Dernier, I presume?" Dr. Anders said in a strong Australian accent as he reached for one of the suitcases at Laurent's feet. "Welcome!"

From her research, Maggie knew that Antoine Anders had a PhD in psychology and came highly recommended for couples retreat experiences by the Institute of International Marriage Counselors and also the Federation of Life Coaches.

They shook hands and the doctor, who immediately insisted they call him Antoine, ushered them into the interior registration alcove.

Maggie was a little taken aback by Antoine's Australian accent. She'd assumed because of his name that he would be French. She realized that a part of her had thought his being French would help smooth over any residual vestiges of doubt that Laurent might have about the retreat and its purpose.

She found herself more than a little horrified at her seriously flawed assumption.

"We've a bit of a walk," Antoine said jovially. "We're doing drinkies on the very top in the Blue Room—nine hundred steps if you're up for it!—but leave your bags on the first level since that's closest to your room."

Unlike the bottom floor where they'd entered, this part of the abbey had clearly had very little renovation except for the electric sconces set every few feet in the stairwells positioned next to wooden holders for torches. At first, all Maggie heard was the sounds of their shoes on the stones as they climbed but soon she heard the sound of the wind too, whistling through the cracks in the walls. She shivered at the thought of the storm now raging outside.

Antoine stopped at the first landing and turned down an even more narrow hallway—also completely lined in stone.

"I think you two are the first ones off the stairs," he said. "Very convenient. I fear the other couples will end up hating you when they realize *how* convenient."

He walked to a door and used a key card to open it before pushing the door open and turning to hand Laurent the key.

"Just set your bags inside. You're the last ones to arrive and everyone else is upstairs and the wine is flowing!"

Maggie took a quick peek into their room as Laurent set their bags inside and was relieved to see it looked as modern as she could have hoped. A large queen-size bed with a fluffy duvet was front and center. There was a window facing the western horizon.

After locking the door behind them, she and Laurent followed Antoine up the stairs, passing two more wide flagstone landings before finally stopping. Maggie had a sense that they had climbed to the very top of the abbey. Her calves felt it too.

"Here we are," Antoine said breathlessly. "*Voila*, the Blue Room."

The stairs emptied into a broad, unfurnished room that overlooked the abbey's cloister. Antoine stepped quickly inside.

"I try to have everyone on the first night experience the western terrace," he said. "The view is fantastic but of course with all this rain, no can do. But this part of the abbey is lovely too."

He began to lose his breath and Maggie realized he must have made this climb at least twice today.

"No elevators I guess?" she said.

"My dear girl!" he said with a laugh. "I wish! No, but as I

told the others, I can confidently promise you a lighter heart going into whatever you think your marital difficulties are after this weekend—and possibly a stone or two weight loss!"

He laughed at his own joke and Maggie was left feeling uneasy at how blithely he'd talked about marital difficulties.

## 6

From where they stood in the cavernous room, and in spite of the storm outside, Maggie could see that the marsh view from the Blue Room was astonishing. The surrounding bay encompassed the whole back side of the abbey. Even with the encroaching darkness and fog, Maggie could see that the tide had already rushed in, cutting the island off from the mainland.

"Amazing, isn't it?" Antoine said as he paused at the plate glass window overlooking the garden. Beside the window were ornately carved French doors that led to the cloister.

"In the old days the monks would grow vegetables and their medicinal herbs here," he said. "They'd meditate and read the Bible. Sadly, I fear this isn't the weekend to enjoy it."

He turned away.

"Come along and meet the others."

Inside the Blue Room was a long table covered with an assortment of wine bottles, soft drinks and appetizers. Five people stood with little plates and drinks in their hands beside a window that overlooked the small square of straggling hedges set in a carpet of pale lawn that was the cloister garden.

"Allow me to introduce the people who are going to help you forge a new emotionally-connected empowerment with your partner. The people you break bread with today are the same people who will advocate for you as you reset your emotional compass in order to restructure your behavioral and emotional engagement—to yourself."

Maggie frowned at Antoine's words but when she glanced around the room, she saw that everyone else was smiling in confirmation of them.

Antoine gestured at a thin balding man who stood with a heavy-set, smiling woman.

"This is Paul and Esmé Georges," he said. "From Liverpool."

"Like the Beatles!" Esmé said, grinning so broadly her eyes disappeared into cheeky folds of flesh. She had short, greying hair and wore no makeup that Maggie could see. Her face was pricked with a ruddy mien.

Unfortunately, when Maggie and Laurent shook hands with them, Maggie felt her heart sink. They weren't French either.

"This is Maggie and Laurent Dernier," Antoine said. "From Provence. Laurent owns a vineyard."

"Oh, I love wine!" Esmé said. "You'll have to tell me all about how you do that!"

"And over to my left is Hadley and Alex Davis, all the way from Toronto."

Maggie smiled at the couple who frowned back at her. In looks, Hadley appeared to be Esmé's complete opposite. She wore a snug form-fitting knit dress over an obviously toned body. She had permed hair and dramatic makeup. She held a glass of water in one hand with a slice of lemon in it. Maggie's first thought was that—trim figure notwithstanding—Hadley might be pregnant.

Alex wore a blank expression that was in direct contrast to the garish pink tie he wore sprinkled with ruby hearts. Maggie wondered if Hadley had picked out the tie for him. It hardly looked like the sort of thing Alex—who appeared at least dour if not morose—would have chosen for himself.

Maggie caught a glimpse of Laurent's face as he shook their hands, but as usual she couldn't read his expression. She tried to imagine how things could be worse.

*Well. They could all be American.*

"So you're our resident Frenchman, I see," Hadley said, smiling appraisingly at Laurent. She ran her tongue over her lips as she regarded him, her lashes lowering demurely.

Maggie was used to women lusting after Laurent. At six foot five he had a bearing and a dark, mysterious handsomeness that most women found beguiling.

But having Hadley point out that he was the only Frenchman was hardly going to help him think more positively about the weekend, Maggie thought with a wince.

"And may I introduce our de facto host, Père Jean," Antoine said, sweeping an arm in the direction of a slight, pasty-faced man wearing a black cassock and looking around the room nervously.

"Père Jean has been the pastor and curator of the abbey here at Mont St-Michel for the past two years," Antoine said. "If there are any Catholics in the group, I'm told that mass is held every morning at seven. Meanwhile please, help yourself to refreshments and get to know each other."

Laurent went to the table and looked at the buffet. Maggie could see from where she stood that there was a decent selection of appetizers. But he didn't reach for anything, which Maggie decided was a bad sign. It wasn't that Laurent was picky. He definitely saw food as a very good thing, even a curative, and the fact that he was rejecting everything on display here—especially after a train trip where he'd eaten nothing—meant he thought the food on the buffet was subpar.

*Not a good sign.*

"The promise of tomorrow begins tonight," Antoine said. "It is the promise embedded in the vow each of you made at one time and it is a promise that must be kept. The assurance of that vow will be seen in the new way you look at your partner by the end of this weekend."

He smiled confidently as he gazed at his audience, pausing with dramatic effect to make eye contact with each person.

"It is a promise that must reside hand in glove with a committal," he said. "A heartfelt committal that each of you will recognize and honor—I promise you!—before you leave this island. I can further promise you that it will be one that you will pledge to discharge to yourself with every ounce of your being, desire and will, both physical and mental. And that committal begins with one very simple step."

He turned and picked up a large wicker basket behind him and turned to face the couples.

"I'm sure I don't need to tell you how seductive the lure of technology is," he said as he walked over to Alex with the basket.

"Please, not my phone," Alex said with a laugh as he ruefully put his phone in the basket.

"It's for your own good," Antoine said as he moved on to Alex's wife. "I wish I could tell you how many of my clients have come to me after these retreats to tell me they intended to limit their screen time when they get home. That's how extraordinary, how palpable, how indelible are the true connections you'll feel once these vampires of your partner's attention are taken out of the equation."

"I feel like I'm putting my right arm in that basket!" Hadley said with a mournful smile. "When do we get them back?"

"You'll get them back as soon as you walk out the door tomorrow afternoon," Antoine assured her. "Meanwhile they'll be snug and sound in a high-security safe—to which only I have the key. Now grab your drinks, everyone and get comfortable! It may be the last time in the next twenty-four hours where you can truly relax."

Everyone laughed. Maggie glanced at Laurent. He had his hands in his pockets and was staring at the floor.

*Not even pretending to be involved.*

"I'm joking, of course," Antoine said. "But before we leave to dress for dinner, I want to give you a little back story about this very unique setting and how I believe it will help you break through whatever emotional barriers you might have unknowingly constructed with your partner."

Maggie cringed at his words. She knew Laurent well enough to know that every word out of Antoine's mouth was exactly the sort of artificially contrived shrink-speak he disdained. He didn't try to catch her eye which she decided was just as well since she refused to give him any indication of commiseration that might be seen as capitulation.

At least until it was clear that was her only recourse.

"So we'll have a fine dinner tonight," Antoine said as he walked around the room amongst the mostly seated guests. "After which time we'll begin the first of several couples exercises designed to give you a perspective and insight into your partner that will allow the kinds of deep-rooted and systematic communication breakthroughs you'd otherwise have no hope of expecting."

He waved a hand to the priest who was now standing nearly hidden by a tall potted Ficus tree.

"We've got the whole incredibly amazing place to ourselves this weekend. Just the good father here and, oh yes! there *is* also a reclusive resident author but she keeps to herself and I doubt you'll see her. Please, no smoking while you're here but otherwise I only ask that you keep an open mind. Not only to any new concepts I might introduce to you over the next twenty-four hours, but indeed to anything you may see that your rational mind might at first reject."

Hadley giggled.

"I'm very serious," Antoine said to her earnestly. "Mont St-Michel has a deeply religious but storied past. For those who've visited before as a tourist, I can tell you that the island is much more than what the guidebooks tell you. For example, how many of you knew that this island had been fortified to withstand sieges?"

Alex raised his hand and when Hadley snorted derisively, he shrugged.

"What? I'm supposed to be embarrassed because I did my research?"

"Not at all, Alex!" Antoine said, smiling broadly at him. "I'm delighted you delved into the past of this mysterious and amazing island. And while today we know Mont St-Michel as, among other things, a place of religious succor, you should know it was also once a place of unimaginable torture. A feared place of desolation and evil for thousands of unfortunate souls—many of whom died within these very walls."

Antoine walked among the couples, his smile in place, his drink unwavering in his hand.

"For those of you who have never spent a night here—and I'm confident that that will be all of you—don't be surprised if you feel as if you are not alone when you lay your head down tonight."

He paused then as he held each person's glance as he looked around the room before breaking the tension with a soft chuckle which generated a responding scattering of laughter among the couples.

Maggie laughed too and was glad to shake off Antoine's ominous words as if she were actually dispelling them. But she was aware that even her laughter didn't take away the fact of the goosebumps that were forming up and down her arms.

# 7

After drinks and meeting everyone, the group was dismissed back to their rooms to relax and change before dinner.

Everyone's rooms were on the same level and off the same uncarpeted passageway so Maggie and Laurent got in line to walk the two flights down along with everyone else.

The drinks seemed to have helped everyone unwind a bit. There was laughter and conversation as the group descended. Maggie realized that she wasn't the only one feeling awkward and out of place.

She reminded herself that every couple here had something they were hoping to work through. No wonder most of them had been less than friendly up to now.

The room she and Laurent had been assigned was indeed the first room around the corner from the stairwell. She nodded at Hadley and Paul as they passed them while Laurent unlocked their door.

Once inside, Maggie felt a sudden release of tension as if, alcohol or not, she'd been more anxious than she realized.

She was pleased to see that, as dramatically authentic as the rest of the abbey was, at least the guest rooms didn't appear to be from the twelfth century. There was a thick jute rug next to the bed that looked new, plus two nightstands and a good-sized dresser and, best of all, a door that led to a private bath.

A window over the bed, recessed into the thick stone walls, was big enough to provide a glimpse of the fury of the storm raging outside.

"You know," Maggie said as she looked out the window. "With this weather and all the creepy stonework everywhere, if I didn't know better I'd say we'd landed in a Halloween horror film."

Laurent grunted but said nothing.

It was clear to Maggie that Laurent wasn't interested in debriefing on the retreat or the people here. She thought that might be because he was annoyed at having been tricked—*had she tricked him?*—into coming.

She stopped just short of asking him if he wanted to leave. What would she do if he said yes? Was she ready to give up? Before they'd even started?

Instead she held her tongue and laid out her outfit for dinner. Antoine had said that they would be in the hallways of the abbey for their exercises and should wear something warm but not so cumbersome as a coat. Maggie opted for wool slacks and a cashmere turtleneck.

Glancing at Laurent on the bed reading one of his books, Maggie went to the bathroom to shower and dress.

By the time she came out, she had already half decided to tell Laurent that they would leave in the morning. That sounded like a good compromise and she hoped he would see it as that. She hoped he would see her meeting him halfway. Besides, they might as well leave. She knew her husband. There was no way he was going to respect anything that happened here.

The fact was, as soon as she'd met Antoine Maggie had begun to lose confidence herself. Her first impression of him was that he would be just as happy doing stand-up comedy as dispensing marital advice to unhappy couples.

*Is that who Laurent and I are?*

She tried to remember what she'd read about Antoine that had made her feel he might be able to give her—and Laurent—the perspective they needed at this point in their lives.

No, she thought, feeling her throat constrict, this whole idea was a disaster and the sooner they cut their losses and returned home to Domaine St-Buvard, the better.

It was just...if this wasn't going to work, what was she left with?

Maggie looked at herself in the mirror and picked up a lipstick tube, watching Laurent in the mirror on the bed, a book on vineyard management in his hands. She had to bite her lip not to say that he could probably *write* a book himself on vineyard management.

Was he pretending to read to avoid talking to her?

"Are you ready to go up to dinner?" she asked.

"You go on," he said. "I'll be there in a moment."

Instantly she felt a stiffness develop in her neck at his words.

*Great*, she thought as she tossed her lipstick down on the counter and picked up her pashmina shawl.

Because nothing says *couple unity* like showing up to a couples dinner twenty minutes apart. She wrapped the pashmina around her shoulders and left the room.

∾

Towering stone-block walls crowded the narrow stairs that led from the residence floor to the Knight's Hall situated in the heart of the abbey. Flagstone flooring led to a large room opposite a dramatic set of wooden French doors.

The room was punctuated by a series of columns that formed four aisles. Except for a display of swords fanned out on one wall and a wall of unlit torches and lanterns, the space was as minimally unfurnished as the Blue Room had been.

In the center of the room was another buffet table, this one wider than it was long, shoved up against the far wall. On it were arranged a dozen or more clean glasses, at least two dozen wine bottles, both red and white—already opened—and several water bottles.

Maggie watched as trays of *pâté*, raw cut vegetables and *gougères,* along with little china snack plates, *serviettes*, silverware and glassware were carefully set out by two of the waitstaff—a pair of glum twins in somber dark dresses.

She was the first to arrive, which suited Maggie fine. Maybe people would think Laurent was outside smoking or in the restroom. She waited patiently until the two women had put the last touches on the table. When they finally slipped out of the room, their eyes never raising above knee level, Maggie walked to the table to pour herself a glass of wine.

In the time it had taken her to walk upstairs she had talked herself into staying for the weekend after all. It occurred to her that the only real benefit to leaving early was to please Laurent, and while that might help in the short term, once they were back at Domaine St-Buvard nothing would have changed. Laurent would be just as uncommunicative and evasive about the reasons for his black mood as before. And Maggie would be just as clueless as to what to do about it.

While she recognized that she didn't hold out a lot of hope that this weekend would change anything for the two of them, she knew that doing nothing wouldn't help at all.

As she took her wine and walked back to one of the looming floor-to-ceiling windows that looked out over the marshes, Maggie spotted a woman who had not been present in the Blue Room earlier.

The woman was short, even shorter than Maggie. She wore her hair in a dark bob, and was wearing black leggings, ballet shoes and an oversized man's sweater.

Because this woman hadn't been in the Blue Room earlier, Maggie realized she must be the author in residence Antoine had told them about.

Maggie felt a sudden impulse to speak with her.

Prior to the crisis with Laurent, Maggie had recognized the onset of a very uncomfortable empty-nest syndrome brought on by Jemmy's leaving for college in the fall and Mila getting more involved with her own projects.

She'd published a book the summer before she'd had kids. While the publisher's advance had not even been enough to pay for a decent celebratory party, it had been the arrival of her children that had made Maggie stop writing.

It was true that for years Maggie had written a popular expat newsletter promoting their part of the world to travelers in the UK and the States. However, these days social media influencers were younger and more aggressive about getting and keeping their backers to support their blogs. Maggie had found it hard to compete with their energy and corporate backers.

While she still kept up the newsletter, she'd gone to quarterly instead of monthly issues. Laurent made more than enough money at Domaine St-Buvard through their vineyard. They certainly didn't need whatever minimal revenue she brought in from her little expat newsletter.

"Hello," Maggie said, smiling as she approached the woman. "I'm Maggie Dernier. I understand you're an author?"

The woman turned and smiled and they shook hands.

"Guilty as charged," she said. "Jenny Jacobs. I assume you're a part of Ander's latest group? Welcome to Mont St-Michel."

"Thank you. I was really excited to hear that we were sharing our weekend with a published author," Maggie said.

Jenny's face reddened at Maggie's words and she turned away to avoid eye contact. For whatever reason, Maggie could see that her comment had upset Jenny. Her mind sprinted for some way to change the subject and bring Jenny back to their initial level of comfort and ease.

"So can you tell me about this room?" Maggie asked.

"The Knight's Hall," Jenny said, nodding, quickly seeming to regain her self-assurance and poise. "Although nobody thinks any knights actually congregated here. It dates back to the founding of the Knights of Saint Michel by Louis XI."

"It's beautiful."

"It was originally used as a Scriptorium where the monks would spend their days copying and illuminating precious manuscripts." She hesitated and dropped her voice. "The monks used to think that the more secluded they were, the closer they were to God."

Maggie got the distinct impression that Jenny was referring to herself. The woman stared off into the middle distance as if in a trance.

"It's so cool that you live here," Maggie said softly.

Jenny shook herself out of her reverie and smiled at Maggie.

"Well, it gets a little creepy at night when all the tourists clear out," Jenny said with a throaty laugh. "But you get used to it."

"I'll bet you're able to get a lot of writing done?"

"You could say that."

"What's it like living in a tourist mecca?"

"You'd think you could never get lonely," Jenny said wistfully. "Which is especially surprising since that was the whole point when I first came here—to get the solitude I craved. But even with a swarm of Nikon-clicking tourists each month, I end up experiencing more solitude than is good for me."

Maggie detected a sadness in the woman that was hard to isolate. She smiled and even laughed, but something was wrong inside her.

"Père Jean is determined to continue to make the place available for retreats and private functions," Jenny said. "Even though, as you can imagine, he loses money every time he closes the gates to tourists."

"Very commendable of him," Maggie said, although she guessed that the price per head that Antoine was charging for the retreat this weekend would go a long way to making up the difference.

Jenny snorted and then smiled diffidently. "Don't mind me. I'm not the biggest fan of Anders' little projects but that's just me."

"Oh?"

Jenny waved her hand as if dismissing her own comments.

"Let's just say I'm exactly where I need to be in the world. *Removed*."

That comment seemed to confirm to Maggie that she'd been right about the sadness she'd detected in the woman.

"I wish I'd known you were going to be here," Maggie said. "I would've read a few of your books before I came."

"That's kind of you," Jenny said. "But I've only written nonfiction in the past few years and honestly I've been having trouble finding a publisher for them. And I'm not techno-savvy enough to figure out how to publish them on my own."

"What kind of nonfiction do you write?"

"Oh, God don't get me started!" she said with a laugh. "I wrote a history of the social development of women's participation in the Industrial Age that I'm sure you've never read."

Jenny was literally bouncing from foot to foot, her eyes sparkling with excitement. "I find the subject absolutely fascinating," she said, "but I'm afraid it doesn't have a happy ending. People like happy endings, you know?"

Jenny filled her wineglass to the rim and sipped it.

"Did you know that women's roles in historic events were typically not even mentioned in academic texts? Nor were they taught in school. You know that, right?"

Maggie frowned.

"Remember the consciousness-raising era way back when? Women's liberation? Ever heard of it?"

Maggie nodded again but it was clear that Jenny didn't see her. She was in her own little world.

Jenny rubbed her hands together and spoke in a louder voice.

"I mean when you look at the history of discriminatory hiring and wage practices against women in the last forty years," Jenny said, "it's chilling to see how little progress we've made. Chilling and heartbreaking."

Maggie nodded again. It wasn't that she didn't recognize the fact that women's equality was still something to achieve. But in her view, life was what it was and not likely to change regardless of what she did. She knew how fatalistic that sounded and accepted that she might be part of the problem. But then there was the distinct possibility that recognizing the truth on a regular basis could make her depressed. And what good would that do? As a result, Maggie had long ago and without conscious thought, adopted a fully entrenched get-on-with-it attitude.

Plus, she thought, ruefully, it probably didn't help that she was married to one of the biggest chauvinists on the planet.

"So are you a writer too?" Jenny asked suddenly, as if aware that she had gone into a tirade. "Or are you here for the couples counseling?"

"Both actually," Maggie said.

"Oh, I'm sorry! I didn't mean it to sound like that. Seeing you out here on your own without a partner I didn't think you…it doesn't matter. Besides, it's not you or the others who are the problem. It's Anders."

"Really, why?"

"You do know that whatever he's charging you he's only paying a fraction of that to the Mont St-Michel Foundation, don't you?"

"I didn't know."

"Of course you wouldn't. Why would you?" Jenny said and drank the rest of her wine before turning and refilling her glass. "But listen, let's keep in touch after you leave. I'd love to talk to you in six months to see if you're still married."

Maggie's back stiffened.

"Oh, God! I didn't mean that!" Jenny said, clapping a

hand to her mouth in mortification. "Sometimes I appall even myself. I spend too much time alone. Forgive me?"

Maggie nodded, a little woodenly.

"Although I do find Ander's practice vaguely predatory. He's basically taking advantage of these poor women who turn to him for help. I mean there are a lot of very good *women* psychologists in the world, you know? Makes you wonder why a woman—who's being made miserable by a man—would turn to another man to fix the problem!"

"You might have a point," Maggie said politely. "He is highly accredited though."

"Oh, I'm sure he is. But tell me honestly, was this retreat your idea or your husband's?"

When Maggie hesitated, Jenny nodded, satisfied.

"I thought so," she said. "It was your idea and he's here to pacify you. Same old story."

"That's not the case," Maggie said with a frown.

Although of course it was. And why was that? Laurent was clearly as miserable as she was, both of them trapped in their communication gridlock. Why did *she* have to be the one to desperately seek out this ridiculous retreat?

*Because he knows it's hopeless.*

"Anyway," Jenny said. "I hope I haven't ruined any hopes you had for the weekend but I won't apologize for trying to keep your feet on the ground. And I'm sorry because I do hope you're still married this time next year." She paused. "That is, if you really want to be."

On those words, she turned with an apologetic shrug and took her drink, spilling a little on her hand as she moved, and slipped away down the nearest corridor.

# 8

As soon as Maggie left, Laurent swung his legs off the bed and tossed his book down. He walked to the window and stared out into the bleak landscape.

The sky was too dark to make out very much but he saw the torrent of pellets bouncing off the windowpane.

*This is madness,* he thought as he watched the rain batter the window. The storm was sitting directly on top of the island seeming to pound at its very foundation. Even if he convinced Maggie to leave, they'd never make it to the mainland before being drowned like kittens in a bag. And while they may not actually expire from the experience, it would likely be something she'd remember from this weekend for a very long time.

Which was the last thing he wanted.

It was his own fault. In more ways than one.

He should never have agreed to come. He could tell she'd been surprised that he had. But he'd wanted to give her something before it all came crashing down on them.

So here they were, trapped on an island in the middle of

what promised to be a once-in-a-century storm, their marriage in tatters. He rubbed a hand across his face. It wasn't like him to exaggerate. That was Maggie's provenance.

But this weekend was definitely going to make everything worse. And until this moment he didn't think that was possible.

He clenched his jaw and turned away from the window and went to his jacket. It was still wet from the walk to the abbey hours earlier. He pulled out his phone and scrolled to the phone call he'd refused thirty minutes earlier. His gut tightened at the sight of it.

He tasted a bitter tang in his mouth as he thought of her.

The wretch had called twice yesterday and both times Maggie had noticed. He'd told her lies to cover. But whether she'd believed him or not...no, she hadn't believed him.

He felt a thickness in his throat at the memory of the lie. It was an unfortunate hallmark of their marriage that they had a history of playing fast and loose with the truth. Usually it hadn't mattered, a simple short cut, an innocent roundabout to where he needed to go.

Their secrets—their secrets on top of secrets—it's what their relationship was built on, wasn't it? How could Maggie not see that? Did she forget every uncomfortable fact she'd ever learned along the way in order to live with the scenario of her choosing? That would be so like Maggie.

He looked at his phone and saw that Élodie had left a voice message. Just seeing it sent a splinter of fury through him. He debated not listening to it. A part of him wanted to just delete it. As if he could delete the caller in the same way. But deleting the voicemail wouldn't erase the problem. She would just keep calling. He clicked Play.

"*I know you're dodging my calls but it won't help. Now or*

later there's no way out. Call me back or you're not going to like what happens next."

Heat rushing through his body in building fury he deleted the voicemail and sat holding the phone, staring at it. He should have dealt with this before now. He flexed his fingers. He felt like hitting something. Punching a wall. Something. Someone.

He knew how much Maggie was counting on this trip. As hopeless as only he knew it was, he'd agreed to it. How could he not? How could he deny her anything she asked? And once she found out the truth?

He grimaced and tossed his phone onto the bed.

It was easy enough to tell Maggie yes when she'd asked, especially when he could see she thought it would solve everything. And so he had. Which was just delaying the inevitable. Worse, it was getting her hopes up, making her believe they might get better. When in fact the worst was yet to come.

He ran a hand over his face. It wasn't like him to put off doing something unpleasant. It wasn't like him to hesitate to do what was necessary.

It was a philosophy he'd pounded into the boys—both Jemmy and Luc—and even Mila to a certain extent.

*Mila.*

He ran a hand over his face and felt the pain in the back of his throat return. Just the thought of his daughter made his stomach churn with crushing guilt. He took in a long breath, then stood up and pulled on his blazer, wishing more than anything that he could walk down the stone steps that led to the front door and just walk away.

Walk away from all of this, from the hurt and pain he was going to see in Maggie's eyes, the shame he was going to see every time he looked in a mirror.

Instead, he put his phone in his jacket pocket, stepped outside the room and shut and locked the door behind him.

As he did he tried to think if he'd ever done anything in his life that he dreaded more than the conversation he would need to have with Maggie.

Soon.

# 9

Maggie walked across the hall to the dining room a glass of Cabernet Sauvignon in her hand, to see if Laurent had shown up yet, but she couldn't see him.

She fought down a shiver of annoyance at his continued absence.

*Is there a way not to take this personally?*

She swallowed down her anger and turned her attention to the activity in the room. The dining room was set for dinner although no one was yet there. Maggie glanced back across the hall to the Knight's Hall from which she'd just come. The other couples had arrived to load up on aperitifs and hors d'oeuvres.

Esmé and Paul stood side by side at the narrow buffet their backs to the others. Esmé wore a nylon dress that appeared strained at the seams. Maggie could see she was piling her plate high with *gougères*.

Maggie glanced around the room and saw Hadley's husband Alex standing in the corner glowering, a glass of wine in one hand. His eyes were on his wife who was doing a masterful job of ignoring him.

Well, Maggie thought, that *is* why we're all here, because we've got issues to work out.

She caught a fleeting glimpse of the priest's long cassock disappearing down the long corridor, his hands shoved into his sleeves like a medieval monk.

Maggie frowned. He'd literally come from out of nowhere. He hadn't been in Knight's Hall. So where had he come from? With images of secret staircases and concealed rooms filling her mind, she shrugged and sipped her drink. She was about to go back across to Knight's Hall to talk with Paul and Esmé when she spotted Antoine entering the dining room and heading straight for her, a glass of red wine in one hand. She smiled in greeting but her smile faded with his first words to her.

"I see you've met the resident nut case," he said, his eyes dancing.

Maggie was struck speechless by the comment, her mouth falling open in shock.

"Oh, come on," he said at her reaction. "I'm just keeping things light. It's shrink humor. But seriously I'd keep my distance if I were you. Our Jenny has quite the unsavory backstory."

As Maggie stared at him, the thought occurred to her that it was a little soon, even for her, to make up her mind that she didn't like someone—especially when that someone was supposed to be helping her regain her equilibrium in her marriage.

"She seemed very nice to me," she said.

"Well, she would, wouldn't she? It's only men she hates. She can barely suffer the good padre, and Jenny is a committed Catholic. Trust me, if she had her way she'd ship

Père Jean off and install Soeur Thérèse in his place. Have you met Soeur Thérèse? The nun? She's just as whacked out as Jenny."

Maggie's face must have revealed her horror because he hurriedly continued.

"Oh, come on," he said, making a face, "I'm not telling tales out of school. Five minutes with an Internet connection and you'd discover the whole story for yourself."

"What story?" she asked in spite of herself.

Although they were the only ones in the dining room Antoine dropped his voice and leaned in closer.

"About ten years ago, Jenny was engaged to marry. As these things sometimes go, about a week before their wedding, she caught him with another woman. Her sister, in fact."

Maggie winced. Yes, that was terrible and she found herself feeling sorry for Jenny. But on the other hand, if Antoine was saying that as a result of that experience Jenny decided to sequester herself away, then Maggie was a little less sympathetic. Jenny was still relatively young. Going to live in a remote island abbey because you were disappointed in love sounded like an overreaction.

"I can see by your face you're not impressed," Antoine said with the expression of someone revving up to deliver a very big punchline.

"And neither was the jury," he said, pausing dramatically to take a sip of his wine, "when they convicted her of her fiancé's murder."

## 10

Maggie gasped in astonishment.

"She killed her fiancé?"

"She did," Antoine said with relished delight. "A steak knife across the jugular." He demonstrated the whole terrible business by drawing a ruthless finger across his throat.

"It was considered a crime of passion and you know how *that* is in France. Her twenty-year sentence was reduced to eight. As I understand it, after she got out she bounced around from country to country before ending up here two years ago. She never leaves the island and pays Père Jean for her room and board."

Maggie stared out over the dining room without seeing it. Instead she was envisioning the gruesome drama of murder and outraged betrayal, juxtaposing it with the impression that she'd gotten of Jenny: a sweet if mildly obsessed loner who just wanted to be left alone with her various writing projects—and evidently her heartbreak.

"What happened to her sister?" Maggie asked abruptly.

"Ah," Antoine said cheerfully. "Well, not surprisingly,

the two are not on speaking terms. Again, if you Google *Jenny Jacobs' sister*, you'll see she's married with three kiddies and living in New Zealand. Oh, and you'll also see that Jenny's whereabouts are presently unknown so I'm sure she'd appreciate you not blogging about having met her here."

Maggie felt a brief flinch of guilt at knowing Jenny's disturbing history. Would her face give it away if they were to meet again during the weekend? Maggie wasn't good at dissembling. She would be sure to reveal by her expression alone that she knew Jenny's secret.

*Damn Antoine! Why did he even tell me?*

Antoine reached out to touch Maggie's arm before turning away.

"Excuse me, will you, Maggie?" he said. "I think I see a little friction between Paul and Esmé that I'd like to head off at the pass. Go ahead and seat yourself. They'll be serving dinner in a moment."

He turned and hurried across the hall toward Knight's Hall where Esmé and Paul were standing in the doorway, their heads close together. Paul's face was working furiously as if he was attempting to say ugly things but not so anyone else could hear.

Esmé appeared to be crying.

Maggie felt a flutter of sadness in her chest at the sight. She supposed it was perfectly expected for people who were having trouble in their marriage to behave like this. Regardless of the drinks buffet, the *gougères* and the *pâté*, this wasn't a cocktail party or a spa retreat. This was a weekend's effort to get to the truth behind why she and Laurent were not communicating. It was *supposed* to be uncomfortable!

As Alex and Hadley came into the dining room, smiling briefly at Maggie before looking for their seats at the table,

Maggie felt her stomach clench. Laurent still hadn't showed up.

She fought down a surge of anger.

How was his agreeing to come this weekend doing either of them any good if he didn't participate?

*If he didn't even pretend to participate?*

She went to the place at the table with her name card and sat down, flapping out her napkin.

The scent of sautéed garlic and onions combined in the air with an odor of fryer grease and also perfume.

Maggie knew she needed to keep some level of confidence in the process. It was bad enough that Laurent was clearly going to be an unwilling, non-participant in all this but she needed to believe it might help! She watched as Hadley and Alex set their drinks down and took their seats.

Paul and Esmé were now standing at the entrance to the dining room with Antoine. Esmé was scowling, her tears had left long black rivers down her cheeks. Maggie hated to stare and hated worse that her first thought when she saw Esmé was that the poor woman looked like a mime with a painted face.

Paul stood stiffly with his arms folded across his chest, refusing to look at either Antoine or his wife. Antoine was speaking intensely to both of them in a low voice.

The same two village women who had set up the drinks and snacks in the Knight's Hall appeared and walked around the table filling water glasses and putting butter pats on bread plates beside each place setting.

The priest appeared briefly in the entranceway, standing behind the three people blocking his way into the room. He seemed to be debating whether or not to enter. Maggie thought she caught a glimpse of someone standing behind him and she leaned forward to see if it was Laurent.

But Laurent was a big man and it was difficult to mistake him for anyone else. Whoever was standing behind the priest was short and doing a masterful job of staying out of sight. When Père Jean finally entered the dining room, Maggie caught a glimpse of a small dark shape behind him twist away in a flurry of black clothing and retreat into the hallway.

Mystified, she watched the priest as he came to the dining table. Antoine had mentioned a nun was also on the island this weekend. Could that have been her? If so, why wasn't she having dinner with the rest of them? Maggie had every intention of asking Père Jean about it, but he sat in a seat the full length of the table away from her, making conversation impossible.

The servers filled her water glass and put a basket of fresh bread in front of her as Antoine, Paul and Esmé finally came into the room to take their seats.

And still Laurent hadn't shown up.

Maggie bit her lip and felt her mouth go dry.

*Was it possible he left?*

Maggie's stomach clenched as she glanced at the entrance to the dining room and tried to imagine her humiliation if he never came. What would she say to the others? It was one thing to have an angry tête-à-tête and tears before dinner like Paul and Esmé had.

But at least they were both present!

Maggie straightened her silverware and smiled politely at Hadley and Alex, neither of whom seemed interested in engaging in small talk.

By the time the servers returned to the room rolling a cart with the fragrance of savory *gigot d'agneau* emanating from it, Maggie's stomach was in knots. She could no more eat dinner than dance naked down le Grand Rue. Just as she was about to get up from the table with an apology and an excuse of stomach upset, Laurent appeared in the entrance of the dining room.

His face was inscrutable as usual, although his eyes did go to the dinner cart with a hint of his usual interest in food. Maggie watched him as he made his way to his seat beside her. Not once did he attempt to catch her eye. Not once did he even affect to know her, let alone greet her. Or apologize for being late.

Maggie dug her nails into her palms as the servers set a plate of lamb in rosemary and Madeira in front of her. The scent of it wafted around her and for a moment she thought she might be sick. She could feel Laurent as a solid palpable presence beside her. She told herself she was being too sensitive. After all, he was here before dinner had been served. Was she overreacting?

She stole a glance at him but he was focused on his plate of food.

Yes, he took food seriously. Yes, he often preferred to eat in silence in order to give his food his full attention.

And yes, he tended toward laconic. But no, this wasn't normal. Even for him.

It wasn't normal for him to not acknowledge her. It wasn't normal for him to seat himself beside her without touching her shoulder, her arm, for his eyes not to meet hers with silent messages of a suggested mutual perception or understanding.

*Nothing about this was normal.*

Maggie forced herself to turn her attention back to Paul and Esmé. Esmé's tears were dry and a tremulous smile was now on her lips. Paul had even turned to say a few words to her.

It occurred to Maggie that this obviously broken couple

was actually behaving in a much more loving and connected manner than she and Laurent were.

The thought was accompanied by a sensation of cold fingers tracing down her spine and she shivered uncomfortably.

Then, as she glanced around the table—from Paul and Esmé and their fragile détente, to Alex and Hadley—who was still only drinking sparkling water—to the priest who was already eating without saying grace, and past Laurent who was studying his food as if it would talk to him, Maggie's eye rested on Antoine.

For some reason, she stopped and really looked at him as he sat at the table gazing about the couples with a self-satisfied smile on his thin lips. He turned and caught her watching him and winked at her.

Maggie turned her attention back to her own plate and found her confidence seeping away—for this weekend, for anything that might happen to change what was happening between her and Laurent, and for this odd duck marital counselor who would happily and wholeheartedly reveal another person's secrets to a total stranger.

## 11

Roses and peony centerpieces anchored the starched linen tablecloth at both ends. The silver and crystal place settings looked generic, and upon closer inspection, only silver plate and cut glass. But the china and thick cloth napkins gave a formal, vibrant tone to the dinner. A background of baroque music played through a hidden speaker system—somber but pleasant enough.

The lamb was fragrant, its sauce delicate yet distinctive, as was the buttery risotto, the grilled *courgettes* and bottomless baskets of warm bread.

Maggie did a fair job of moving her food around on her plate but her appetite was still affected by Laurent's late arrival. She felt she was overreacting to his tardiness but knowing that only made her stomach clench worse. That self-knowledge just confirmed to her that she was behaving in a way that had somehow turned Laurent away from her.

*What other answer could there be?*

She had worked herself into such a state of self-recrimination that by the time the two women who waited on them had placed the dessert courses in front of the diners, Maggie had practically convinced herself that Laurent's distant and cold behavior was her fault. It had to be a direct result of something that she had done.

Or worse, hadn't done.

Laurent spoke to her briefly during the course of the dinner—asking her to pass the mustard and even commenting once that the lamb was good. But he'd not given her any significant eye contact or made a single personal comment in her direction. Maggie had been married long enough to know that when loving couples were among strangers or in a new environment, eye contact was the main way they communicated.

*Loving couples.*

By the time coffee was served and the dessert plates whisked away, the six bottles of wine had gone a long way toward relaxing everyone—with the exception of Maggie who'd only sipped her wine and time after time eschewed Antoine's eager offer to refill her glass.

Hadley and Paul, seated side by side, were talking animatedly to each other. Esmé, who was seated next to Père Jean and who had obviously forgotten her earlier altercation with Paul, was giggling and talking loudly to the priest.

The twins who'd helped set the table and serve the meal were now huddled in the outer vestibule just visible through the dining room entrance. They wore rain gear and appeared to be talking to someone whom Maggie could see was the diminutive nun she had seen earlier with the priest.

A short woman with a floor-dusting black habit and her hair pulled back into a bone crunching coif, the nun spoke briefly to the twins, then disappeared with them out of sight.

It was hard—but all too tempting—to try to guess the

problems of the two couples with whom Maggie and Laurent were sharing their weekend on the island. On the face of it at least, Paul and Esmé looked like a bit of a mismatch. She was noisy and loud, obviously desperate for attention. He was thin, stern-looking, quiet and basically ignoring her.

Plus—and Maggie hated to note this fact even in her own thoughts—even balding, skinny Paul wasn't bad looking whereas Esmé had clearly dropped the flag as far as trying to keep herself maintained. The streaking mascara had been evidence that she'd at least tried tonight, Maggie thought. But still, the too-short dress, the awkward shoes and the unkempt hair told the real story.

Alex, on the other side of Hadley, was still wearing his ridiculous pink hearts tie. He might have talked to Laurent, except Laurent clearly wasn't open for conversation. Antoine—seated on the other side of Maggie—was too far away for Alex to talk to, so he sank, for lack of better company, into his wine.

As a couple, Maggie thought Alex and Hadley made more sense than Paul and Esmé. While Alex did appear somewhat vapid, he was not bad looking. Hadley on the other hand was decidedly the more exotic creature. She was attractive but it was the sort of prettiness that had to be worked at. Her dress, makeup and hair had obviously been the result of many hours of attention and money in hair and cosmetician salons.

Like a lot of women who in Maggie's opinion spent too much money on their appearance, Hadley presented herself to the world as if she was putting on a performance.

As far as her interaction with her husband Alex, she seemed pleasant but essentially unconnected, as though they were strangers at a party. Civil and nothing more.

Maggie watched her for a moment as she giggled over something Paul said, quickly showing more animation than she had all evening.

A loud squeal from Esmé made Maggie and everyone else at the table turn their heads. Esmé had scooted her chair so close to Père Jean's that she was nearly sitting in his lap. Maggie glanced at Antoine to see if he would manage the situation. She was surprised to see only mild interest on his face and certainly no hint that he was about to step in.

"Père Jean just told the dirtiest joke!" Esmé said in an earsplitting voice, followed by a donkey bray of a laugh. "Tell them, Padre!"

Maggie grimaced at both the laugh and the look on Père Jean's face.

"Tell them, Father!" Esmé said again, looping one arm through the priest's and leaning so far into him that her breasts were pressed against his arm.

*Père Jean's face was red with embarrassment. He looked around the dinner table as if for escape.*

Maggie glanced at Laurent who was studying the wine in his glass with a concentration it definitely didn't warrant, and she wondered what the other couples thought of the two of them. She wondered if it was obvious to an outside observer that Laurent did not want to be here. She wondered if the fact that he *was* here meant that even he knew that something needed fixing between them.

She felt a sliver of discouragement at the thought.

*If he's not here solely to pacify me it means he knows we've got a problem. And he doesn't know what to do either.*

Maggie tried to remember a single time in her whole entire life with Laurent when he didn't know what to do at any given time.

"How was your lamb?" she asked him.

"Fine," he said.

"Mine was good too," she said pointedly.

His eyes flashed to hers for just a moment before looking away.

"Let's both try harder," Maggie said to him. She realized with a start that she hadn't intended to say it. She didn't even know why she did.

His face clenched in tension and he leaned back in his chair, his eyes scanning the table as if to find something—anything else—to look at besides Maggie.

"You can't even look me in the eye," she said.

"Do not make a scene," he said in a low voice.

Her heartbeat was suddenly racing as she gripped her hands into fists.

"Is it something I've done?" she said, feeling the desperation mutilate her words as they came out of her mouth. "Whatever you think I've done—"

"Maggie, stop it," he said in a fierce whisper, pushing his chair from the table as a threat to leave if she said more.

"Okay," she said softly and turned away, her eyes brimming with tears, her vision blurring.

*So I was right. It is something I've done.*

She reached for her wine glass and drank the contents down before reaching for the bottle on the table and refilling her glass.

She could feel Laurent literally vibrating with indecision next to her which was something else that Maggie hadn't felt before.

Laurent was never unsure.

The fact that he appeared to be struggling with how to go forward was positively terrifying to her.

## 12

Maggie looked around the table at the wine and water glasses sparkling under the single large chandelier that hung over the table in spite of the scattering of lighted tapers on the table. She could see the effort that Antoine had gone to so that they all might be comfortable their first night in the abbey. She glanced at Laurent and knew he wasn't seeing any of it.

"I think from a distance Mont Saint-Michel looks like a wedding cake," Esmé said with a giggle. "That's what I told Paul. Don't you think, Father? When you first see it?"

"Very good, Esmé!" Antoine said as he swirled the wine in his glass. "Mont St-Michel is actually one of the most visited sights in France and probably one of the most photographed too."

He picked up the wine bottle and refilled everyone's glasses near him.

"In fact its unique top-down design was done deliberately for religious purposes. On the very top you have God in the form of the abbey church and the refectory which today houses the religious members who live here full time.

"Below that are the great halls: Knights Hall, where we met for cocktails before dinner tonight, and this room, which is called the Breakfast Room and which you can see is really a large meeting room, although we will in fact be meeting here for breakfast tomorrow."

Antoine smiled at the faces looking at him from the table.

"That is," he said, "if our ladies from the village are able to make it back inside after the storm. I just heard on the radio that we're in for a serious storm."

He glanced at Père Jean as if for confirmation. Esmé was still leaning against the priest, her hand gripping his arm possessively.

"Anyway," Antoine continued with a shrug, "in the old days this room was used for meeting dignitaries, which in a way is what you all are. It was very lush indeed, complete with gorgeous, handmade tapestries, acres of stained glass and the most lavish, expensive furniture."

"And the bottom floor?" Esmé asked, snuggling even closer to the priest. "Is that where the clergy lives? Because Monsieur Secrets here won't tell me."

Maggie frowned at Esmé's behavior. She decided it was probably a good thing Esmé was such a poor listener since Antoine had just said where the clergy live in the abbey.

Esmé giggled and touched the priest's nose with her finger. The priest flinched and pulled his face away with a moue of distaste. Even so, Maggie noted, he didn't leave the table and she assumed that was an option.

"The bottom floor houses the Chaplaincy," Antoine continued, unperturbed, "which at one time was where the priests and monks would interact with the village people, offering them food and succor and such. Today it's where the registration and gift shop is."

"Oh, we saw that coming in!" Esmé said shrilly. "Didn't we, Paul?"

"What about the dungeon?" Paul asked, ignoring his wife. "There is one, isn't there?"

"That would be the *Cellier*," Antoine said, a flicker of annoyance crossing his face. "But it is closed to the public."

Paul turned to Hadley.

"I read that they used to put prisoners down there," he said. "So when the rising tides came in through the dungeon windows, well, let's just say the water did the executioner's work for them!"

"That's ghastly!" Hadley said with a delighted gasp.

"Yes, well," Antoine said, his lips pursed in a flat line. He was clearly not pleased to have the limelight shifted from him. "There are many stories about the abbey at Mont St-Michel and some of them, depending on how ghoulish you are, are a little less savory than others."

If there was a rebuke in Antoine's words, Paul didn't seem to notice.

"Is this all there is people-wise on the island?" Alex asked, waving a hand at the table "Is it just us here tonight?"

Maggie thought he already seemed a little drunk.

"Well, as I mentioned earlier over drinks," Antoine said, "we have our host Père Jean who will be on the premises the whole time. And our lovely servers will be back in the morning to make our breakfast. I'm told there are in fact four other religious members living in the abbey but they are away this weekend. As for the island itself, the village population is a scant forty-four. So yes, Alex, we are on our own tonight."

"And with the storm moving in," Paul said, directing his comment to the priest, "I imagine they've all battened down their hatches for the night in the village!"

"If they're smart, they have," Antoine said. "Now, if I may continue?"

He began to pass out a small stack of laminated pages and as he did, he cleared his throat.

"You may not be aware that Mont Saint-Michel was originally called Mont Tombe," he said. "In the eighth century, it was renamed Mont Saint-Michel after Saint Michael."

"Mont Tombe?" Hadley said rubbing her arms and looking around. "So is it haunted?"

Antoine smiled at her. "After your visit this weekend," he said mysteriously, "I hope you'll tell me."

"The bay was chocked full of sheep when we drove in," Esmé said in a loud voice. "Do they all drown when the tide comes in?"

"The sheep are owned by the villagers," Antoine said, "and I am happy to say they survive the tides. In case you hadn't noticed lamb is an area specialty."

"Poor little lambs!" Esmé said, pouting her lips and looking at the priest. "That makes me sad."

Maggie was surprised Esmé hadn't realized they had been served lamb tonight.

"But thank you for reminding me, Esmé," Antoine said. "I'm meant to warn everyone not to walk in the marshes because the tide can come in very quickly and without notice. And there are pockets of quicksand."

"Quicksand?" Hadley said, unhappily, looking at Paul as if for comfort.

"Not to worry," Antione assured her. "You will all be kept way too busy for impromptu scampers through the marsh. And now—"

"What about the author you mentioned?" Esmé said. "Will she be joining us?"

"This is a private function," Antoine said, now seeming

to visibly force himself to smile at the interruption. "It's very likely you won't see Jenny at all this weekend although Maggie met her briefly. She tends to keep to herself."

"At what point do we drink to your success for being asked to host the International Counsel for Marital Harmony Association?" Esmé asked in a loud voice.

Antoine's face froze as he stared at her. His mouth was open and he was blinking rapidly.

"What's this?" Paul said. "There's a reason to break out the champers and you didn't tell us?"

"You know how shy Dr. Anders is," Esmé said. "Am I right, Dr. Anders?"

Maggie was surprised to see the normally effusive Antoine redden and look down at the mention of what sounded like recent and notable achievements but decided she didn't know him well enough to make a judgment one way or the other.

"Thank you," Antoine said tightly. "Now, if you will look at the laminated maps that I have just passed out, you'll see the areas of the island that you are allowed to walk through in fulfillment of your exercises. Please keep in mind that while we do have most of tomorrow, the island will once more be besieged by tourists. Tonight is our only time to really make some headway without any distractions."

The map was a laminated card with text and a crude schematic of the abbey on one side. Maggie saw the evening's two exercises were numbered.

She also noticed that Laurent didn't pick up his map.

"There *are* several secret passageways not shown on this map and that's just as well since you're not allowed to use them should you stumble across one," Antoine said. "And yes, Paul, there are even a few torture rooms also not shown on the map although the main dungeon—the Cellier—will be the destination for our first bonding exercise in just a few minutes."

Laurent snorted and Maggie turned to look at him and she began to feel her irritation with him swell.

It was so obvious that he had no intention of doing any more than the bare minimum to get through the weekend. She crossed her arms and looked away, determined to focus on anybody or anything else.

Suddenly the sound of a chime—muffled from inside a purse or pocket—made everyone turn their heads in search of the source.

"Hey! I thought we weren't supposed to have phones!" Hadley said. "Not fair! I want mine back!"

Maggie felt a sudden stab of nausea when she realized that the chime was coming from Laurent.

Everyone turned to stare as he pulled his phone from his pocket.

"Now, our Monsieur Laurent here is being very naughty," Antoine said, shaking a finger at Laurent. "These retreats always work better without the distraction of electronics and it is in fact the foundational tenet of my methodology. I will ask you, Monsieur, to please hand it over."

Antoine was smiling but Maggie was not.

The fact that Laurent had kept his phone when he knew everyone else had given theirs up underscored to her in big block letters his resistance to what she was trying to do here —*save their marriage*. Whether or not that was an exaggeration, at this point, she was done fretting the minutia of what was or wasn't happening between them.

Maggie snatched his phone out of his hand, her muscles quivering with fury.

"Let me help you with that, dearest," she said tartly as she stood up to hand the phone to Antoine.

As she turned with the phone in her hand she saw a green text message on the screen. While she hadn't intended to, she found herself reading the short message.

When she did, she sat back down hard as a jolt of electricity seemed to slam into her. A sudden feeling of cold penetrated her gut and expanded through her chest.

"Maggie?" Antoine said. "I'll take that phone now, please."

Still holding Laurent's phone, Maggie stared at the message, reading it over and over again, her mind whirling with shock and disbelief.

<You have proof of paternity, Papa. Now either pay up or I tell your wife>

## 13

The rain had started up again, leaving a dismal, flat white sky to contrast against the brilliant flashes of scarlet and yellow of the maple and horse chestnut trees that lined the driveway.

Grace stood at the kitchen sink drying the last of the dinner dishes as she watched the wind outside gust up, rattling the panes. She was mildly surprised at herself and wondered when she'd started enjoying the natural world.

*Probably when Laurent gave me Dormir to run,* she realized. Before then her interests were only clothes, jewelry, and anything having to do with herself. It was true that the last ten years had been hard the hardest of her life—but they'd also been the best.

She smiled in memory as she wiped up milk from the counter and heard Philippe's laughter coming from the living room where he was watching television with Danielle.

*And me without a man,* she thought, shaking her head in bemusement. *Will wonders never cease?*

Life was definitely slower these days when it wasn't whirling by so fast in a whirlwind of big jobs and little chores—all the things necessary to run a successful bed and breakfast. Sometimes she couldn't remember what happened between standing in the garden with her first cup of coffee of the day and standing at the sink, finishing the last of the dinner dishes.

Everything else in between was just a blur.

A very satisfying, comforting, blur.

She dried her hands and glanced at the kitchen clock. She was expecting someone to come tomorrow and give her a price on pulling up a very old and nearly dead crepe myrtle in the garden in order to make room for another installation. Laurent would pay for it, of course, but it was a matter of pride for Grace that she track down the best price. The pool that Laurent had put in last year had single-handedly been responsible for a dramatic uptick in five-star reviews on all the more popular travel sites.

Plus, it was always nice when there were a few days without guests when just she, Danielle and Philippe could relax and imagine for a moment that there weren't five cottages to be cleaned, with sheets to be washed, and a bushel of chestnuts to peel or an hour's worth of emails from potentially interested guests to answer.

Grace was seconds from tossing down the dishtowel and joining Danielle and Philippe in the other room when she saw her phone vibrating on the counter.

Hoping it might be Zouzou, she picked it up to see the call was from Gregor. A tiny seismic shift trembled through her as she pushed *Accept*.

"Hi, Gregor," she said. "I was just thinking of you."

Why did she say that? Guilt? Because he was the last thing she was thinking of?

"Oh yes?" he said, his voice smooth and courtly. "I am always thinking of you, *mon cher*."

Grace turned and sat in one of the kitchen chairs.

"I really enjoyed last night," he said. "Very much."

"Me, too," Grace said, wondering why she wasn't able to come up with anything more demonstrative.

Last night had been dinner and a bit of shy fumbling in Gregor's car until Grace remembered she had an early day the next morning.

She wondered if he could tell it was a fib.

"I was hoping to talk you into a weekend away in Nice," he said.

"Oh!"

Panic grabbed Grace as she tried to think how to avoid the trip and then stopped herself, realizing that this was the first time with Gregor that she was really vividly aware of how she felt.

"Um, when?" she asked, knowing because of how she made her living, there was every possible excuse in the book at her disposal. In fact, it would take a true miracle to allow her a full weekend off even if it were George Clooney asking.

"Perhaps mid-month?" Gregor said. "Or just whenever is good for you."

That makes it harder, Grace thought, trying to quell the feelings of panic in her breast.

She didn't want to hurt him. She didn't want to lose him. She didn't want to spend a weekend with him.

"Can I let you know?"

"Of course."

There was a moment of silence in which Grace managed to stuff every second of it with the leviathan guilt she was feeling.

"Oh, I think I hear Philippe calling," she said.

"Yes, of course, *chérie*. Tell him hello from me, yes?"

"I will."

"Goodnight, Grace."

"Goodnight, Gregor."

She disconnected and sat back in the chair hearing the laugh track of the show Danielle and Philippe were watching. She suddenly felt too weary to get up from her chair to join them.

## 14

Maggie heard a dull buzzing in her ears as she sat there staring at the phone. She felt like the floor had abruptly fallen away and taken her stomach with it.

*Laurent has a secret child?*

She stared at the text message, rereading it again and again as if the words might somehow reform and change into something else. She shook her head in disbelief, then rubbed her eyes.

"Maggie," Laurent said in a low voice.

Out of the corner of her eye she saw his hand reaching for his phone or perhaps for her. She looked at his face, praying that when she did, she'd realize that what she'd read on the phone was easily explainable. In fact, couldn't possibly be what it looked like. She'd be able to tell with one look at his eyes.

He gazed at her, his face unnaturally still, a face literally laced with guilt. His normally enigmatic expression was gone as he searched her eyes in blatant shame.

*It's true*, she thought numbly.

"*Maggie,*" Laurent said again, although now he'd dropped his hand.

He didn't want the phone back. He clearly could no longer hope she might have misunderstood the text and that they could somehow carry on from here.

"I'll take that from you, Maggie," Antoine said, rising from his chair.

Maggie flung the phone at Laurent. He didn't flinch when it hit him in the chest before it fell to the floor. Alex leaned down and scooped it up.

She let out a forceful breath and felt a sudden sharp pain in her lungs. She could barely form the words rolling around in her head as she stared at Laurent. But her questions were unnecessary. One look at his face told her that.

*He has another child. He's had a baby with someone.*

She felt dizzy. Tears were threatening and she used anger to push them back. Her vision blurred as she did.

"I'll take that, Alex," Antoine said as he walked around the table with his hand out. Alex gave him Laurent's phone.

"I want to move my room," Maggie said to Antoine, her gaze at Laurent still unbroken. "I want a private room."

"I'm sorry, darling," Antoine said as he slipped Laurent's phone into his pocket. "But we've only booked the one block of rooms for the weekend and there are none to spare. In truth, it would defeat the purpose of your time here."

"Fine. Then I'm leaving," Maggie said standing up.

"Maggie," Laurent said with a heavy sigh as if even the effort of saying her name was too much.

"That too is impossible, I'm afraid," Antoine said. "The last bus has left and the tide is rising with the impending storm. There is a bridge but it's a long walk in very bad weather."

"Not to mention," Paul added, "last time the bridge was

completely submerged."

Knowing how much Laurent would hate her making his secret public and before she had a moment to think better of it, Maggie stood and faced the group.

"I have just discovered that my husband has an illegitimate child that I knew nothing about. Am I truly expected to sleep in the same room with him?"

Esmé and Hadley both gasped, their faces wreathed in guilty delight.

"The little scamp!" Esmé squealed happily as she looked at Laurent and eased away from the priest. "I'll switch rooms with her!"

"Now, now, everyone," Antoine said. "We'll all of us keep our own beds for now and Maggie, thank you for your honesty. While I appreciate what a shock this must be for you, it does underscore how much you and your husband have to discuss. Am I right?"

He looked around the table at Esmé and Hadley, both of whom were nodding their heads.

"Now for our first activity, we'll pair off boy-girl to begin our trust exercise. And I think that's just in time. Am I right? Okay, everyone? Coffee and desserts finished? Ready to find the best your marriage can be?"

Maggie sat down hard in her chair and folded her arms across her chest.

"Fine," she said. "But I'm not doing it with him."

"Maggie," Laurent said again in a low voice.

Esmé jumped up from the table and ran over to Laurent. She latched onto his arm.

"If she doesn't want him, I'll take him!"

Maggie stood up, tossing down her napkin.

"Be my guest," she said, as she turned to stride from the room.

## 15

Laurent watched Maggie leave the dining room, his shoulders hunched in misery. He had only himself to blame for this travesty. He'd wanted to pick his own time for telling her, but he'd waited too long.

He'd planned to deal with it when he got back to Domaine St-Buvard—deal with his daughter Élodie—

*No, I won't call her that. Mila is my only daughter.*

"Ooooh, how big are you?" Esmé giggled from where she stood next to his chair and squeezed his bicep. "I bet people ask you that all the time."

Laurent removed his arm from her clutches and stood up so suddenly that the woman started to topple over. Quickly, he put a hand on her elbow to keep her on her feet. He glanced around the room to see Esmé's husband Paul had quickly paired off with Hadley—presumably since Maggie had broken the husband-wife pattern—and they were scurrying out of the room leaving Alex, who would now be Maggie's partner, still seated.

Antoine stood at the door, his eyebrows up in exaggerated questioning in Laurent's direction.

"You two need to get going," Antoine said. "It's a timed exercise, you know."

Alex stood up looking flushed and drunk.

"Works for me," he said. "The little Yank is hot as hell."

Laurent took two steps toward him and pushed him hard against the table. Drunk as he was, Alex fell back into his seat and looked up at Laurent in surprise and mild alarm.

"Now, now, Laurent," Antoine said hurriedly, hurrying to insert himself between the two men. "The ladies have made their choices and we will respect them, yes?"

Laurent narrowed his eyes at Alex and quickly deduced that the man was no threat to Maggie—even in the mood she was in. He briefly debated going back to their room to wait for her. His eyes flicked back to Alex, who burped loudly as Antoine pulled him to his feet.

But no, it was probably best to deal with it now. She was angry but she would still listen to him.

*Waiting is what got me into this situation in the first place.*

His self loathing seemed to tighten all his muscles at once.

"Let's go, you lot," Antoine said. "Chop, chop! Especially you, Alex. You're Maggie's partner and she can hardly learn anything beneficial all by herself."

Alex glanced at Laurent and licked his lips and Laurent felt like drilling his fist through the bastard's face just for whatever thoughts he *wasn't* expressing out loud.

Antoine must have read Laurent's mind because he pushed Alex ahead of him through the door. When he did, Laurent saw Maggie standing in the outer foyer with her arms crossed, waiting for Alex. Laurent started in her direction when he felt Esmé wrap both her hands around his arm.

"Slow down, big boy," she simpered. "With those long legs of yours I can barely keep up!"

Laurent grimaced as he reached the hallway with the woman hanging onto him, just in time to see the back of Maggie as she led the way with Alex in tow.

This of course was the least of what he deserved, as he had no doubt Maggie would be the first to agree. It was clear that she had been long-suffering and understanding right up to the point when she realized just how in the wrong he was.

Whatever was waiting for him now, no matter how pernicious, was well-deserved.

Every damn bit of it.

## 16

It was late by the time Grace had read the last five stories to Philippe and finally gotten him to sleep. A full day romping in the garden had helped a bit, but Philippe was an active child, and at seven, he needed a lot of stimulation to tire him out.

*Just my luck*, she thought with a weary smile.

She closed his bedroom door and went to the living room. Danielle had turned off the television and retreated to the little alcove off the kitchen. It was a much smaller room, but was furnished with a sofa, chair, and bookcase which, along with a Franklin stove, made it the coziest room in all of *Dormir*. As she came in, she found Danielle digging through her knitting basket.

"He finally go down?" Danielle asked with a smile.

"Yes, thank God," Grace said. "He has so many more questions about everything than I ever remember Zouzou or Taylor having."

Taylor was Philippe's mother. A difficult if brilliant child, she had dropped her son off with Grace when Philippe was not quite two years old. First Grace had to rename him since he'd come with *Zircon* on his birth certificate. Two years later Taylor tried to shake Grace down for money by threatening to reclaim her son—with whom she clearly wanted nothing to do—and Grace had succeeded in becoming Philippe's legal guardian.

Yes, he was often a handful yet Grace could not imagine a life she could call good without him in it.

"How about a toddy?" Danielle asked with a smile.

"Sounds good. Sit still. I'll get it."

*Speaking of Godsends*, Grace thought as she went to the kitchen to get down the French press to make the toddy. How did someone like herself who'd used up every inch of good grace from the Almighty possibly rate the twin joys of Philippe and Danielle in her life? And of course there was darling Zouzou, and Maggie and Laurent.

*Face it,* she told herself as she measured the coffee out into the press, *you're blessed and that's all there is to it.*

Lonely. But blessed.

She poured the boiling water over the grounds and then set the timer, going to get down the bottle of Calvados in the meanwhile. She heard a shutter banging in the distance, guessing it belonged to one of the cottages. Somewhere from far away came the sound of a barking dog. It seemed to echo down the valley until it was swallowed up by the rising wind.

Once the coffee was ready, she poured it into two glasses with a shot of Calvados and a heaping spoonful of sugar. She put the glasses on a tray with a small plate of butter cookies and returned to the alcove where she set it down between the two easy chairs. Danielle had her small radio on. Grace quite liked the old-fashioned air of depending on the radio instead of finding out the news from a computer or cellphone.

"We've got weather coming," Danielle said as she reached for her warm toddy.

Grace smiled.

*Why do older people always say weather was coming when surely they had weather all the time?*

*It's like when people ask you if you have a temperature when what they really mean is do you have a fever?*

"I heard the shutter thumping all the way across the garden," Grace said. "Gabriel said he fixed it but it's clearly still loose."

"Well, there's always tomorrow," Danielle said with a shrug.

*So French,* Grace thought with a resigned smile, blowing on her drink.

"...once in a hundred year storm off the coast of Normandy..." the radio announcer intoned.

"Wait," Grace said. "What's that? That's where Maggie and Laurent are this weekend."

Danielle turned the volume up on the radio.

"...declaration of emergency in preparation for late season storm which is centered around Pontorson and specifically the island of Mont St-Michel..."

"That's where they are!" Grace repeated in dismay.

"...six thousand people are presently in the eye of the storm which is stalled over the popular tourist island for the past two hours. Although the village itself only has a population of forty-four, the bridge linking the island to the mainland is submerged under at least fourteen meters of sea water and the winds are eleven knots, making communication with the island impossible..."

"Oh, my God," Grace said. "They're stranded there."

"I wonder if they have electricity," Danielle asked,

frowning at the Franklin stove as if thinking she might light it.

It was only October and although they'd had plenty of cooler nights and days, normally it would be mid-November before they kept the stove going all day and evening.

A booming crack of thunder—sounding more like a cannon firing than any natural phenomenon—shook the house, and Grace reached for a wool throw to put around her shoulders.

"We're not doing so hot ourselves," she said, rubbing her hands up and down her arms before reaching for her drink. "Did you know this front was coming?"

Danielle shook her head.

"I have been watching *Petit Ours Brun* most of the evening," she said with a smile. "But there were no warnings on the program. It is just a storm. Nothing to worry about."

"I guess so," Grace said, pulling the throw tighter around her. She was glad they didn't have any guests coming for a few days. Things always slowed down after summer but the rains tended to bring mud which always made her job—and Danielle's—that much harder when it came to keeping everything clean.

"Did I hear you get a phone call earlier?" Danielle asked.

"Yes. It was Gregor. He wants me to go away with him for the weekend."

Danielle raised an eyebrow.

"I'm going to put him off," Grace said. "We get pretty busy in the fall."

*Well, now she knows I'm lying since fall and winter are our slow times.*

"Nobody is talking you into going, *chérie*," Danielle said. "Unless Gregor is pushing you?"

"No. He's being a total gentleman."

"Is that the problem?"
Grace burst out laughing.
"Oh, my gosh, Danielle. You always surprise me. No, that's not the problem. There's just no...spark."
"Ah."
"I'm probably being too picky."
Danielle didn't answer but she gave Grace a look of admonishment. Grace was well aware that Danielle thought Gregor was too old for her and too...stodgy? But that was fine for Danielle, Grace thought with frustration. *She* was happy to live here in the bosom of a family knitting socks. But Grace was still young!

*I'm lonely! I still want love.*

Suddenly the doorbell rang and both women froze and stared at each other. Grace glanced at the clock again. It was nearly midnight. Even if they were expecting guests —which they weren't—a midnight check-in was unheard of.

"Are you expecting any—?" Danielle started to say.

"No," Grace said, picking up her phone and handing it to her. "It's probably just someone lost."

"In a storm?"

"If you hear me shout, push one one two."

"Oh, *chérie*, maybe you shouldn't answer the door?"

"And wait for them to break in through the back window?" Grace said biting her lip in agitation. "Just be ready to call the police."

Danielle dropped her knitting and held Grace's phone with both hands, her eyes round with apprehension.

Grace walked through the kitchen—grabbing one of the chef's knives from the butcher block holder as she did—and walked to the front door.

Whoever it was had started to knock on the door.

Feeling her adrenaline spike, Grace took in a long breath and tried to let it out slowly.

"Who is it?" she called through the door. "We're closed!"

The voice was muffled under the sound of the rain pounding on the overhang over the porch. Through the top of the transom Grace saw the evening sky ignite in brilliant flash of lightning.

*Who in the world could be out there?*

What if it was someone lost? Someone wet and needing help?

She took in a long breath and slowly unlocked the door and the deadbolt, holding the knife ready by her side. Wishing she'd made Gabriel put a safety chain on the front door, she opened the door and eased it open just far enough to be able to see, her muscles primed to slam it shut if he charged her.

He didn't charge her.

Grace swung the door open all the way and stood there, dumbfounded, her knife now clasped to her chest like a bouquet of flowers, her mouth open in astonishment.

The rain was pouring down and the lightning flashing, framing the sight of her ex-husband standing on her doorstep.

## 17

Maggie stormed down the corridor, so angry and hurt and yet full of questions that twice she stopped with the intention of turning and confronting Laurent, and twice she forced herself to surge on ahead, determined not to give him the satisfaction of a showdown.

At least not yet.

She marched down the stone corridor with Alex trotting behind her.

Antoine had said the exercises were to be held in the Dungeon and the Chaplaincy—both on the bottom floor. Maggie resisted the temptation to go back to the room instead. But Laurent had the key and she would be damned if she would ask him for anything at this point.

The stairwell was well lighted and wider than the stairs that Maggie had used to climb to the Knight's Hall. She took the steps down to a lobby which featured a dramatic high-arched ceiling of rock hovering over a slate flooring with dingy stone walls. The connecting passageway was narrow.

As soon as she left the lobby, the cold seemed to leap out at her from the very walls and drill its way under her sweater.

Sounds began to creep into her awareness, pushing past her fury to demand her attention. She slowed her steps and heard the clink of metal nearby. She stopped and turned but there was only Alex hurrying behind her. He still wore that ridiculous pink tie which now seemed to vibrate obscenely in the harsh hall lighting. She turned away and instantly heard the ominous sound of steel sliding into a scabbard.

Beads of sweat formed on her forehead and she stopped again and placed a now clammy hand on the stone wall. When she did she felt the cold shoot into her hand and up her arm. She snatched it away and rubbed the palm of her hand.

"Where are we supposed to go?" Alex asked. "It's bloody freezing down here!"

She heard the tread of heavy boots behind her and turned around again. Glancing at Alex's feet, she saw he wore athletic shoes.

*What am I hearing? Is Antoine playing some sort of public address sound effects?*

"Give me the map," she said. She'd left hers on the table.

As soon as Alex handed it over, Maggie again felt an overwhelming urge to go back upstairs and confront Laurent.

She needed to know if it happened while they were married so she could go ahead and get a divorce attorney on the phone tonight.

"I think Antoine said we're supposed to go to the dungeon for this," Alex said. "Which way is the dungeon?"

*This is stupid,* Maggie thought in frustration. She wasn't sure she didn't say it out loud. The cold seemed to be worse when they were just standing.

*Can this temperature really be normal?*

She rubbed her arms to try to warm them and Alex tugged the map out of her hands.

"It says here we're supposed to give our partner instructions for a task—he has a list of examples here—and then blindfold each other—"

"Can you just stop talking for a single minute?" Maggie snapped.

She continued to rub her hands up and down her arms. She wasn't wearing a coat, only a thin pashmina shawl and it was sorely deficient for the job. She turned to peer down the long passageway. Electric sconces lit the way but also illuminated the details of rat droppings and tourist litter in the corners.

*What are we doing?* she thought in mounting despair. *This is crazy.*

*Worse, this is useless.*

"Do you hear noises?" she asked Alex.

He frowned and pulled a small flask out of his jacket, offering it first to her. She shook her head.

"What kind of noises?" he asked.

She didn't want to say she'd heard the sound of a sword coming out of its scabbard, or hobnail boots marching behind her. She didn't want him to think she was as hysterical as she'd already effectively demonstrated tonight when she ran out of the dining room like some kind of psychoneurotic when she forced everyone to switch partners.

*I hope Laurent is petrified of what I'm thinking right now. I hope he's frantic with worry!*

She ground her teeth and rubbed her arms with her hands faster and faster in manic, short jerky movements.

The thought of him worried about how angry she might

be was a comforting one. It reinforced to her that the last thing she needed to do was go looking for him.

She turned to look at the map again and began to walk down the hall. Up ahead she saw two people. It occurred to her that they probably weren't supposed to fraternize during the exercise so she hesitated just long enough to see the two people come together in an embrace.

Her breath caught when she saw that. Instantly she stepped into the shadows of the passage. When she did, she recognized Hadley and Paul. She frowned. There was no way they could've gotten together after having just met each other!

Maggie supposed a sex addiction might easily be a reason why at least one of them was here this weekend. She turned to see if Alex had seen them too.

But when she did she saw he was no longer behind her.

## 18

The cold seemed to go straight into her bones as she stared down the stone passageway where she'd last seen Alex. There was only a long empty tunnel of stone. She took a few tentative steps back, feeling a cold fluttering sensation in her stomach, but there was only darkness. She rubbed her forehead.

"Alex?" she called.

Maggie stopped and listened and heard what appeared to be a roaring sound coming from beneath her feet. Stupefied, she looked down and then staggered back. At her feet was a skeleton crouched against the wall.

Maggie screamed and fell backwards, her hands clawing at the wall behind her for purchase, her eyes riveted to the sight in front of her.

The skeleton's bones were a bleached bright white, glowing nearly fluorescent in the dark. The skull had dark holes for eyes and grinned at her, its head tilted toward her. Maggie swallowed hard and shook her head to clear her vision.

Her heart now pounding, she closed her eyes tightly and

pressed her spine deeper into the wall, feeling its solidness against her back, and taking some comfort from it. When she opened her eyes the skeleton was no longer there.

*What is going on?*

She pushed herself off the wall and hurried past the spot where the skeleton had been. One of the electric sconces had gone out. The other one flickered uncertainly. As she rounded the corner, she was suddenly immersed in complete darkness. She shot both hands out to touch the wall for support.

Instead she felt warm flesh.

She screamed in terror as she felt fingers wrap around her arm and pull her.

"*Chérie*, it's me," Laurent said.

Maggie's relief was obliterated immediately by her fury at having been so badly startled. She wrenched her arm from his grasp.

"Let go of me!" she shouted, hearing her voice as if it was being broadcast from a jumbotron at a football stadium.

"You're shaking, *chérie*," Laurent said in a low voice.

"Leave me alone!" she shrieked.

Her pent-up emotions, incubated in the uncertainty and fear of the past few minutes—and compounded by her doubts—exploded into a blast of fury that felt as liberating as a free fall off a very high cliff.

"You betrayed me!" she shouted at him. He appeared as a wavering shadow in front of her. "You betrayed our wedding vows! You…you—"

"*Chérie*, I am sorry."

He reached out again to pull her to him.

"Don't you *chérie* me!" she said, slapping at his hands. "And don't touch me!"

He held up his hands as if to mollify her. He was backlit

by a single electric sconce. His shirt was stained and disheveled, his hair wild around his face. His jacket appeared wrenched half off his shoulder.

"Maggie, you are acting like a madwoman," he said in a calm tone.

"Are you serious?" she said, her nostrils flaring. "Do you *know* what a madwoman is? A madwoman would be clawing your eyes out. A madwoman would have bitten your ear off and spat it back at you."

"Very colorful, *chérie*."

"How dare you mock me!"

She slammed her hands against his chest but didn't succeed in even rocking him back on his heels. He ran his hands down her arms and held her steady, making sure she couldn't twist away from him. He lowered his head to make eye contact with her.

"Listen to me, *chérie*. It happened before you and I met," he said. "Years before."

That took a little of the wind out of her sails but she wasn't ready to be appeased just yet. It felt too good to be angry.

"I don't believe you."

But the problem was, she did believe him. It made sense. Honestly what *hadn't* made sense—the thing that had made her go so immediately crazy—was the unfathomable notion that Laurent had cheated on her.

"When?" she said, jerking her arms out of his grip.

She realized that he seemed to have grown several inches since dinner. He seemed to literally tower over her.

"When did it happen?"

"I was seventeen. I don't even remember who she was."

"And you didn't know she'd gotten pregnant?"

"Of course not. Don't be ridiculous."

"Don't tell me not to be ridiculous! Don't you dare tell me...!"

Laurent put his hands up, hands looking like big round softball gloves to her, to calm her.

"Yes, okay, okay," he said. "Sorry."

Maggie felt her whole body vibrating as she stood in the stone passageway and faced him. There was a steady hum that she hadn't been aware of before that now seemed to come from behind him.

As much as she was trying to focus on Laurent—suddenly so massive that he seemed to be like part of the stone walls that surrounded her—she was distracted by a purple hawk perched in a recessed shelf behind him, staring at her, its eyes glittering like opals. It opened its beak and an operatic aria poured out.

Her legs felt weak as if they would collapse under her at any moment.

"Something's wrong," she said breathlessly.

"We will fix it, *chérie*," he said.

"No, Laurent. Something's wrong right *now*!"

Maggie waved her arms to indicate the place where they stood. She watched his eyes widen at her words as if he suddenly realized what she was saying.

The hallway was suddenly flooded by an eerie yellow light.

"What's happening?" she asked, the panic thick in her voice.

Behind Laurent, Maggie saw something move but when she looked at it, she couldn't find it. A groan came as if out of the very walls. A man's groan. A groan of pain and hopelessness.

"Don't you hear that? The screams?"

"I hear...other things."

The groans turned into bloodcurdling screams which rose and fell, their intensity ebbing and tightening. Were there other people on the island? Were people being held captive here?

"What is happening?" Maggie said, reaching out for Laurent.

But he was far away now. She saw him standing with his hands by his side, his arms long and touching the stone floor. The stone floor that Maggie suddenly realized was wet. She took a step back as she saw the hallway filling up with water.

"Maggie, no," Laurent said, his voice a long way away. "Stay calm."

"The place is flooding!" she shouted. "Don't you see it?"

"It's not. It's not there," Laurent said, his voice a tiny dot a thousand miles away.

Maggie was hearing his voice through her brain, through her memory. She looked around the hall and saw the walls begin to move like they were breathing. They inhaled and exhaled, sucking in and out in time with the screams of the prisoners captive in the walls.

"Laurent, where are you?" Maggie screamed, looking wildly around for him.

But he had gone too.

The water was nearly to her knees now and it was clear it was meant to drown her—to drown them all. She turned and sloshed through the deluge, through the filthy water toward the stairwell. A man's torso floated past, face down, but from the hair and shirt she could see it was Alex.

Maggie shrieked and fell against the wall to avoid the corpse, then fell to one knee, sloshing in the water, tasting the salt foam as it splashed up into her face.

She scrambled back to her feet and clutched her head to

block out the screams of the abbey prisoners, squeezing her eyes shut tight as she did. She heard her name being called as if from a long way away. At first she thought it was Laurent but then it sounded like the prisoners had begun to chant her name.

"Maggeeee! Maggeee!"

She turned and ran, realizing the water had suddenly gone and there was now nothing impeding her. She felt an abounding joy suffuse her then and when she did, all the lights in the hall blinked on in a golden halo of grace and goodness. She felt encompassed by it.

She still ran, with her mouth open in awe at the electrifying show around her, as stardust—literal stardust—sprinkled down from above coating her hair and shoulders.

Then the music that had always been there in the background suddenly came to the foreground in an almost mystical crescendo of horns and percussion. Maggie slowed to stare in awe at the golden avenue the passageway had become.

It looked as if it was lined in gold, glittering from every stone, every surface. As if goodness itself was imbedded in the walls. The walls pulsed around her in a shower of love and goodwill.

She was still moving forward, still in wonderment, as her foot hit something solid and she stumbled. She reached out for the walls to break her fall but they moved away from her. She fell, slamming painfully onto the stone ground, her hands in front of her in an involuntary attempt to catch herself. She lay there feeling the cold of the floor emanating up into her legs, her hips and her hands. Her legs rested on something soft, the impasse that had tripped her.

Maggie lay immobile, her body humming with expectation, and saw the last and final dusting of gold dust sprinkle slowly down onto her hands. She felt an incredible sadness come over her.

Slowly, she turned to look at the thing she had fallen over.

And started to scream.

## 19

Maggie panted in her desperate attempt to scream but no sound came out of her mouth. She stared at the body in the dim light.

It seemed to fluctuate and mutate but it didn't disappear. It was a woman's body, Maggie realized. It looked like...she reached out and touched it. It was firm and warm.

Her adrenaline rocketed. She snatched her hand away and tried to crab-crawl away from the thing.

"Help!" Maggie whispered, her voice only a croak. "Somebody, help me!"

"I am here, *chérie*," Laurent said, suddenly beside her.

She looked at him in bewilderment. Had he always been there?

"Is it real?" she asked loudly as if trying to be heard over the thundering rush of the waterfall that was nowhere to be seen but obliterated all other noise in her world.

Behind Laurent's shoulder she saw Alex. His hair seemed animated, moving on its own accord, dancing and waving at her. He was staring at the body, his eyes so big and comical that a nervous laugh welled up inside of her.

*Is any of this real?*

"Is she...is she...?" Alex said.

He leaned forward to touch the body and lost his balance and began to fall forward. Laurent shot out an arm and thrust him away from both Maggie and the body. He put a hand on Maggie's shoulder but she jumped abruptly.

"It is only me," Laurent said. "Can you stand?"

Maggie shook her head but not in answer to his question. It was in denial of what she was seeing and hearing. She crawled nearer to the body and lifted its hand to feel for a pulse. The body was warm but there was no heartbeat. She withdrew her hand and saw that it was shaking.

"What's wrong with us?" she asked as Laurent pulled her to her feet.

"We've been drugged," he said.

Laurent knelt beside the body pulling a long strand of hair out of its face. Maggie let a moan escape when she realized who it was.

"Oh, my God, Laurent," she said, biting down on the scream that wanted to come out.

"Antoine! Is that you?" Alex shouted as he whirled around in the corridor. "Who's there?"

Antoine appeared from out of the darkness, his eyes round and blinking. Maggie saw his tongue flicker out of his mouth like a snake's and she emitted a horrified gasp.

"What's happened?" he asked. "What's all the yelling about?"

He looked from one to the other and then finally to Esmé on the ground before the shock registered on his face. He looked up at Laurent.

"What did you do?" he said.

Before Maggie could respond, Laurent stood and slammed Antoine up against the wall. The smaller man made a strangled sound but before he could put his hands up to protect his face Laurent punched him.

Maggie ran to Laurent and pulled at his arm to stop him although she was fairly sure he was finished. She turned on Antoine who was cowering and covering his face with both hands.

"You *drugged* us?" she said to him. The wall he was pinned up against was moving again, breathing. It made Maggie dizzy to look at it.

"It's...I...it's in the waiver you signed," he whimpered, putting his hands to his nose. He pulled his hand away and stared at the blood on his palm. "I'm going to throw up."

He turned away and made gagging sounds into his hands.

Alex again edged over to the body.

"Is...is it Esmé? Is she okay?" he asked.

"*No*, she's not okay!" Maggie said as she watched Alex's tie with its shimmering hearts begin to gently pulse and vibrate in a way that fabric design should not.

"Somebody needs to give her mouth to mouth!" Antoine said, wiping his hands on his slacks. Even from where Maggie sat she could see the perspiration on his face. "Does anyone know how to do that?"

Alex sidled past Laurent, looking warily at the bigger man, and knelt by the body.

"Does anyone have a light?" he asked, patting his shirt pockets before pulling out his own lighter. His hand shook as he ignited the lighter and held it over the body.

When he did, it was quickly evident that mouth-to-mouth would not be necessary.

The six-inch slice across her throat made that very clear.

## 20

"Are you going to let me in, Grace?" Windsor said, hunching his shoulders against the rain that was splashing up onto the porch.

Grace's eyes widened as she stepped away from the door. "Yes, yes. Of course! Omigosh, Windsor, what are you doing here?"

Windsor stepped into the foyer and looked around while Grace held her hand out for his raincoat. Later she would wonder at that gesture. She would wonder why she assumed he would be staying. It was late. Was that a normal assumption?

She hung his coat on the coat rack in the foyer and turned back to him.

Barrel-chested with honey brown hair and blue eyes, Windsor didn't look like he'd changed a bit since she'd seen him last. He smiled at her in that embarrassed way of his, one that Grace hadn't seen in years. Before the divorce, before the angry bickering over custody and how to deal with Taylor and her constant trouble-making, before his second and third marriages, before the relentless and heartbreaking agony over what to do with Philippe.

"Grace?" Danielle called worriedly from the other room.

Windsor nodded at the knife in her hands.

"I see you came prepared," he said. "Wouldn't a security camera be less stressful?"

Grace laughed and felt the tension leave her body in a sudden whoosh.

"Yes, well, after tonight, I'm pretty committed to shopping for one. It's fine, Danielle!" she called as she led Windsor back to the cozy alcove.

"Oh, my goodness!" Danielle said when she saw him. "Good evening, Windsor."

"Hi, Danielle," Windsor said, leaning over to kiss her on the cheek. "Sorry to freak everyone out. I underestimated the time to get here from the Marseille airport."

Before this moment, Windsor had been at *Dormir* only once for a very tense and awkward handover for a summer visit with Philippe. Windsor's second wife Susie had been with him and their toddler (whose name Grace could not for the life of her recall but assumed it was something trendy slash weird like Lebanon or Bluebell).

"What brings you here at this time of night?" Danielle asked as Grace stepped into the kitchen to get the bottle of Syrah she and Danielle had had with dinner.

"Well, I was hoping to spend some time with my grandson," Windsor said. "For starters."

He didn't go on from there which Grace found very odd. First and mainly because while she was delighted that he wanted to spend time with Philippe, the fact that he didn't call and arrange it with her was disconcerting to say the least.

*He's having marital problems.*

Why he might want to fly from Indianapolis to Marseille and then drive four hours in a thunderstorm to visit his estranged ex-wife in the middle of the French countryside was harder to fathom.

She'd already considered and dismissed the possibility that he had some kind of terminal disease. He was too jolly for that to make sense.

She came into the room with the bottle and three glasses. Windsor had seated himself on the settee nearest the unlit stove.

"How's the baby?" Grace said as she handed him a glass of wine.

"Peoria?" he laughed. "Hardly a baby anymore. She's in the second grade. *Tempus fugit*."

"Oh, my goodness, it certainly does," Danielle said, but waved away Grace's offer of wine. "I'm off to bed," she said, getting up and putting a hand on Windsor's shoulder. "And will we see you at breakfast?"

"Yes, if that's..." He looked at Grace. "If that's all right."

"Sure," Grace said, just beginning to realize how very glad she was that he was sitting here in her house. "Philippe will be ecstatic."

## 21

The library annex inside the refectory was situated adjacent to the church. As cozy and intimate as the rest of Mont St-Michel was austere and grand, the library appeared well-used and comfortable and was more luxuriously furnished than any part of the abbey that Maggie had seen so far.

Facing leather sofas flanked a tall stone fireplace in which Laurent had started a fire. Plump pillows and wool afghans were on the sofa. Soft lighting from the many table lamps helped give the room a feeling of warmth and security.

Antoine had gathered everyone together in the library where he explained that the effects of the synthetic hallucinogen he'd drugged them all with had a very short life.

"You should all be perfectly yourselves again," he said to them, "in a matter of minutes if you're not already."

Maggie sat next to Laurent. Like the others, she was shaken, but slowly feeling her wits come back to her.

Antoine had placed bottles of water—and also whiskey—on the coffee table. He sat separately from them in a leather wingback chair, his hand holding a towel to his nose. It was no longer bleeding, not broken after all.

"I just want to add for the record," Antoine said scanning the room clutching his towel, "that what happened was not my fault."

Hadley and Paul sat at the far end of the sofa. Hadley looked pale and stunned. Paul sat with his hand over his mouth, his eyes wide and staring but clearly not seeing. Across from him sat Alex, Jenny and Père Jean.

"You drugged us! Without our permission!" Hadley said.

"Which is illegal," Maggie added angrily. "In fact it's a criminal offence!"

Antoine shook his head.

"No, now, what I gave all of you was a designer drug. And *not* an illegal substance."

"That has to be bull," Paul said hotly. "France is very intolerant of designer drugs."

"You can't even smoke pot here!" Hadley said.

"Yes, that's true," Antoine said, his face glistening with sweat. "But my chemist uses a compound that is entirely unique and has not been prohibited. It's not illegal."

"Not yet, you mean," Jenny said with a snort.

Maggie was astounded that Antoine could drug them without their consent with something his chemist cooked up in his basement...and couldn't be prosecuted?

"I want to know why," Paul said, shaking his head. "Why did you drug us?"

Maggie reached for a water bottle and hesitated. It hadn't been opened but still...She saw Laurent nod so she twisted off the cap and drank, quenching a thirst she didn't know she had until then.

Stress and fear, she realized. *She turned to glance at Paul.*
*His wife has been killed tonight and none of us will be able to*

*tell anyone a damn thing about what happened because we were all incapacitated.*

"It is a growing and highly endorsed trend in the field of couples counseling," Antoine said petulantly, crossing his arms and hunching his neck into his shoulders like a turtle.

"The breakthroughs that are possible when one is able to completely abandon not just inhibitions and social mores but the ingrained tendencies to—"

"Stop," Maggie said sharply, feeling her anger bubble up. "Quit trying to justify what you did. *How* did you do it?"

Antoine licked his lips and glanced guiltily around the room. She imagined he was already considering the possibility of several lawsuits against him. She glanced at the priest. And maybe Mont St-Michel too?

"It was in the wine," Antoine said. "But it's gone now. All the bottles here are fine."

"As long as they're unopened," Hadley said pointedly.

"I can see why you might say that," Antoine said, clearly offended. "But may I remind you that trust is the cornerstone of every successful relationship. I'm going to ask all of you to attempt to overcome whatever prejudice or preconceived judgment you may have made as the result of what happened tonight."

"Prejudice? You're referring to Esmé's death?" Maggie said pointedly.

Antoine visibly winced.

"He wants to make sure he doesn't get a bad Yelp review," Hadley said with disgust.

"That's not true!" Antoine said, the front of his shirt flecked with blood. "I consider that comment singularly unhelpful and...and very hurtful."

Maggie glanced at Jenny and found it somewhat surprising that the woman—recently so opinionated—

had yet to comment. She'd clearly been roused from a dead sleep and looked muddled and confused, her face creased by her pillow, wearing only a heavy overcoat over her pajamas. If Maggie remembered correctly, Jenny had also helped herself to the wine at the Knight's Hall.

"Look, we've all had a terrible shock," Antoine said nasally. "But if we just stay calm we'll get through this."

"That's more than Esmé can say," Hadley said as she reached for Paul's hand.

*Did I imagine them kissing in the hallway?* Maggie wondered as she stared at the two of them. *Am I imagining what I'm seeing now?*

Antoine held up his cellphone. "I've already attempted to call the police. But unfortunately, with the storm bearing down on us, we've lost cell reception. I'm assured by Père Jean that this is typical and will undoubtedly be reestablished in the morning."

"Give us our phones back," Hadley said.

"What did I just say, Hadley?" Antoine said in frustration. "There's no point. You can't call out."

"I don't care! I want my phone!" she said hotly.

Antoine turned away, refusing to look at her.

"I suggest we all go back to our rooms and try to get some sleep," he said. "Meanwhile, Paul, I know the rest of the group joins me in saying how very sorry we are that this has happened and I feel sure that when the police get here tomorrow—"

"You were the last one to see her alive," Paul said abruptly to Laurent. His eyes were dull as if he was having trouble focusing and he chose his words haltingly. "We all saw her leave with you."

Laurent glanced at Paul.

"Your wife left me before the exercise began," Laurent said.

"You're lying!" Jenny burst out. "Men always lie to save themselves!"

Maggie leaned toward the author and bared her teeth.

"Why would he kill her?" she said to Jenny. "We didn't even know her."

"Men don't need a reason for the heinous things they do," Jenny said, her eyes on Laurent like she half expected him to grow horns and a tail at any moment.

"What did Esmé ever do to you?" Hadley asked Laurent

"He's already told you he wasn't with her," Maggie said, crossing her arms and glaring at her. "He found me and then Esmé joined up with Alex."

"That's not true," Alex said, shaking his head. "Esmé never came to me."

"There's no way Esmé wouldn't follow him," Hadley said, nodding at Laurent with a jerk of her head. "She wouldn't just stay in the creepy hallways all by herself."

"I handed her off to Alex," Laurent said, tilting his head as if mystified as to why Alex wasn't confirming this.

In the dim and flickering light of the few lamps around the room, Maggie noticed again that Laurent's clothing and hair were rumpled. Plus, she could see he was missing a shirt button. She frowned in consternation. It must have happened when he roughed up Antoine in the corridor.

"Is that true, Alex?" Antoine asked. "Did Esmé join you?"

"No! I'm telling you I never saw her once we entered the passageways."

"You're lying," Laurent said coldly. "I pushed her into your arms."

"Sorry, man," Alex said, shaking his head. "I can see why

you'd want people to think she wasn't with you but we all saw her leave with you."

Laurent took a step toward Alex but Maggie grabbed his arm. There was certainly no benefit to punching anybody else tonight. She felt his arm tense and unyielding beneath her hand.

"Look at him!" Hadley said, pointing at Laurent. "He's clearly violent! First, he cheats on his wife, then he beats up poor Antoine, and now he's threatening Alex!"

"Nobody is threatening anyone," Maggie said angrily.

Hadley turned toward Paul who put an arm around her. Maggie was astonished that Alex, who was sitting on the other side of his wife, didn't appear to notice what she and Paul were doing.

"I think we should all cool off," Antoine said. "And for everyone's safety..." he glanced at Laurent, "let's go to our rooms, lock our doors, and wait for the police."

Antoine looked at the priest who stood watching the group as if unsure whether or not he was watching a staged production.

"Yes," Père Jean said. "The Pontorson police will visit us in the morning to see if we suffered any damage from the storm. We can tell them then what happened."

"Great," Antoine said. "So we'll disperse until morning. We'll leave poor Esmé where she is for now—I'm sorry, Paul."

Paul nodded to indicate that he understood and accepted the need to keep the sanctity of the crime scene.

As they all filed out of the library to head to their rooms, Maggie's mind was buzzing uncomfortably. The accusations against Laurent were alarming. They had clearly all made up their minds that Laurent had killed Esmé. That's what they would tell the police.

Suddenly Maggie saw clearly what needed to happen before then. She saw what she needed to *do* before then.

She needed to find evidence *before* the cops showed up and possibly decided to take the easiest route to solving Esmé's murder—the route that led straight to her husband, the person who, as far as anyone knew, was the last person to see Esmé alive.

## 22

As soon as they got back to their room, Maggie went to her overnight bag and rummaged around until she found what she was looking for: a penlight. She tucked it into the pocket of her slacks and then went to the door and eased the door open.

Her head was pounding to match the thumping of her racing heartbeat.

"*Chérie?*" Laurent said. He reached for her but she easily evaded his grasp.

"Shhh!" she hissed before turning to look down the hallway. It was empty. "I'll be back in a minute," she said as she slipped out the door, closing it softly behind her.

She walked down the hall toward the stairs. The cold hit her as soon as she stepped outside but at least this time she wasn't hearing sounds or voices. All she heard was her own heartbeat pounding in her ears.

She kept to the shadows, creeping silently down the steps and up the narrow half stairs, now slick with the rain that had been tracked in. The sensations brought on by the drug in her system seemed to activate as soon as she put herself back in the same scene—darkened corridors, the cold damp stone walls—and she tried to remember as she walked to discern what was real—what she'd really experienced—and what was an aftereffect of the drug.

She and Laurent should sue Antoine for drugging them! Fine print or no fine print. That was unconscionable that he would do that without their knowledge or consent! Paul should definitely sue him since it was his wife who died.

*Unless of course it was Paul who killed her.*

Maggie slowed her breath and her pace as she approached the spot where she and Laurent had stood and argued and when she did, she heard the sound of a soft tread behind her. The hairs on the back of her neck seemed to stand at attention and a needle of cold shot down her collar. There was no door or window near this spot. There was no explanation for a sudden cold draft.

Slowly she turned on her heel to stare behind her, sure she was about to see—drugs or not—the apparition of any one of the hundreds of poor wretches who had died of torture and starvation in this place over the centuries.

Laurent stood, dark and looming in the shadows. Maggie let out a breath. It had always amazed her that someone so large could walk so silently.

"What are you doing, *chérie*?"

"Oh, so after three weeks of silence, *now* you're talking to me?" she said as she turned back to take the half dozen steps around the corner to where she'd found the body. She could feel Laurent behind her and when she turned the corner she stopped.

Esmé's body was exactly where they'd left it.

"Stand at the corner and let me know if anyone comes," she said in a low voice.

She walked over to the body. She heard him as he took

his place at the corner. She knelt by the body and pulled out the penlight and shone it on Esmé's neck. The wound was long but ragged. And definitely lethal.

Maggie noticed a dark stain on Esmé's jacket lapel. It was a smear not seemingly connected to any rip in her clothes or slashed neck.

*The killer wiped the blade off here.*

Maggie flicked her beam of light along the floor and up the walls in case the murder weapon was visible but she found nothing. The blood from Esmé's neck wound had coated the top of her blouse in gore. Maggie poised the light over Esmé's face and neck and then inched the light beam down her body, stopping at her right hand.

Esmé's hand was balled into a fist, already made stiff by rigor mortis. Maggie hesitated to touch the body but then slipped her fingers into Esmé's fist and eased her fingers apart.

A button fell onto the stone floor from Esmé's grip making a soft pinging sound as it did. Maggie picked up the button and shined her light on it in her hand.

She felt her skin tingle and a light pressure filled her chest.

It was the missing button from Laurent's shirt.

## 23

Maggie stared at the button and felt a cold wave of nausea ripple through her.

"What did you find?" Laurent asked.

"Nothing," she said before she knew she was saying it.

Knowing that she shouldn't tamper any further with the crime scene, she slipped the button into the pocket of her slacks and rocked back on her heels and stared at the corpse.

What did this mean? Why did Esmé have Laurent's button? Clearly she must have ripped it off his shirt.

During some sort of struggle?

Another cold current filtered down from the tops of the stone walls. Maggie shivered and became conscious of Laurent watching her. It dawned on her then that she was registering a feeling of vague uneasiness at Laurent's presence.

She further realized with a start that the sensation wasn't new. It was one that had been steadily growing in her over the last few weeks. She fought not to succumb to it. She told herself it was the residue of the drugs. He was her husband. He was *Laurent.* Jemmy and Mila's father.

She wiped a hand across her forehead and realized that even in the cold of what was virtually a rock quarry she'd begun to perspire.

It was true she *hadn't* seen him push Esmé into Alex's arms, but if he said he did, she told herself, then he must have done it.

But even with that thought in her mind, the feeling of the button in her pocket burned like a hot ember. She was so alert to it—indicting, incriminating—that she felt an overwhelming urge to throw it into the sea and get rid of it forever.

But no matter what she did with it, the question of *how* it ended up in Esmé's hand would still be there.

She scanned the stone floor around the body. It was sticky with blood.

"Why didn't we notice the blood when we found the body?" she said more to herself than anyone.

"It is difficult to see with all the mud," Laurent said.

Maggie focused the beam of her light over the floor again. He was right. There was mud here. Not much but more than she would've thought this far from any external door.

There was no way a CSI team would be able to pull footprints from this mess. Everyone had been walking around here. Maggie knelt and looked closely at the ground around the body and thought she even saw what looked like animal prints. A small dog? Maybe a raccoon? She blinked her eyes and the prints disappeared. She felt a rush of fury at Antoine. How long before the effects of the drug were gone completely? How much could she trust about what she was seeing? What she was feeling? She felt suddenly very thirsty.

"Someone's coming," Laurent said.

Maggie got to her feet and looked around. There were two deep alcoves tucked into the bend of the stone corridor. She caught Laurent's eye and nodded toward the hiding spots. Quickly they both slipped into the separate hidden recesses.

Maggie held her breath and waited as the sound of the approaching footsteps became louder. Soon the shadows shifted and morphed into a form as Antoine appeared in the hall.

He was no more than three feet from Maggie. She was sure he could smell her perfume and hear her breath caught in her chest. But he didn't look in her direction. She squinted to make out what he was doing and saw he carried a flashlight and held his phone to his ear.

*I thought the phones didn't work?*

Antoine stepped over to Esmé's body but didn't focus his flashlight beam on it.

"Okay," he said into the phone. "Since we don't have cellular reception inside the abbey at the moment I'm recording my initial observations for the police."

He directed his beam to his feet which Maggie thought very strange. It wasn't like he was looking for something. It almost appeared that he was trying very hard *not* to look at the body at his feet.

"I've put all couples under lock and key until you, the police, arrive in the morning," he said with a slight tremor to his voice.

He paused and looked around. Maggie saw his face, saw the sheen of perspiration coating his forehead and top lip.

She saw the tremble in the flashlight beam where he couldn't hold it steady.

He turned and for a moment Maggie thought he was staring right at her.

"While I'm happy to give a full biographical rundown of all the workshop participants," he said into the phone "the one you need to pay close attention to is Laurent Dernier."

Maggie ground her teeth and felt the heat flushing through her body at his words.

"The man is at least six foot five—maybe larger. He's unstable and, in my professional opinion, violent. He already attacked me once but I was able to subdue him."

Antoine eased a few steps away from Esmé's body, his back to Maggie but she could still hear his words clearly.

"I have proprietary information," Antoine continued, "about Dernier's past actions which I assume will prove helpful to you. The fact is, he's been cheating on his wife and while I know that isn't a factor in a murder investigation it does speak to the man's propensity for deceit."

He was quiet for a moment while Maggie's stomach churned in fury and indignation. It was all she could to hold herself back from jumping out and confronting Antoine on the spot but angry or not, she recognized that Laurent wasn't bursting out of *his* hiding spot. She figured she should probably take her cue from him.

After all, when it came to clandestine behavior, Laurent was the expert.

"In my professional opinion," Antoine said again, "when you add the fact that the man is violent *and* that he is a proven liar—" He dropped his voice. "Note to self—see if Maggie will confirm this. She certainly looked mad enough tonight to do it." He cleared his throat. "Where was I? Oh, um, if you combine the fact that he is a proven liar with the fact that he was the last one to see Esmé alive, I'd say it's safe to say that Laurent Dernier is your killer."

## 24

Antoine ended his conversation abruptly after that and then turned and fled the passageway. Maggie waited until the sounds of his footsteps had vanished before she stepped out of the recess. She stared down the darkened tunnel where he'd disappeared.

It was clear that Antoine hadn't come to this spot to report on anything that was here. Nor had he come to answer a question for himself about how Esmé had died. He'd merely come here because he felt this was the one place on the island where he could be sure of having a private phone conversation. Or so he thought.

Laurent stepped out of the shadows.

Maggie's fears that Antoine and the others would attempt to make Laurent their scapegoat had been proven real. At least the police were being held back from immediately coming. It gave her some time.

She glanced down at Esmé's body. There was nothing more to learn here. Whoever had killed her would have all night to get rid of the murder weapon—if they hadn't already disposed of it. In any case, with a crime scene surrounded by water—and even more pouring from the sky every minute—there was no way the police were going to find it now.

There was also no way that *she* was going to be able to find it. And even if she did? The killer would surely have wiped his fingerprints. And her being in possession of the knife that had killed Esmé would hardly benefit her case for Laurent—Esmé's presumed killer. If anything it would just help her be seen as an accessory to murder.

Laurent reached out and touched her arm. The contact made her jump, it had been so long since he'd physically connected with her.

"Come, *chérie*."

She shook her head and felt another wave of hopelessness come over her. She tried to tell herself that it was the late hour, the emotional hyperdrive she'd been operating under all night, or the remnant effects of the damn drugs.

"I hate that we're just leaving her here," she said. "It feels so wrong."

"*Je sais.*" *I know.* "Come."

Maggie turned to look at him, but once more found it impossible to read his face. She removed her arm from his grip and turned to lead the way back to their room, careful to stay in the shadows, the shirt button burning in her pocket the whole way.

Once back in the room, Maggie shrugged out of her jacket and kicked off her shoes. She sat on the bed, suddenly feeling more tired than she ever remembered feeling in her life.

Laurent pulled his sweater off and stood in the middle of the room staring at her.

"Tell me how it happened," she said without preface. "Starting with why you kept it secret from me."

He sighed and tossed his sweater on the chair next to the bed.

"I only found out myself last week."

"That's seven days longer than you should have kept it to yourself."

"I am not like you, *chérie*."

"You mean because I'm not a big fat liar?"

Something flinched in his face but he didn't respond to the attack.

"Of course I was going to tell you," he said. "She is trying to blackmail me."

Maggie stared at him. That meant that the only reason he would tell her the truth was because he knew the girl was going to blow the lid off anyway. Maggie could lash out and accuse him of wanting to keep the girl a secret but what good would that do?

The bottom line to all this was the part that was the hardest to accept: *If he could have gotten away with not telling me he would have.*

That's just who he was. A flicker of memory from decades past fluttered into her brain. It was a sensory memory of the heat and glitz of Cannes in the height of summer and both of them so much younger. Before children, before Domaine St-Buvard.

Before she knew the true extent or ease of his lies.

"Who is she?" she asked, tamping down the urge to scream at him, to blame him for being the man she knew she had married. She looked away unable to hold his gaze.

"Her mother's name is Inès Tresor. I knew her through Gerard. We met at a party."

Maggie frowned at him when he mentioned Gerard's name. Laurent's brother was dead now, but in his life he had been the author of nearly every misery and catastrophe in their lives including, indirectly, the cause of Maggie's sister Elise's death.

Not to mention the death of Elise's child Nicole.

The *real* Nicole.

"This is just what you do, isn't it?" Maggie said, feeling her anger ramp up. "You keep secrets."

"Maggie..."

"You kept the secret about Nicole not really being Elise's child, remember?"

"We both kept that secret."

"I only did because I had to continue the lie once you started it!" she shouted. "You know that! You let me believe that Nicole was really my niece, really Elise's daughter and all the time she was dead! My mother still has no idea that Nicole is not her granddaughter! And what about Luc? He has no idea he's your nephew. None! Another secret! Another lie!"

"This is different and you know it," he growled.

She saw the frustration and annoyance flit across his face.

"How is it different? This, I'd love to hear." She stood up in front of him, her legs planted wide, her chin high and defiant.

"What happened to me with Inès was nothing more than youthful indiscretion," he said. "I am impressed you never had one of those."

"None that ever developed into a whole human being! How dare you try to minimize this?!"

"You are determined to be angry."

"You don't think I have a right to be?"

He lifted his shoulders in that confounding and silent articulation of Gallic expression which could literally mean anything.

She moved to the other side of the room and forced herself to take a breath. A part of her brain knew what he said was true. He hadn't betrayed her. Not really. He hadn't cheated on her or lied to her. But he had delayed telling her.

Would he have told her? Eventually?

"You said you were seventeen?" she asked, forcing her voice to remain calm.

"*Oui.*"

"And you're sure it was you that got this Inès pregnant from that one night? It *was* one night?"

"Yes, *chérie*. One night. That is often all it takes."

She slapped her hands against her thighs.

"Do not be flip with me, Laurent! I'm really not in the mood for quips!"

"Yes, yes, *je suis* désolé, *chérie*," he said, running a frustrated hand through his hair. "She sent me proof of paternity a week ago."

She took in a breath and recovered as best she could.

"Look at me, Laurent."

He turned to face her, the misery and guilt distorting his normally handsome face. The look she saw in his eye now was one of hope of rapprochement.

"If you keep making me drag this out of you," she said, "I swear I will divorce you. *How* did she get access to your DNA?"

Laurent scratched the back of his head and stood up. His jaw was clenched, his posture rigid. Maggie saw how much this tortured him because he would have to reveal over and over again that he'd known for too long before revealing it.

*Correction,* she thought bitterly. *He didn't reveal it. I found out.*

"She didn't," he said, his face flushed with shame and

also irritation. "They sent me a sample of the child's DNA—"

"How did you know it was really the child's?"

"It was certified."

"Okay," Maggie said, feeling a crippling weariness descend upon her. "And then?"

"I provided a sample of my own DNA and had it tested at a genetics lab. I sent it together with the child's and it came back as a match."

For a moment neither of them spoke. The air seemed heavy with despair. Maggie felt her whole body sag.

"Okay," she said finally, her voice heavy with grief. "So that's that. You have another child. What is it?'"

"What do you mean?"

"A son? A daughter?"

"A daughter."

The word hit Maggie square in the gut and she could see Laurent reacting to her reaction. But he'd had time—at least a week—to digest the information himself. And she was getting it all in one heart-wrenching, stomach-lurching conversation.

Suddenly, the room lights snuffed out, plunging them both into darkness.

## 25

Maggie rooted blindly in her bag again for the penlight and snapped it on.

"There are matches and candles in the top drawer of the bureau," she said.

She waited for him to find them and light two candles, setting one on the dresser and holding the other in his hand.

"We once said we would never threaten divorce," Laurent said as he held the candle, his face a mask of gentle reproach. The light flickered against the stone walls creating an ominous, menacing effect.

"Well, I guess that gives you an idea of how pissed off I am," she said tightly. "Please *continue*."

"She called me—"

"Who? Inès or your...daughter?"

"Don't call her that," he said, his eyes flashing in the candlelight. "Inès called and said we had a daughter and that she would send proof. After that she would require money to keep the knowledge from you."

"I see. Were you tempted?"

He gave her a baleful look as though he would not deign to answer the question. Even after holding back what he'd known for a week, it was still a cheap shot and Maggie knew it.

"After the DNA confirmed the match, she demanded fifty thousand euros for her silence," he said.

"When was this?"

"Two days ago."

Maggie knew it wouldn't do any good to get indignant or irate over the fact that Laurent had been doing all of this while Maggie had been busily putting together their couples retreat and thinking how much better things were going to be between them.

It wouldn't do any good to think of how he had been interacting with the blackmailing mother of his child between taking calls from Luc and Jemmy and Mila in the States, running domestic errands, managing the household with her, writing up family menus and grocery lists, and interacting with Grace and Danielle. He'd been going through the motions of his daily round at Domaine St-Buvard—and with Maggie—as if nothing else was going on in the background.

Except of course he hadn't quite been able to manage that, Maggie reminded herself. He may have attempted to go through the normal motions of farm and family life, but his so-called attempt only served to announce blatantly—at least to Maggie—that something was very badly wrong.

"I told her I wouldn't be blackmailed," Laurent said. "That's when Élodie began texting me."

"Élodie, that's...the daughter?"

"*Oui*. When I didn't respond to her threats, she said she would call the board of directors of Domaine St-Buvard."

Domaine St-Buvard was the boutique winery that Laurent owned and operated.

"She did her research," Maggie said cynically.

"Maggie, it was a long time ago."

"Funny. It feels like only seven days to me."

"I should have told you."

*Did it help hearing him say it? A little.*

She watched his face and tried to see the truth in it. She had never known Laurent to have a cowardly bone in his body. She'd seen him nonplussed last year when he didn't know how to deal with Mila and her tantrums. She'd seen him discouraged over Jemmy's lack of interest in the family wine business. She'd seen him disappointed when Eduard Monceau—along with someone Laurent considered a friend—had burned down almost eighty percent of his fields at Domaine St-Buvard twenty years ago.

But she had never seen him face trouble and simply refuse to deal with it.

That's what she was having trouble forgiving.

"What are you going to do now?" she asked.

"Nothing. I've told her I won't pay. The next move is hers."

"You're not going to call the police?"

"I can handle this."

Maggie was well aware that Laurent's experience with the police was a long and rocky one. In his past as a con artist working the Riviera, he'd eluded, paid off and even befriended many policemen over the years. But in all the time she'd known him, Maggie had never known him to willingly reach out to the police for any sort of assistance.

"You don't want to meet her?"

He looked at her in genuine confusion.

"What for?"

"I don't know. To see what she looks like? To...get to know her?"

Laurent frowned and then gave her a blank look as if he didn't understand the question.

"I know all I need to know about her. She is a blackmailing *morveuse*."

Maggie hadn't heard that word before but assumed it wasn't very nice. She stared at him, trying to decipher the expression of his face.

"Are you sure?" she said.

Laurent stood up and went to where Maggie sat on the bed. He knelt beside her.

"*Chérie*, what happened is just biology. It doesn't make her special to me in any way. She has attempted to threaten the well-being of my family. I want nothing to do with her."

"You're angry now but perhaps later..."

But Laurent was shaking his head.

"There is no *later*. She is *un voleur*. That moment with her mother was a fleeting moment of weakness."

Maggie stared into his eyes and believed him. She believed he didn't want to know this young woman who must be in her early thirties by now. He wasn't even curious.

Laurent could be hard, Maggie knew. And in this case, even the fact that this woman had twenty-three chromosomes from him was no argument in his mind to forgive her for what she was threatening.

One thing Maggie knew about Laurent was that, once crossed, he was unlikely to forgive.

Maggie couldn't say that she herself wouldn't have been curious if the roles had been reversed but she believed Laurent when he said he was not.

She got up and walked to the dresser, her back to him.

"They're going to say it's you, Laurent. In the morning

when the police come, they're going to lay this murder at your feet."

She turned and held out the button in her hand.

"I found it clutched in Esmé's hand."

He barely glanced at the button, then his eyes went to hers, probing. But Maggie was staring at his chest where the missing button should be.

"So however it was that she got this button off you," Maggie said, "people are going to wonder how she could've kept it clutched in her hand while you dragged her down the corridor, threw her into Alex's arms, and then all during having her throat cut."

"I suppose it makes more sense for her to have ripped the button off during a fight for her life, *non*?" he said.

His eyes bore into Maggie's, his face hard and unreadable.

She sighed. "More believable anyway," she said.

Maggie knew it was entirely likely that Esmé hung onto the button once she ripped it off Laurent in an attempt at an embrace. She had been a desperately silly woman looking for attention and affection.

It was also entirely believable that Esmé might have wanted to keep the button as a romantic talisman of her moment with Laurent—even one that had been mostly him attempting to peel her off him.

Yes, to any normal, rational person—even if you'd only known Esmé for five minutes—that likelihood was completely plausible.

But to someone who was trying to find the person who killed her?

To that person, and anyone else without a bias, the button looked a whole lot like evidence.

## 26

The wind was blowing in sharp angry gusts that flapped the wooden sign that read *Dormir* on the front of the house. The rain slashed sideways and thunder rattled the windowpanes in the cozy little alcove.

Grace tried to remember if it had ever stormed this badly in their section of Provence before.

She was sitting in the corduroy club chair with her legs pulled up under her. For it being so late, she was surprised at how wide awake she still was. Even more surprising was the fact that Windsor was so awake too, especially after a seven-hour international flight and a four-hour drive.

She remembered when they were younger how Windsor was always the first to collapse from jet lag. She used to tease him about it. She found it so strange that jet lag didn't seem to bother him now. She wondered what other changes had happened in him that she hadn't been around to witness firsthand.

"I only wish there was some kind of baseball or football outlet around here for Philippe," Windsor said. "It just seems strange that a grandson of mine won't know anything about American football."

"I don't know," Grace said. "Jemmy has lived here his entire eighteen years but he seems to know all there is to know about football. Did you know he's going to Georgia Tech in the fall?"

"Really? That's great. So he's not going to stay on the farm, so to speak?"

Grace smiled. "I think he loves Domaine St Buvard and growing up there, but no, the vineyard isn't his passion."

"You love it here, too," Windsor said. "Provence, I mean."

They had moved on from the leftover wine at dinner to drinking Calvados. Grace was drinking mostly water now and only sipping at her Calvados but she was feeling mellow and relaxed. For once she wasn't running all the chores she had to do the next day in her head. She was happy to just *be*.

"I do," Grace said. "I was pretty lucky that Laurent thought of me for *Dormir*."

It was much more than luck as Windsor well knew, since at the time Grace was systematically blowing up every worthwhile relationship she had.

Laurent had even reached out to Windsor at the time to help facilitate a sort of intervention. Just the thought of it made Grace cringe. She'd come a long way since then. She'd singlehandedly—well, with Laurent's help—pulled herself out of the mire, but then, she'd been the one to burrow herself into the mire in the first place.

"Well, you've done an amazing job with the place," he said, looking around the room and nodding approvingly. "I read some of your reviews online and everybody raves about it."

"You read my reviews?" Grace felt a surprising boost of pride.

As long as she'd been married to Windsor, he had been the breadwinner and she the one who spent the money. Yes, she had style and good taste, but she hadn't really contributed to their family beyond that in any real sense.

For him to be proud of her, gave her an unexpected and very sweet sense of gratification.

The sounds of the rain drumming against the window of the snug alcove produced a soothing background noise to the cocoon of tactile comfort they'd created tonight. She felt mellow and relaxed.

"Philippe will be out of his mind when he sees you tomorrow," she said.

"Me, too," he said.

"But I can't help but wonder why you're here. Is everything okay...at home?"

Windsor looked at her for a moment and blinked and then looked away.

"You always could read me so well."

"What's going on?" she asked.

"I think we're over," he said with a helpless shrug. "Me and Steph."

"Oh, Windsor, no," Grace said. An involuntary warmth infused her body at his words. Her face stayed frozen in an expression of concern but her heart was singing.

Why? Was it because she was so lonely and Windsor had never been lonely for five minutes after their divorce? Is that why she felt shamefully happy at his news?

*Or was it because she wanted him to be available for her?*

Grace straightened her legs out and put her hand to her hair. It was a mess. She'd even laid down with Philippe at one point when trying to get him to sleep tonight. And she hadn't bothered putting makeup on today.

"She's seeing somebody," he said.

"A...a boyfriend?" Grace said.

"No, I mean, like a counselor."

"Oh."

"And I think he's telling her to dump me."

"I'm sure that's not true, Windsor. Counselors work to keep couples together."

"Not always. Not if they think it's not the best case for one party."

Grace shrugged.

"I cheated on her," he said.

Grace was careful not to react but Windsor dropped his chin to his chest in shame anyway.

Windsor had never cheated on her but they'd broken up anyway. They'd broken up even though it was the last thing Grace wanted and she knew it was the last thing Windsor wanted.

"Why?" she asked softly.

"I met someone," he said with a shrug. "Nobody important. Not even somebody I'm still seeing. So it's my fault."

Grace hesitated because they were getting along so well and what she was about to say would take them into dangerous waters quickly.

"I believe that there's usually a reason for why people stray," she said.

"Was there a reason with you?" he asked, his eyes meeting hers directly.

*This is exactly why I should've stopped while I was ahead.*

She swallowed and looked away. "You know there was," she said. "As selfish and stupid as it was."

"I wouldn't call Zouzou a selfish or stupid reason," Windsor said gently.

Grace had cheated on him one reckless night after months of fruitless attempts at seemingly endless fertility treatments.

One night when she was ovulating and he was inconveniently drunk.

Now it was Grace's turn to stare at her hands in shame. She sighed heavily.

"Windsor, what is the point of this? Are you still angry at me? Because you know Zouzou loves you as the only father she's ever known."

"Does she know the truth?"

She threw her hands up in a helpless gesture.

"I don't think there's any point, do you? Connor's dead."

He held her gaze for a moment and then smiled sadly.

"I want you to know I don't blame you," he said. "I know you didn't love Connor. I was just hurt. And now we have Zouzou, our amazing daughter."

Grace pressed her lips together and glanced into the fire in the stove, her shoulders falling.

*A daughter we were not able to share or raise together because of the circumstances of her birth.*

*Or, rather, her conception.*

"And I don't blame you for wanting out of the marriage," Grace said, smiling sadly. "At least, not anymore."

"What a pair we are," he said but his eyes were happy when he said it.

They were the eyes Grace knew so well. They were the loving eyes of the old Windsor who'd adored her beyond reason and who had once vowed never to let her go. They were the eyes of the man she had once thought would forgive her anything and who would always be there for her.

So many years ago.

"I guess I just needed some distance from the whole thing," he said, leaning back into the sofa and dragging his hands through his hair.

Grace wasn't sure whether he was talking about their marriage a decade ago or his current one.

"I'm glad," she said. "A change of scenery can often give you the perspective you need."

"Exactly. So I was wondering, do you have many guests at the moment?"

She was surprised at the change of topic but decided he was probably tired and ready to call it a night. He'd already said he'd stay for breakfast and so likely he was going to make this a proper visit. They still had plenty of time to talk.

And the talking felt so good. Talking with Windsor felt like swan-diving into an oasis after years of bone-dry thirst.

"No, this is our shoulder season. I've got a Canadian couple coming in later in the week. So I've got plenty of room. Laurent built another cottage opposite the pool last year. Did Zouzou write and tell you about the pool?"

She knew she was talking too much about nothing and she knew that was because something had shifted between them in the last few minutes. They'd touched on the very worst and most tender issue between them—and forgiven each other for it—and they were still relaxed and comfortable with each other on the back end.

In one breathless moment, the realization made her see everything she'd been missing in not being with someone who knew her. And loved her anyway.

"She did. I ask because while I'm hoping to stay long enough to spend some quality time with Philippe..." He took in a long breath and stretched his hands out on his knees as if steeling himself. One leg was tapping nervously and he ran his hands through his hair again.

Grace realized she was holding her breath.

"I'm hoping I can talk you into getting back together."

## 27

Maggie and Laurent stared at each other from across the room. She knew that this was the moment when it would be so easy to slip into his arms and tell him she knew it wasn't his fault. It would be so easy to let it all go and tell him they would sort it out together.

A part of her wanted to do just that. She wanted to tell him she believed him and that she knew Esmé hadn't ripped the button off in a death struggle with him. Surely he knew she didn't think he killed Esmé!

But the fact remained she was still mad at him. He'd put her through two months of confusion and worry and one week of downright agony when he'd essentially turned away from her.

She felt the embers of anger being stoked in her chest. She looked away and the moment to come together passed.

"I need some air," she said.

"Esmé's killer is still out there."

"You don't know that," she said putting her shoes on.

"More than likely he's in his room waiting for the cops to come and arrest *you* for the murder."

"I need you to stay here in the room," he said firmly.

"Don't tell me what to do!"

"I only want what's best for you," he said in frustration.

"Well, that's a relief!" she said sarcastically. "Because for the last two weeks you've acted as if I did something wrong! You've barely spoken to me! You've barely looked at me!"

"I am sorry, *chérie*," he said helplessly.

"So, yes, I get it now. You were ashamed. But those two weeks when I couldn't get through to you and I didn't know what the problem was—I nearly drove myself mad! I imagined all kinds of things wrong with us! As evidenced by this stupid, ridiculous weekend I dragged you to!"

Somewhere in the back of her mind, she realized she'd exaggerated the time from one week to two but she didn't care. And he didn't correct her.

"Maggie, please, you have every right to—"

"Don't tell me what my rights are! I know I have every right! I don't need your permission to be pissed as hell at you!" she shouted. "And I need some air!"

She jerked open the door and slammed it behind her. As soon as she stepped outside into the frigid hallway, her flashlight beam darting spasmodically up the granite walls, she felt an instant relief from the overwhelming guilt and anger that swelled behind that room door.

Anger because he'd put her through hell these last days and weeks when it all could've been resolved so easily by just talking with her. And guilt because she knew she should forgive him and get on with it.

And she just couldn't.

Maggie walked down the hallway away from the stairs they had taken to reach the Knight's Hall until she came to another threshold of stairs. These were a set of slick stone steps that twisted downward in a stomach-lurching spiral. Unlike the stairs she'd seen in the abbey so far, this was a Ranulphe staircase, and much more typical of the sorts used in medieval castles and other defensive buildings from that era.

Halfway down the staircase, a vertical slit window gave her a glimpse of the bay on this side of the castle, confirming to her that these stairs led to a perimeter of some kind as well as giving her a sense of how high up their room was. The window wasn't big enough however to allow much of a view. The cold seaward air seemed to flow off it into the stairwell.

She wasn't even really sure where she was going. She just knew she needed to get out. She needed a few minutes where she didn't feel as if she were being buried alive between multiple levels of stone crypts beneath her and several tons of towering rock above her.

She remembered the little stone chapel they'd passed on the way to the abbey earlier this afternoon. If she remembered correctly, it was just around the corner from the main entrance, so probably even closer to where this staircase would let her out.

She pulled the hood up on her rain jacket, knowing it would prove relatively useless in the storm outside but not caring.

She tread as close as she could to the wall of the spiral steps, leaning her shoulder against the wall as she did. A misstep on the more narrow, interior side of the steps would send her tumbling to the bottom. It was amazing to her that monks past of Mont St-Michel managed to live in this place without regularly breaking their skulls. Her shoulder felt the cold of the night transmitted through the castle wall.

There were no lights or torches on this staircase so she used her flashlight to find her way down. The stairs ended abruptly before a rounded wooden fairy door with a modern bar handle and a garish sign that read EXIT. She pushed open the door and stood frozen for a moment staring at the lightning storm exploding in front of her, illuminating the village cobblestone streets and sharply outlining the swinging sign of the sandwich and crepe shop across from her.

The rainwater poured down the center of the street in an aggressive flood, carrying debris and trash. Blinding jags of electricity snapped around her, lighting the scene before her like it was full daylight before plunging it once more into darkness.

She hesitated for a moment and then stepped into the street. She knew the chapel was close. Ten steps at most. The wind grasped her and pushed her down the uneven surface of the village street, the cold rain soaking her hair and face in spite of her hood.

She made it to the door of the chapel and stepped into the vestibule in front of it, breathing hard. Instantly she felt better. It was exactly what she needed.

She had to admit it was heartening to have Laurent switched back "on" but why did it take a family crisis—not to mention a murder—to do it? She felt the threads of anger —the ones that had slowly quieted since she left the abbey —begin to vibrate again.

He had made her think there was something intrinsically wrong with *them*! With their marriage. And all along it was his guilt and indecision over a situation that had happened over thirty years ago. How senseless was that?

But knowing Laurent, it made all kinds of sense. He was a man who cared strongly about protecting and providing for his family. That *he* would be the one to bring turmoil and discord into the union would be particularly agonizing for him. But unfortunately the way he chose to react to it had made it all worse.

Maggie pushed open the heavy wooden door to the inner chapel, unsurprised to find it unlocked.

Inside, the space was as small as she'd imagined. A truncated stone-lined atrium led to a narrow aisle flanked on both sides by four rows of wooden pews. A holy water font in a stone basin was set to her right. Maggie dipped her fingers in and crossed herself before entering.

The altar was spare. There were no windows, no stained glass, no statuary. Just a barebones table and two tall candle holders on it.

Someone was kneeling before the altar, his back to her, the scent of incense drifting lazily around his head. Maggie walked closer, her wet shoes making soft squishing sounds on the stone flooring. Père Jean half turned around but didn't look at her.

She hesitated and then took a seat in one of the pews, her sopping coat creating puddles on the pavers around her. She wouldn't let the priest's presence prevent her from getting what she came for—a little serenity and peace.

She took in a long breath and tried to sort out her feelings. She still wanted to cry and scream and go running out into the storm. But mostly she was angry. The more she thought about it, the more she thought her anger at Laurent was less about him keeping secrets from her and more about him shutting down and keeping her at arm's length when there was a problem that affected them both.

She knew he operated from a different mindset but did

twenty-one years of marriage count for nothing? Had he learned nothing about her in all that time?

She brought his face to mind, the image of his eyes searching hers for forgiveness—the forgiveness she couldn't give—and she tried to see in his face the words he couldn't say out loud to her. When she concentrated, she saw his message to her as clearly as if he had spoken them.

"*I need to protect you.*"

Maggie felt her shoulders slump with the realization. It wasn't something Laurent would ever say to her in words. He would never give any kind of excuse for his behavior. But that didn't make it any less the truth.

Laurent's driving force in life was to protect her and the children. Maggie knew that. In fact, if she knew nothing else about him, she knew that. He was not a coward. He'd kept the blackmail a secret because he was hoping to find an answer that would protect her from having to know and deal with a painful, senseless reality.

If he'd been successful she would never have had to think of Laurent creating a child with someone else. She would never have to think that Jemmy and Mila had a half-sibling that had nothing to do with her.

She smiled sadly. It was classic Laurent. In every way it could be.

Abruptly, Père Jean got up and walked over to her. She noticed his hair was wet. He hadn't been in the chapel long. She wondered what he was doing here. If he was just praying, why didn't he do that in the Mont St-Michel abbey?

"May I ask what you are doing here?" he asked coldly. "Everyone is to be in their rooms."

"And yet *you're* not," Maggie said, stung that he wasn't welcoming, even though she'd just as soon be left to herself.

She saw his face coil into a grimace of displeasure. He

hesitated for a moment and, as if he could read her mind, reluctantly sat down in the pew in front of her.

"Do you want to talk?" he asked, his mouth twisting into a moue of reluctance.

Actually Maggie preferred the silence but she didn't want to be rude.

"It's all pretty upsetting," she said.

He snorted derisively and Maggie couldn't help but wonder if maybe he'd been doing this job too long. He definitely appeared sour about having to give succor to the flock. He turned away from her and stared at the front of the altar for a long moment. She was sure he'd forgotten she was there when he spoke again.

"He brings them in one after another," he murmured. "The crowds of gawking tourists are easier to endure."

She assumed he was talking about Antoine although she wasn't completely sure.

"Easier than what?" she asked, realizing she didn't want to break whatever reverie the priest had retreated into.

His face flushed and he licked his lips as if the words were stuck in his throat.

"The noise," he said. "The incessant, relentless...chatter."

Maggie got a sudden image of Esmé at dinner last night —her mouth full of food as she talked, braying and yammering ceaselessly about some television show she'd watched or some reality star she liked, clinging to Père Jean like a demented sloth.

Maggie hadn't been close enough to get the full brunt of what Esmé had been saying to the priest, but even from the other end of the table she'd gotten the picture and it was hardly pleasant.

"It's enough to make you go mad," he said. "And it's worse when the rest of them are gone."

Maggie assumed *the rest of them* referred to the crush of tourists who helped pay for the upkeep of Mont St-Michel along with the assorted vendors and souvenir shops who fed off them.

"And then the clothing," he said with a shudder. "Or should I say lack thereof? Whorish flaunting, garish makeup—every bit as loud as the relentless noise."

He rubbed a hand over his face and seemed to come out of his trance.

"It's enough to make you go mad," he said again, darting an embarrassed glance at Maggie.

Suddenly he twisted in his seat and Maggie saw that he'd spotted what she hadn't until just this moment. A woman, dressed all in black, stood in the shadows of the chapel vestibule. Maggie leaned forward and when she did she saw her face—a flash of white framed by a dark veil. The nun. Soeur Thérèse.

Now that she got a look at her, Maggie realized this was definitely the woman she had seen standing behind the priest before he went to dinner. The woman was tiny, probably less than five feet.

Maggie nodded at her and tried to smile but it wouldn't come. And that was probably because the nun was staring at Maggie with an intense loathing that made her blood freeze.

## 28

In a very big way Grace felt like she was acting in a play on stage. The whole situation was that surreal. It was that dramatic. It was a moment in life building to a specific denouement. Maybe even one she'd been waiting for her entire life.

Windsor's words rang in her head like the final wonderful pronunciation the main character delivers to thunderous applause from an audience begging for a happy ending.

Was this her happy ending? Finally?

She got up from her chair and came to sit next to him on the sofa. Instantly, his hands were around her waist and he pulled her close and into a kiss that neither of them had planned.

His lips were warm and knowing. The touch of them on hers was like coming home. It was like falling into the familiar warmth of a cozy den—one that she'd been looking for month after month, year after year.

She pulled away, her breath literally stolen from her, and looked into his eyes. His kind, brown, Windsor eyes.

"I can't believe you're here," she said in wonder.

"I can't believe you let me kiss you," he said, his eyes glittering on the verge of tears.

"I've missed you so much, Windsor," she said, feeling her throat close up with emotion. "So much. My past is your past."

She ran her hands down his sleeve and felt the hardness of his arms. That was new. This Windsor worked out. This Windsor was strong.

"I've been thinking about you," he said, "about this, the two of us, for a long time. I think it's half the reason Steph and I...well, I don't want to talk about that. But I swear I'm always trying to find you. In everything I do. In every woman I meet. I've been looking for you since the day I let you walk away."

"Oh, Windsor."

And now the tears did come and yet he kissed her through them.

"I can't believe this," she murmured.

He pulled her deeper onto the couch and she melted into his embrace, his touch, his kiss.

"I can't believe I've found you again," he said, his voice struck with wonder.

"I was here all along," she whispered.

As he leaned in to kiss her again, Grace couldn't help but think that all the terrible dates and stilted conversations and all the Gregors of the world were all behind her now.

Her family was complete now that Windsor was back. She would never have to think about settling again.

She listened to the rain drum on the rooftop over her head and let herself meld into this man she knew so well and loved so dearly, realizing she was finally home and safe for the first time in a very long time.

## 29

Maggie left the chapel, her shoes soundless against the cold slate pavers of the little chapel, past Soeur Thérèse, past the baptismal font, past the outer foyer's recessed statuary of Mary, and outside to the street once more braving the icy rain.

She hurried up the cobblestone road before entering the island fortress through a side door that took her directly to the Chaplaincy by way of a chillingly cavernous hall of stark white stone and soaring arches. She moved quickly to another set of stone stairs.

Breathless, she stood at the top of the landing, surrounded by stonework that seemed to drill the cold of the night straight into her bones. She glanced at the staircase she'd just taken which would take her back to her room and she realized she wasn't ready for Round Two with Laurent.

More precisely, she still wasn't ready to forgive him.

She looked at her watch. It was one in the morning. She didn't feel tired. But she could do with a drink, she decided.

Wondering if there was any unopened wine in the Knights Hall, she made her way back up the Ranulphe staircase and moved quietly, keeping to the shadows in case Antoine was out patrolling to ensure they were staying in their rooms.

Torches flickered along the hall, which surprised her. Who had lighted them? It must have been Père Jean. After all, if losing electricity was that common, he likely had a routine he enacted each time.

Maggie walked down the eerily quiet and dark hall and as before felt the same icy cold pierce her—the same odd cold draft when there was no obvious source for such a thing.

Suddenly she heard a moan. She froze and snapped off her flashlight. Standing in the dark except for the flickering torches, she strained to hear the sound again. She didn't, but she did hear something that sounded like movement across the stone flooring.

Unlike what she thought she had heard during the couples exercise on the dungeon level, this sound of movement was real, she was sure of it.

Taking another tentative step down the hall, she reached the lip of the alcove just before the entrance to the Knight's Hall. Just inside the entrance into the alcove, Maggie spotted Alex sitting with his back against the wall and a bottle of wine between his knees.

Maggie stepped into the alcove. On the table by the door she found a sealed bottle of water. Keeping one eye on him on the floor, she opened the bottle and drank thirstily.

"What do you want?" Alex said sullenly.

"Nothing from you," Maggie responded tartly.

"Hey!" he said angrily, getting to his feet. "What is your problem?"

It *had* been an ugly thing to say and if she hadn't been so tired and upset, she likely would never have said it. On the other hand, she was mildly surprised that Alex was sober enough to register the insult. Was he faking how much he'd drunk?

She turned to him, resting her weight on one hip. She studied him coldly. Alex was the main impasse to Laurent going free tomorrow when the police arrived.

"You were the last one to see her alive," she said.

Alex visibly whitened. He made two tries to put his bottle on the table before he finally succeeded.

"That's not true! I can see why you don't believe me but your husband is lying. I never saw her."

"Laurent was with me. He has an alibi. You don't."

"It's his word against mine. They'll believe me," he said earnestly. "After all, I'm Canadian."

"Are you drunk? Or are you so deluded you think the French cops wouldn't lean in favor of their own countryman against the word of a *Canadian*?"

Alex wrinkled his brow and his eyes darted around the room.

"Why isn't anyone looking at Paul for this?" he said in a whiny voice. "He's the husband. He's the one with the most to gain by Esmé's death!"

"How so?"

He wiped his hands on his pants and reached for another bottle of wine.

"Hadley told someone on the phone last week that Paul had a million-pound life insurance policy on Esmé. Plus there was a prenup that he told Hadley was impossible to break."

Maggie frowned. "A million pounds? Are you serious?"

"He definitely had more motive than anyone else," Alex said, burping wetly.

"Hadley knew about the prenup last week. So you all knew each other before coming to Mont St-Michel?"

Alex looked away to avoid looking into her eyes. "We'd met a time or two."

"Why would Hadley tell a friend about Paul and Esmé's prenup? Why would she think her friend would find that of interest?"

"I don't know why women do the things they do!"

"It's almost as if Hadley had a stake in the prenup. Because why else would she care?"

"What are you talking about?" he said angrily. "Why would Hadley care about Paul and Esmé's prenup? I can see you're desperate to pin this on someone except for the person who did it—*your husband*—but you're nuts if you think my wife had anything to do with Esmé's death!"

"I don't think that," Maggie said.

"I should think not."

"I'm more concerned with why *you* would lie about having been with Esmé. That's the sort of thing a guilty person does."

He took a step toward her, his eyes glassy with anger and fear.

"You'd better stop saying things like that," he said in a low, threatening voice.

Maggie took an involuntary step backward. If Alex hadn't been drunk—if he truly was—she wouldn't have worried, but she knew the restraints that lifted with the application of alcohol.

"If you keep saying stuff like I was with Esmé," he said, taking another step forward with one hand grasping the neck of the wine bottle, "something bad might happen to you."

He took another unsteady step toward her.

"In fact, you might end up just like her," he said menacingly.

## 30

The chill Maggie had felt before was gone and hot blood now throbbed in her face as panic welled up inside her. Hemmed in by the table on one side and the wall on the other, she turned to sprint past him. She made it two steps when she heard Alex's shout of horror followed by the sound of a wine bottle falling and smashing to the stone floor.

She turned and saw Alex gazing at something behind her. His mouth moved as if he was trying to speak but nothing came out.

"Nooooo!" he whimpered before pushing off from the table and careening away from Maggie, knocking her to the ground in the process.

A piece of splintered glass sliced into her palm. But she still turned to see what it was that had so terrified Alex.

The corridor was deserted. One of the torch lamps had snuffed out and a cold, withering breeze slithered down the hall and wrapped its tendrils around her throat.

Swallowing hard, Maggie gingerly tossed away the large shard of glass whose point had sliced into her slacks at the knee but hadn't cut her. She carefully pulled herself to her feet and took a quick inventory. Except for her hand, she was unharmed.

Reaching for a stack of paper napkins on the table to wrap around her hand, she stopped for a moment to listen to the overwhelming silence all around her and looked again down the darkened corridor behind her.

What had he seen? What had made him run away?

*He's drunk and seeing things.*

She took in and let out a long breath to steady herself but felt a frisson of fear pierce her. She was suddenly overcome with a nearly irresistible urge to run. She inhaled again deeply and gripped the edge of the table to anchor her in place until she could recover her equilibrium.

*What did he see that made him run?*

Within seconds of taking in long measured breaths, Maggie found she was no longer convinced Alex had meant to attack her. Yes, he'd appeared threatening. But he was drunk.

*She wondered* briefly about the possibility that he was much more unbalanced than anyone really knew. As she was considering this, she became aware of voices from across the hall. It seemed that she and Alex weren't the only ones flaunting Antoine's edict to all stay in their rooms.

Maggie shakily drank the rest of her water before crossing the hall to enter the dining room and the source of the voices. When she entered, she was astonished to see not only Laurent sitting in one of the dining room chairs, his leg across his knee and a glass of whiskey in one hand, but everyone else there too.

Like it had been at dinner, the room was basically unfurnished except for the dining room table and eight Parsons dining chairs set around it. There was no carpet or wall tapestries in the room to add warmth to the austere stonework or muffle voices or chairs scraping on the stone floors.

Maggie had no doubt that this room would give her goosebumps even in the height of summer. In autumn on a rainy cold night, it was just short of macabre.

Someone had lighted more candles and positioned them around the room. Alex was now slumped in a chair in the corner with yet another bottle of wine in his hands. His face was white and he was moving his lips as if talking to himself.

Hadley and Paul sat at the dinner table across from Antoine.

"Please join us," Antoine said as Maggie stepped into the room. "It seems nobody wants to be alone tonight."

Maggie walked over to the table and was surprised to see that Père Jean and Soeur Thérèse were also in the room, their dark clothes blending with the dark tapestries and paneling of the room.

Maggie walked over to Laurent and took a seat beside him. His eyes flicked to her bandaged hand, but his face was intractable. He made a barely discernible movement with the hand that held his drink—an invitation—but Maggie shook her head.

"We were just talking about the argument that we all heard your husband and Esmé have last night," Paul said as he locked eyes with Maggie.

"I heard it, too," Alex said, slurring his words. "I heard Esmé shouting at him to leave her alone."

"You're lying," Maggie said. "You're trying to distract everyone from the fact that you were the last one with her."

"You're the one who's lying!" Alex said heatedly.

"Alex, don't," Hadley said. She looked at Paul and then back at Alex, her face showing her dismay.

"Hadley and I definitely heard the two of them arguing," Paul said.

"Then you must have been closer to where Esmé was killed than you've admitted to up to now," Maggie said.

Paul blinked in surprise and his eyes tracked back and forth as if trying to think of what to say to that.

"Your husband was shouting at Esmé," Hadley said. "We heard it from a long way off."

"My husband doesn't shout," Maggie said.

"Even so," Antoine said as if attempting to play the peacemaker. "Noises carry in this place."

"No kidding," Jenny said as she stepped into the dining room from the hallway. "I thought we were all supposed to be in our rooms until the cops came?"

"Plans change," Antoine said brightly. "Take a seat, Jenny. It looks like we'll be keeping an eye on each other until morning."

Jenny went to where Alex sat with his bottle.

"Do you mind?" she said sourly.

He handed her the bottle and she went to the table and poured wine into one of the water glasses. She sat at the table and ran a tired hand across her face.

"Okay," she said. "So now what?"

"Now we get our phones back," Hadley said to Antoine.

"Hadley," he said. "I told you—"

"Just give them back, Antoine," she said tiredly.

"Look, I can't, okay?" he said, looking around the room. "I...I lost the key to the safe."

There was a penumbra of silence before Hadley spoke. "You're lying."

"I'm not!" Antoine said indignantly. "I swear."

Hadley stood up. "Then give me your phone. I know you didn't lock *it* up."

Antoine pulled his phone out and set it on the table.

"The battery's dead," he said.

*And we have no electricity to charge it*, Maggie thought.

"I don't believe this," Paul said as he gaped at Antoine. "How did you lose the damn key, for God's sake?"

"Look," Antoine said, appeasingly, leaning forward and getting eye contact with each of them. "We'll get a locksmith in the morning. It's nothing but a minor complication."

Suddenly the room was rocked by a deafening explosion of thunder. Everyone jumped and Hadley and Jenny both squealed in panic. The candle lights flickered as if a wind had swept through the room.

"This is inhuman!" Hadley said petulantly. "I can't believe we have to endure this!"

"It's just a storm, darling," Paul murmured to her.

Maggie watched Alex turn his head to Paul and Hadley as if seeing them for the first time. He seemed to struggle to focus on them, his face creased in a baffled frown.

"Is there any food?" Hadley asked, turning to look at Père Jean and the nun.

The priest looked surprised to be addressed and looked around the room hopefully for someone else to take the question.

"The housekeeping staff attends to that," he said.

"Yes, but the housekeeping staff isn't here, are they?" Paul said.

Maggie watched Père Jean and Soeur Thérèse from where they sat in the near shadows, the flickering candle-light moving across their faces. In spite of that she noticed their twin expressions of revulsion as they listened to their guests.

"This is ridiculous!" Hadley said petulantly. "So we're just going to stay here all night without food? With a murderer on the loose?"

"You and Paul are welcome to go back to your room," Antoine said, his tone light.

Since everybody with the possible exception of Alex had to be aware that Hadley and Paul had effectively paired off, all heads turned to Alex to see how Antoine's words would be received.

Alex blinked in confusion and drunkenness. "What's that?" he said.

"Antoine was just pointing out that your wife and Paul want to be alone," Laurent said, surprising everyone including Maggie.

Alex looked at Laurent and then a shaft of awareness broke through the fog.

"You bastard!" he said to Paul, sitting up straight, his eyes glassy with anger. "I should kick your ass!"

"Oh, calm down, Alex," Hadley said, glaring at her husband. "You're embarrassing both of us."

"No, no!" Antoine said excitedly, scooting his chair closer to the table and leaning toward Alex. "Go with that, Alex. Tell us how you feel."

"I feel like punching you in the nose!" Alex said, turning to Antoine, his face twisted in anger.

"Why are you encouraging this destructive macho BS?" Jenny said to Antoine. "Do you *want* bloodshed? Or are you just a sick voyeur?"

"Don't speak to me like that," Antoine said, his face stitched in angry indignation. "You are not a part of this."

"Well, it certainly feels like I'm a part of sitting up all night waiting for the cops to come since one of your party killed another one of your party!" Jenny hissed.

Père Jean stood up. After a brief hesitation, Soeur Thérèse stood too.

"Please," Père Jean said. "This behavior is unseemly. You forget where you are."

"And *you* forget that evidently one of us is a killer," Hadley said hotly.

She turned and pointed her finger at Laurent.

"Still waters may run deep but I know what I saw," she said. "Everyone saw it! Esmé was climbing all over you. Tell them, Paul."

Paul made a face as if embarrassed.

"Yes, well, Esmé *was* very needy," he said.

He glanced at Antoine. "It was one of the things we...she was trying to work on."

"I'm not saying Esmé was asking for it," Hadley said, twisting in her seat to nail Laurent with a cool, indicting gaze. "But she was definitely asking for *something*. And I think we can all agree that the last person to lay eyes on her was the one who gave her a little more than she bargained for."

## 31

For a moment the only sounds in the room were the inexorable battering of the storm outside. There were no windows to reveal the inescapable lightning outside over the marsh but the crash of thunder continued to thrum ominously under the layer of panic and fear in the room.

Maggie was also aware of the combined smell of stale food, alcohol and body odor in the room. No, it wasn't unwashed bodies she was smelling, she realized. It was fear.

"*Nobody* knows what happened," Maggie said to Hadley. "Except for the killer. So unless you want me to bring a suit of slander defamation against you when the cops come, I'd shut the hell up."

"How dare you speak to me like that?" Hadley said shrilly, looking at Paul as if expecting him to step in.

Paul rubbed his face with both hands and leaned his elbows on the table in a picture of exhaustion. He had, after all lost his wife tonight, Maggie reminded herself.

"Look," Antoine said as Père Jean and Soeur Thérèse

made their way out of the room as silent as two wraiths. "We should all go back to our rooms and try to get some rest."

"I think that's a great idea," Jenny said, picking up the half full wine bottle. "And in case the killer is listening, I have a double deadbolt on my door."

"Nobody wants to kill *you*, Jenny," Antoine said with a sigh.

"Yes, well, the *killer* would say that, wouldn't he?" she said, arching an eyebrow at him. She backed out of the room slowly before turning and hurrying down the hall.

"I suppose we should try to get some sleep," Paul said, standing up.

Hadley got up too and looked over her shoulder at Alex, who had done a miraculous transformation from being on the verge of punching Paul in the face to falling into nearly an unconscious state, sprawled in his chair, his head bobbing unsteadily on his shoulders.

"Leave him," Antoine said to Hadley. "He'll sleep it off."

"But what if...?" She looked at Paul and then Antoine before looking meaningfully at Laurent.

"You can't be serious," Maggie said to her. "What possible reason would Laurent have for wanting to kill your moron husband?"

"Maggie, please," Antoine said, grimacing. "It's not an indictment of Laurent. But it will make everyone more comfortable if you would both go to your rooms."

"Thank you, Antoine," Hadley said as she hugged Paul's arm tightly.

The two of them stopped long enough to gather up a couple of wine glasses.

Wordlessly, Laurent got to his feet and Maggie impulsively touched his arm. He turned to look at her and reached out to put a hand to her cheek.

"However you get there, I don't care," he said in a low voice. "Just as long as you end up where you belong."

"Excuse me, you two," Antoine said, clearing his throat. "I'll feel better if I can confirm to the police that I saw everyone go to their respective rooms. It's for your sake as much as anyone's."

Maggie turned to Laurent. "You go on," she said. "I want a word with him. I'll see you back at the room in five minutes."

She could tell Laurent didn't like that and she saw the force of will it took for him not to argue with her. But he nodded, giving Antoine a not-so-veiled look before leaving the dining room.

Antoine blew out a few of the candles on the table and stood waiting for Maggie at the entrance. She walked over to him at the door but didn't exit.

"I overheard you make your recording for the police saying you think Laurent is the killer," she said, her voice tight.

Antoine took a step back and blinked rapidly.

"How could you possibly..."

Maggie watched him put the pieces together to come to the realization that she must have been near when he revisited the crime scene.

"Look, I'm sorry you heard that," he said, "but I only said what I believe to be true."

"So you saw Laurent kill her?"

"Of course not. But he was the last one with her."

"He told you that he swapped Esmé for me before the exercise began."

"Alex denies that."

"Well, he would, wouldn't he? If he killed her?"

"Why would Alex kill Esmé?"

"Why would Laurent?"

Antoine clenched his jaw in frustration.

"Look, I appreciate your position, Maggie. Of course you'd defend your husband. But ask yourself, how much do you really trust him? Did he not have a secret love child that he kept from you?"

Maggie felt her body tense in fury.

"How dare you? Maybe I'll come to this international symposium of yours as a walking testimonial of your crackpot methods! Secret-drugging, name-calling and shaming—all obviously acceptable tools in your marital counseling toolbox. Wonder what your peers would have to say to that?"

His face whitened.

"I trust my husband," she said. "Let's leave it at that. You, however, drugged us without our knowledge, lied about there being no cell phone reception, and instead of letting the evidence speak for itself, implicated Laurent in a murder you know nothing about. That is, unless you know more than you're saying?"

"What is that supposed to mean?" he said, a dribble of perspiration forming on his top lip.

Maggie realized that his affect had changed dramatically in the last few seconds. He'd gone from affable charismatic leader to guilt-ridden, suspicious victimizer in just the time that they'd stood talking.

*Good. Let him stew about it.*

"Oh, by the way," she said. "I think I have a phone charger in my bag." She held out her hand for his phone.

His face tightened.

"I'm sorry, Maggie," he said. "I can't let a suspected murderer have access to a phone."

"I told you! Laurent was with *me*. Esmé was with Alex."

"I know that's what you said but that's not what I saw with my own eyes. We all saw Esmé leave with your husband."

Maggie could see Antoine was unmovable on this point and something nagged at her to wonder why.

Why was he so determined to believe that it was Laurent who killed Esmé? If he really knew nothing about what happened, why wouldn't he be open to hearing all the evidence before making up his mind?

There was something under his words—something that, when Maggie had touched on it, he'd reacted as if burned. But what that something was, Maggie could only guess.

And unfortunately, guesses were not going to keep Laurent from being arrested tomorrow morning for first degree murder.

## 32

When Maggie tapped on their room door Laurent opened it as if he'd been standing on the other side, waiting. She stepped inside, but not before noticing how tired he looked. His shoulders were rounded, looking like he was bearing up under the weight of a tremendous burden. She hesitated at the sight of him, her heart reaching out to him in spite of herself.

Her emotions must have shown on her face because he reached for her and pulled her into his arms. When she felt his arms, firm and secure around her, Maggie realized with a shock that it had been weeks since he'd held her. She knew the reason for that was because he'd been ashamed and the easiest way around *not* feeling that way was to keep her at arm's length. She should know him by now.

She should have understood before now what she'd been seeing in his behavior. How could she be married to him for so long and not know how to handle his occasional tendencies?

The strength of his arms around her made her want to

collapse into him and let him carry the weight, just carry the full weight of the responsibility for fixing them.

But that's exactly what he *had* been doing. And that was partially why they were in the spot they were in right now. To some degree this whole mess was the result of Laurent deciding he didn't need anyone's help.

She knew him that well. He'd wanted to fix the problem without her involvement because he felt it was his fault. And he didn't want her hurt.

She pulled out of his arms and looked up at him.

"Sometimes I try to imagine what marriage might be like with someone who actually spoke to me," Maggie said. "I try to imagine how things would be different if I didn't always have to interpret your grunts or decipher your silences."

He stepped away from her and then turned his back.

"You see? Just like that. *I* see that we're having a conversation but *you* only see that you're being attacked. And so you retreat."

He stopped at her words but didn't turn around.

"I can't believe you have a child that we don't have together," she said. "I can't believe I have two kids and you have three."

She knew there was no point in saying these things but if communication was their main problem how wrong could talking be? Unless she was talking just to hurt him? She felt a sliver of guilt and then weariness.

How could two people be so different? She would always say the things that didn't need to be said and he would always keep inside all the things that did.

"Whatever," she said, knowing it was a trigger word with him.

She found she really wanted to pull the trigger.

He turned and looked at her, a frown on his face.

What was he thinking? That she had every right to be angry? He'd already said that and she'd taken his head off for it. That the words she spoke were factually true? Again, not an argument. That she was trying to lay a belief at his feet that wasn't his? He'd already said he didn't regard Élodie as a real daughter, biology or not. So why had she stated that she was?

*Because I'm angry and I'm hurt.*

And maybe Laurent was right not to speak. Because what was there to say when your wife was just lashing out to inflict pain without really trying to communicate?

Maggie turned away, not ready to hear the truth—even when it was her own conscience speaking it.

"I talked to Père Jean," she said instead, walking over to the bed and kicking off her shoes and stripping off her outer jacket.

He sat down on the bed. "Yes?"

"He sounds pretty bitter," she said. "There's a story there."

"Where did you speak to him?"

"At the Chapel of Saint Peter on the main drag of the village."

"You left the abbey?"

She glanced at him. "I thought I'd go pray for the state of our marriage."

It was only a gentle jape and, to Laurent's credit, one edge of his lip twitched in a hint of a smile.

"He really hates all the noise that Antoine's groups bring to his sanctuary," she said.

"Then why not kill Antoine?" Laurent said.

Maggie blinked at the idea. "Good point, but a better one might be why *only* kill Esmé? I would've thought living in a place full of tourists all day long would be enough to drive anyone to murder."

Laurent watched her as she slipped out of her slacks and folded them to hang on the back of the room's desk chair. The rip in the knee was barely noticeable.

"What happened to your hand?"

Maggie looked at the cut on her palm. It had stopped bleeding.

"I tripped," she said.

He held her gaze for a moment. She knew he knew she wasn't telling the whole truth. It was a small lie. A lie of omission.

*Laurent's favorite kind.*

"Soeur Thérèse said Père Jean locks himself away when the tourists come," he said.

"You talked to the nun?"

He shrugged. "In passing."

That surprised Maggie. The few rare sightings she'd had of the woman, she couldn't imagine having a conversation with her, even *in passing*. Maggie remembered the glare that the woman had bestowed on her in the chapel.

"You think there's something going on between her and the priest?" she asked.

Laurent arched an eyebrow at her.

"It's just that when I was talking to him," she said, "Soeur Thérèse came in and she *really* didn't like him talking to me."

He narrowed his eyes and he frowned deeper.

"I guess I'm just groping in the dark," she said as she got up to pull a towel down from the shelf in the room's armoire. "Either one of them could've killed Esmé. They were practically the only people in the whole abbey not stoned out of their heads."

"That is not much of a reason for suspecting them," Laurent pointed out.

"I don't know," she said, with her hand on the bathroom door. "I guess I'm not in the mood to give anyone a pass. Even a priest or a nun."

Whatever faint tincture of forgiveness that she thought she'd mustered for Laurent and the problem he'd brought to their doorstep had gone.

She hated that she was doing this but she couldn't help it. Just when she and Laurent really needed to turn toward each other for comfort and support, all she wanted to do was slam a door in his face.

∽

Laurent stared at the closed door for a few seconds and listened to the sounds of the tub being filled. He imagined what Maggie was doing—he'd seen her fill a bathtub many times over the years.

Of course she was hurt. He could only imagine how *he* might feel if the situation were reversed. But he also knew that stoking her reasons for anger only caused the fire to get bigger.

*She cannot doubt my love. This is her hurt feelings speaking. She cannot seriously believe I have interest in being with anyone else.*

Yes, they were different. And always that difference made their passion for each other all the more exciting. She could always surprise him. He loved that about her.

Yes, he was at fault. No question. But part of what he needed to do to fix the problem was to not allow Maggie to explore the full range of her rampant American willfulness.

Not when they would both regret it later and be no closer together.

He stripped off his sweater and tossed it on the bed. He stood by the bathroom door and thought he heard her humming on the other side. He was about to open the door when he heard a gentle tapping on their room door.

Frowning, he went and opened the door.

Soeur Thérèse stood on the doorstep, her eyes wide with misgiving as she stared at him.

Laurent was used to people being intimidated at his size. Normally it worked to his advantage. But at the moment, the woman look frightened.

"Soeur Thérèse," he acknowledged.

"You must come," she said.

The sounds of Maggie in the bathtub seemed to oscillate in his ears as if obliterating all other sounds.

"Now is not a good time," he said.

"You must come, Monsieur," she said earnestly, tugging on his sleeve with a gnarled hand. "Because I know who killed her."

## 33

"Laurent?" Maggie called from the bathroom. "Is someone here?"

Laurent realized too late that the sound of the water running the bathtub had stopped.

"Meet me at the base of the Black Madonna," Soeur Thérèse hissed. "Five minutes! *C'est urgent!*"

She turned and slipped into the dark hallway just as Maggie opened the door of the bathroom.

"Who were you talking to?" she asked, stepping into the room, a large towel wrapped around her.

Laurent closed the front door.

"Soeur Thérèse," he said, eyeing Maggie's state of half dress.

She saw his look and quickly went back into the bathroom.

"What did she want?" she called through the door.

Laurent waited until she reappeared so he wouldn't be talking to her through a door. When she appeared again she was fully dressed.

"You are not going to bed?" he asked.

"What did she want?" Maggie asked again as she pulled on her socks.

He sighed. "She said she knew who the killer was."

Maggie stopped dressing.

"Who?"

"She didn't say. She asked me to meet her at the statue of the Black Madonna." He looked at his watch. "In three minutes."

Maggie slipped on her shoes and grabbed her coat from the chair.

"I'll go," she said.

"She wanted *me* to come."

"Yes, but *you* are not believable," Maggie said and then stopped as if realizing how that must sound. "I mean, whatever she tells you, nobody will believe because at the moment you're the prime suspect."

"And you are the wife of the prime suspect. Why would your word be any more believable?"

"Maybe it wouldn't," Maggie admitted. "But it should be me for no other than reason than I can follow her without being seen easier than you can."

"I don't like you going out without me."

"Duly noted," Maggie said, as she put her hand on the doorknob.

"What you are doing is not helping anyone," he said. "You know that, yes?"

"I'm trying to find out who might have killed Esmé so that *you* don't end up in the back of a police van tomorrow morning," she said testily.

"That's not what I'm talking about as you well know."

He reached out to take her arm but she shook off his grip.

"I don't want to talk about the other stuff right now," she

said. "What I want is to consider the possibility of a future where I'm not visiting you in a maximum security prison for the sole reason that it would be highly embarrassing for me, not to mention hugely inconvenient."

His eyes glittered briefly with amusement as he regarded her.

"What I know," she said, ignoring his smile, "is that Soeur Thérèse seemed super jealous of anyone who gets anywhere near Père Jean and I saw Esmé gushing all over him at dinner last night."

"You think the *nun* killed Esmé?" he said, his tone clearly skeptical.

"I'm not asking you to believe it," Maggie said. "But that's what *I* saw and that makes Soeur Thérèse a suspect in my book. Plus, *she* wasn't drugged tonight *and* she knows all the secret passageways. She could easily have popped up in the dark corridor, killed Esmé and disappeared without a trace."

"Père Jean knows the passageways too."

"Yes, but I seriously doubt Soeur Thérèse intended to lead you to evidence of the killer if it was Père Jean. Although frankly, I suspect him too."

Laurent threw up his hands in frustration.

"*Vraiment?*"

"Think about it, Laurent. Père Jean hates everyone but particularly loud women and their loose morals."

"If that is the case then why not go after Hadley? She is much more provocative than Esmé."

"In your mind, maybe. But it doesn't matter. The fact is, we're grasping at straws. But if I don't go now, I won't find out what Soeur Thérèse wanted to show you."

They stared at each other, at an impasse. Finally, he turned and walked to the dresser where he picked up Antoine's laminated map.

"Do you know where the Black Madonna is located?" he asked.

Maggie held out her hand for the map.

"I'm sure I can find it," she said.

"Be careful, *chérie*," Laurent said, handing her the map and fighting the urge to pull her into his arms and away from the cold, dark corridor outside.

"I'm always careful," she said as she tucked the map in her jacket and slipped out the door.

## 34

The stone castle stairwell seemed colder and even lonelier than it had thirty minutes earlier when Maggie had hurried down from the top floor of the abbey. There was a pervasive smell of blood and something rotting that she hadn't noticed before. She pinched her nose to mitigate the stench but it was still there.

Maggie knew her bravado with Laurent had cost her precious minutes in warmth and comfort in which to study the map but she hadn't wanted him to see her hesitate lest he mistake it for lack of conviction.

She and Laurent had worked as a team on projects before—not the least of which was raising their children—but it had always been an effort to convince Laurent to allow her to pull her own weight. And as wildly unbelievable as it might seem to him, there were actually a few things that she did better than he.

She paused in the hallway beneath one of the torches and shivered. She'd changed into a pair of jeans and a turtleneck under her jacket. It wasn't warm enough but would help keep her dry. She'd only brought two pairs of shoes for the weekend and the more casual ones—a pair of leather moccasins—were still wet from her walk from her walk to the abbey from the taxi earlier. But they were certainly more appropriate for tonight's mission than the kitten heels she'd worn at dinner.

She pulled the map out of her pocket and quickly found where the guest rooms were located. She then traced her finger from them to the floor where a small icon of the Blessed Virgin and Child was drawn. It was on the bottom level of the abbey, just above the main floor, near a chapel called Notre-Dame-Sous-Terre.

Maggie shivered again. Literally translated: Notre-Dame-Sous-Terre meant Our Lady of the Underworld. A caption underneath the icon on the map read: *This is the oldest part of the monastery. From the first millennium.*

Maggie felt her scalp prickle. She jammed the map back in her jacket pocket and hurried around a tight corner to the first set of stairs that led downward. How much time did she have left? Were the three minutes up? Surely Soeur Thérèse would be waiting at the statue of the Black Madonna.

Both the dungeon and the Chaplaincy were on the same level, just below everyone's rooms. Maggie walked down the stairway touching both sides of the walls to keep tripping on the slippery steps.

Once she reached the next level an abruptly frigid breeze sidled around the corner and drilled into her, making her gasp.

Where was the cold coming from? Was she really that close to an exterior door or window? She was tempted to look at the map again but decided she couldn't waste the time. And in the end the source of the mystery breeze didn't matter. Not unless the unseen cold air really was the spirit of thousands of tortured souls attempting to catch her attention, in which case she really had bigger problems than being late for her rendezvous.

She turned another corner and stopped. The passageway forked into two corridors. One led in the direction of the Chaplaincy and the other to the dungeon. Maggie noticed that one of the avenues was still lighted by at least one flickering torch. The other was completely dark.

She pulled out the map after all and studied the position of where the Black Madonna was supposed to be.

*Damn. Naturally, it's down the corridor with no light.*

She stuffed the map back in her pocket and pulled out her penlight. Its beam was too insignificant to properly light her way, but it might at least keep her from falling down a hidden staircase or tripping over any debris. She continued walking, the wavering beam of light weakly probing the darkness before her.

She took several more cautious steps when she was startled to see a large wooden carving appear on one of the walls. She squinted at it. It was a design of some sort. She took a step closer. What was its purpose?

*Was it even real?*

She had no idea how intense or prolonged the residual aftereffects were of the drug she'd taken.

Finally, stepping past the odd carving, she continued on down the darkened corridor and began to feel the corrosive beginnings of unease.

Would Soeur Thérèse really have wanted to meet Laurent here?

Forcing herself to push down her mounting fear, and now beginning to feel like she was in danger of missing the nun altogether, Maggie continued to inch her way down the dimly-lit corridor which, with every step felt more like an abandoned vault or catacomb than a passageway.

She heard a noise that made her stop cold. She stood wavering, one foot down, the other with only her toes touching the floor. She held her breath, straining to hear the sound again, but all she heard was the sound of her own heartbeat thundering in her ears.

Should she call out?

Something told her not to. Something deep in her gut told her to stay quiet. To wait.

Slowly, she depressed the button on her penlight and the light blinked out, plunging her into darkness. She tried to control her breathing as she waited and listened.

Suddenly she heard a rustling sound, the sound that long skirts make in movement—*like a nun's habit*. She let out the breath she'd been holding.

"Soeur Thérèse?" Maggie called softly.

The rustling sound stopped.

The creeping idea that she was in some kind of stand-off came over Maggie, making her turn her light back on and take another two steps forward into the darkness.

*The Black Madonna should be right here!* Maggie thought in rising frustration as she traced her tiny flashlight beam along the walls.

She took another step but suddenly the floor wasn't there. Scrabbling for purchase with her hands on the stone walls, she dropped the flashlight and lost her footing.

She landed hard on one knee. Cursing as the pain jolted up her leg. The cause of her stumble was a missed stair riser, no more than a few inches, but in the dark sufficient to do the job.

She picked up her dropped penlight which was now blinking. Did that mean the battery was running down?

She felt a wave of frustration as she thought of how she'd insisted on going instead of Laurent and now she was going to have to go back and say she hadn't found the nun.

*Stupid!*

She stood up. Her knee was tender and would likely be bruised. She turned to go back when her flashlight beam illuminated the form of something up ahead. She tilted her head as if that would help her see better. After a brief hesitation, she took another step forward.

It was the Black Madonna.

It stood directly in front of Maggie at eye level. Mary, in a sweeping cloak held the Christ Child in her right arm. Both figures were dressed in gold, both held their hands out in welcome or supplication.

Maggie felt goosebumps pebbling up and down her arms. She went to the statue and ran the flashlight beam over both their black-skinned faces, both pairs of eyes looking past her as if staring beyond the secular world into the underworld.

*Mont Tombe.*

Maggie swallowed hard and the prickling sensation on the back of her neck returned.

*Stop it. Stop seeing ghosts where none exist!*

She swept her beam around the base of the statue. It was perched on a small stone stand. There was no sign of Soeur Thérèse anywhere.

*Where is she?*

Assuming the nun must have tired of waiting for Laurent, Maggie cursed the fact that she had missed her opportunity to find out what the nun knew.

Just as she was about to head back the way she came, Maggie realized that instead of the pounding of her heartbeat she'd been hearing in her head for the last several minutes, she was actually hearing sounds of the storm through the thick stone walls.

*Is that possible?*

She ran her light beam along the walls, looking for a window or door or even a fissure that might explain what she was hearing when she saw a recessed wooden door tucked behind the Madonna statue.

The sound was coming from behind the door.

Was it an exterior door? She pulled out the map again and put her finger on the spot where the Black Madonna was located.

No. She was clearly standing in an interior corridor well away from any outside walls of the abbey. Looking more closely at the map she saw that just behind the icon of the Black Madonna was a small box with the letter *C* written on it.

She looked at the map and then at the door.

C for *Cellier*? The dungeon.

She took a step closer to the door behind the statue and when she did the sound she'd been hearing became louder. She caught her breath at the raised volume. What could it be? What was making that sound if not the storm outside—which wasn't possible?

Before she knew she was doing it, Maggie placed both hands against the door. Instantly she felt a vibration begin in her fingers and radiate up her arms. She snatched her hands away as if burned, dropping her penlight when she did.

It wasn't the storm she was hearing.

It was the *sea*.

The modulating sounds of the waves as they came roaring in, crashing against the door, and then receding were now unmistakable.

Suddenly she heard a different noise under the thundering hum of the ocean that made her arms crawl. She jumped away from the door, her heart in her throat.

It was a moan.

A human sound.

A sound of surrender.

Maggie stared at the door. Had it come from behind the door? Was that possible?

She knelt and snatched up her penlight and shined it on the handle of the door. It was rusted iron, and archaic. Its latch was lodged firmly in a metal catch. A key was in the lock but when Maggie tried the handle, she found the door locked.

Why was it locked? Did that make sense? You lock a door from the inside to prevent people from getting in. You lock a door from the outside *with a key in the lock to prevent people from getting out.*

She shook the chilling thought from her mind. It didn't matter how it was locked. If the sound she'd heard belonged to a person she had to get inside.

The sounds of the sea seemed louder now that she knew what they were. The noise seemed to pound in her head matching the waves rising and falling behind the door. She put the penlight in her mouth and focused its beam on the long rusting handle of the door. Her hands were shaking badly as she grabbed the key in the lock and twisted it. It turned easily.

It wasn't until she pulled open the heavy door that it occurred to her that the door might actually be *holding back* the sea. But the sound of that moan, so hopeless and bereft, resounded in her brain and she was already committed with her momentum.

The door pulled open outward nearly yanking her off

her feet—as if something was pushing it open from the other side.

The smell of mold and rotten fish poured out of the room in a thick fetid blanket, settling heavily on Maggie. Her stomach roiled. The dark walls inside the dungeon were cracked and scabbed with mildew. Rusting lengths of chain hung from the walls. Across from the threshold where she stood was a wide window with only iron bars against the wind and rain.

The sea was pouring in.

The freezing cold slammed into her where she stood. Gulping in air and fighting her growing foreboding and the urge to slam the door shut and run, Maggie aimed her light with shaking fingers around the enclosure.

The beam was too weak and only illuminated a small strip of dark water surrounded by the black stone walls which stretched to an invisible ceiling.

"Hello?" she called, hearing the sound of her voice ricochet around the walls before it was drowned in the cacophony of sea sounds as they ebbed and flowed.

She swallowed hard and felt for the door behind her with one hand. The need to run, to bolt from this noise, this place of death, was overwhelming.

That's when she saw it.

Moving in the water. Moving with the direction of the waves as they gushed into the room and dashed against the slimy stone walls.

No, not moving, she realized as she looked, hypnotized by the motion.

She took an involuntary step forward into the room, her shoe sliding perilously on the wet stones. She narrowed her eyes, trying to make out what she was seeing.

Not moving. *Floating.* Like a huge, black amoeba or jelly fish.

She held the penlight out in front of her, her eyes blinking against the sea spray until she could make out what it was she was seeing.

It was the black undulating cloud of a nun's habit.

# 35

Maggie leapt into the swirling water as it churned and crashed against the scum-lined walls. Terror and hopelessness warred inside her as she splashed in the freezing water, reaching for the woman she knew was there.

Her fingers felt the solid flesh of an arm and Maggie grabbed it with both hands, pulling it to her, fighting the water and the billowing, water-soaked fabric that enveloped the body.

Working quickly, Maggie eased Soeur Thérèse into the swimmer's contact tow position. With Soeur Thérèse's head tucked in the crook of one arm, she side-crawled to the stone stairs that led to the door. She had the nun's face tilted up and out of the water but Maggie couldn't tell if she was breathing.

How long had she been in the water?

As soon as her hand touched the stairs, Soeur Thérèse jerked out of her arms. The impact of the wave crashed into them both.

"No!" Maggie shouted, her voice lost in the bedlam noise

of the cavernous room. She floundered desperately in the rippling waters to recapture the body but it was too dark, she could see nothing.

"Maggie!"

She snapped her head around at the source of the voice and squinted into the blinding flashlight beam that Laurent held focused on her. He stood on the steps. Beside him, she saw the motionless form of Soeur Thérèse.

Maggie swam for the stairs as a tremor of emotions and exhaustion rattled through her. When she reached the steps, she found herself too weak to pull herself out. She clung to the slimy steps as a wave crashed over her and she felt her fingers slip. Then she was moving too, but it wasn't the wave that had her. It was Laurent. She felt her body being lifted and dragged up the stairs.

He deposited her away from the edge and gave her hip a pat. She turned her head, too exhausted for speech to see that he was kneeling beside Soeur Thérèse's body.

As soon as he lifted a section of the woman's hair from her face Maggie saw the gash on her forehead. That was when she began to shake, from the cold, the exertion, and the realization of what had happened.

"She was unconscious when she went into the water," Laurent said.

The bile burned in the back of Maggie's throat as she envisioned someone attacking Soeur Thérèse. In her mind's eye she saw the nun pushed unconscious into the dungeon as it filled with water.

And then the door was locked to prevent her escape.

"We have to…we have to give her…" Maggie stuttered as she crawled to where Soeur Thérèse lay.

"Maggie no," Laurent said. "It's too late."

"No, it isn't!" she said, pushing the nun's hair, now free of its cowl, off Soeur Thérèse's face. Maggie saw the wound no longer bled but it gaped like a hideous rouged smile. "I heard her call out!"

"*Chérie, non,*" he said, grabbing her shoulders.

She felt his hands large and warm through her wet jacket.

"She has been dead nearly an hour," he said.

Maggie rubbed her eyes as another uncontrollable shudder swept through her.

"That's impossible!" she said as she stared at the body with its blue lips and unseeing eyes. "She moaned! I heard her!"

Had it really taken her that long to find the Black Madonna? How could it have been so long? Who had moaned? What had she heard?

Maggie covered her face with her hands and burst into tears. Immediately she felt Laurent pull her into his arms.

"I can't have been gone that long," she said in between sobs. "It doesn't make sense."

"You were, *chérie*," he said. "It's why I came looking for you. You've been gone an hour."

Maggie pulled away and stared at him in disbelief.

How could that be? Residue of the drugs? She'd entered the corridor and it must have triggered a flashback of when she'd been in the halls before. She thought back and realized that she'd come down the stairs and seen the carving outside the chapel of Our Lady of the Underground. She thought she'd only glanced at it in passing. Now she realized she must have stopped and stared at it for much, much longer.

"*You* should have gone to meet her," Maggie said, her eyes filling with tears. "She'd still be alive if you had."

"Shhh, *chérie*," he said. "We don't know that."

"They're down here!" Paul's voice shouted out. "I hear them!"

Suddenly Maggie realized how this was going to look to the rest of them—both her and Laurent kneeling by yet another dead body. She gave Laurent a stricken look. But he looked calm. Or was that *resigned*? she wondered with a sinking heart.

Paul was the first to appear. He stopped when he saw them but didn't move any closer.

Behind him came Père Jean, Antoine, Hadley and even Jenny. Père Jean pushed past the others to where Soeur Thérèse lay. Later Maggie would note that he hadn't looked surprised to see Soeur Thérèse dead at their feet.

"This is all my fault," Père Jean said under his breath in French as he knelt by the body and took Soeur Thérèse's hands in his.

"Oh my God!" Hadley screeched. "Oh, my God!"

"Dear Lord," Paul murmured in horror, his eyes riveted on the black unmoving form of the nun.

"Is...is she dead?" Jenny asked as she edged closer, a flashlight in her hand, her face white with horror.

"All right, everybody," Antoine said. "Let's all stay calm."

"How did you know we were here?" Maggie asked them as Laurent pulled her to her feet, his arm warm and supporting around her shoulders.

"Paul and I were taking turns keeping an eye on your door," Antoine said as he glanced at Laurent.

"When I saw your husband head out, I alerted the others and we followed him," Paul said, glaring at Laurent.

The priest was still holding Soeur Thérèse's hand, his head bowed, his lips moving in soundless prayer.

"Is it...do you think she committed suicide?" Hadley

whispered loudly, stepping closer to the body, her eyes round.

"She has a head wound," Maggie said. "She was thrown into the dungeon to drown." She turned to Paul. "Just like the story you told about prisoners being executed."

His body stiffened in indignation. "What are you insinuating?"

"I think I'm being pretty clear," Maggie said.

"You are freezing, *chérie*," Laurent said as he began to prod her down the corridor toward the stairs.

Hadley, shivering in her long cloak, clapped a hand to her mouth and looked in terror at Laurent.

"Oh my God," she said. "Antoine's right! He's done it again!"

"D-don't b-be ridiculous," Maggie said, stuttering in the cold. Her hands and feet were numb. If it weren't for Laurent practically carrying her, she knew she'd never make it back to the room on her own. "He w-was with me the whole t-time."

"That's a lie!" Paul said. "I saw him leave your room *by himself* not twenty minutes ago."

"This is terrible," Antoine said, shaking his head as he looked at the body.

"Wh-where is A-a-alex?" Maggie said.

She was now trembling so violently that she could barely get the words out. Laurent rubbed his hands up and down her arms and continued his progress of easing her toward the stairs.

"Don't you dare try to pin this on Alex!" Hadley said. "He's sound asleep under a table somewhere. How dare you!"

"I...I just can't b-believe any of this is happening," Jenny stammered as she stood with her back against the wall, her flashlight beam on Père Jean and the body of Soeur Thérèse.

"Somebody...one of you...is...is..."

"Settle down, Jenny," Antoine said. "There's no point in over-dramatizing."

"Don't tell me to settle down!" Jenny screamed. "*You* brought these people here! And now they've killed Soeur Thérèse!"

"Everyone be quiet!" Père Jean said suddenly, his voice like ice as he turned to them. "If you're afraid," he said to Jenny, "go to your room. Why do you keep leaving it?"

Then he turned to Antoine. "Help me get her upstairs."

"Are you sure we should move her?" Hadley asked. "Won't the police be unhappy about that?"

"She's already been moved," Paul pointed out staring meaningfully at Laurent.

"We can't leave her here," the priest said firmly. He turned to Antoine. "Help me."

"Yes, of course. Paul?" Antoine said.

Paul knelt by the body and between him and Antoine, they lifted Soeur Thérèse up in their arms. She was weighed down by her water-logged clothing and heavy wool habit. But she was a small woman.

As Maggie watched them, her stomach churning, she wondered if the moan she had heard had been before Soeur Thérèse had gone under for good. She tried to remember how much time she'd wasted from the moment she'd heard that sound until she got the door open.

Was it longer than she thought? Could she have saved her? Was Laurent right and she'd been dead even before Maggie heard the moan?

"I want to know what you're going to do about all this!" Jenny said to Antoine. "There's a killer in our midst!"

"And we know who it is!" Hadley said, looking at Laurent.

"Someone should lock him up!" Paul said, as he grunted under the weight of lifting Soeur Thérèse's body.

But of course nobody would have the nerve to try to take on Laurent, Maggie knew. Laurent was easily a foot taller than any man here and he was fit. If nothing else, the two run-ins he'd had with Alex and Antoine would certainly discourage anyone who contemplated trying to subdue him.

Maggie let Laurent pull her behind him as the men carried the body past them, past the Black Madonna and toward the stairs.

When they passed, Maggie heard Paul ask why they couldn't just take her to the chapel around the corner. But whatever Père Jean said in reply—Maggie hadn't been able to make out the words—had ended the argument.

The three men, turned toward the stairs with their burden and began the long trudge up to the abbey church on the top floor.

As she and Laurent followed them up the stairs, Maggie trembled in the cold. As she watched the three men stagger up the narrow stone steps with their heavy load, she suddenly noticed with a start that, unlike everyone else, Paul's clothing was soaking wet.

## 36

Once back in their room Maggie began removing her wet clothes. As she did she felt a pain develop in the back of her throat as guilt washed over her.

If she'd let Laurent go, Soeur Thérèse would still be alive. Regardless of what Laurent said, she knew that was true. Whoever had lured the nun into the dungeon and then subdued her so that the tide rushing into the room could finish her off—that person wouldn't have dared to hurt Soeur Thérèse if Laurent had been nearby.

Plus he would have gone straight to the meeting place, Maggie thought. He wouldn't have stopped to stare for fifteen unbelievable minutes at a stupid wooden carving—something that probably didn't even exist!

Maggie realized that in addition to the rain pounding against their window she was hearing a shower running. Laurent came into the room from the bathroom, a towel in his hands.

"Come," he said. "Get the rest of those wet things off. God only knows what was in that water."

"It's only seawater," Maggie said dully as she stood up wearily from the chair and walked slowly to the bathroom.

"You couldn't have saved her, *chérie*," Laurent said as she passed him. His hand gently touched her face. "There was nothing anyone could do."

She didn't believe him, but she nodded anyway. He handed her the towel and she went alone into the bathroom.

A quarter of an hour later, Maggie sat on the bed—dressed now in a pair of sweatpants and a sweatshirt—towel drying her hair while Laurent lighted candles on the dresser. They both knew they wouldn't sleep. Not tonight. The police would be here in a matter of hours. And one way or another their nightmare would either be over. Or just beginning.

Maggie tried to determine by the sound if the storm was letting up, but it was impossible to tell. The rain was still coming down in torrents. The lights were still out. Their phones were still inaccessible.

"They really want to hang this on you," she said as she sat on the bed, the damp towel in her hands.

"It's not personal," Laurent said with a shrug. "They just need for it to be someone."

"Who do you think it is? Who would do such a thing? To a *nun*?"

He frowned. "You think the same person killed both Esmé and Soeur Thérèse?"

"Don't you? Seems a little coincidental for there to be *two* homicidal killers in a group of six. Chances are Soeur Thérèse either saw the first murder or the killer somehow found out that she had evidence against him."

"You are sure it is a him?"

"Not at all. On the other hand, there *is* an argument for two killers if the second killer saw his or her chance to kill because there had already been one killing and he or she thought his crime would be attributed to the first killer."

"A logical supposition, *chérie*."

Maggie stared at him and noted again that he looked weary, which was unusual for Laurent. He was always the last one to tire out. In fact, he never did. She patted a spot on the bed. He came and sat beside her and took her hand.

"We've been through so much, Laurent."

He made a noise that she normally found impossible to decipher, but tonight she actually understood it as some sort of concurrence.

"I remember when I found out that you and I were actually related by marriage," she said. "Remember that?"

"Of course."

"And then when I found out that Roger Bentley was scamming my dad? That he knew Nicole wasn't alive but he still took my dad's money?"

*But you knew that too.*

"It was a tragedy," Laurent said. "But our Nicole, the one we love and who is a part of our family..." He held out his hands as if the universe could finish his sentence, so obvious was it that the Nicole they knew and loved was the right one for them.

"Yes, I know," Maggie said sadly. "I love her too. *Our* Nicole as you say."

*But she isn't Elise's daughter.*

Laurent was right about it being a tragedy. Although the real Nicole was dead, nobody had murdered her. Roger Bentley—and to a certain extent Laurent—had merely taken advantage of an existing bad situation. It was what they did in those days.

And the little girl that they'd found—an abused waif belonging to no one—was today the young woman the family knew and loved.

She was the young woman that Mila and Jemmy knew as their cousin. She was also the young woman who would never have had a chance at college or any kind of a decent life if not for what Roger and Laurent had done all those years ago—pawn off a foundling on an unsuspecting stooge with more money than sense: Maggie's beloved father.

She and Laurent sat quietly for a moment while they listened to the relentless rat-a-tat-tat of the rain against the windowpane. She squeezed his hand.

"So many secrets over the years," she said.

*And lies.*

He nodded and then pulled her into his arms. Maggie embraced the familiar scent of him, the comforting strength of his arms around her. *This* was who she married, she reminded herself. A man with secrets. A man who protected his loved ones using those secrets.

"You need to tell Luc," she murmured into his neck and she felt him nod.

"I know," he said. "But not on the phone."

"Go to Atlanta and tell him."

*If you can. If you're not in prison for murder.*

She felt the muscles in her legs tighten at the thought. She had been trying to push that piece of the nightmare away, at least for now. Because in the end, if she accepted Laurent for who he was—and hadn't she always, really?—then she knew his hesitation to tell her about his daughter was not true deceit.

It was just Laurent trying to protect what was his. Maggie and the children.

"We've come so far, you and me," she said.

He pulled back to look into her eyes. One end of his mouth twitched.

"If Mila didn't succeed in driving us to the brink of madness," he said, again leaving the rest of his thought clear if unspoken.

"And now she wants to be a part of the wine business," Maggie said, shaking her head in wonder. "And all we had to do was not kill her for the year that she was such a little monster."

"I am sorry, *chérie*," he said.

Tears stung her eyes.

"It's not your fault. It was just...I hated your having something that we didn't have together."

"*Je sais*," he said. "But we are not going to adopt this puppy, eh?" He narrowed his eyes at her. "This is not like Luc. This is a cancer to be kept away from our family. Far away."

Maggie tried to read his eyes, so dark and unreadable.

"If you're sure," she said.

"I am."

"Where does she live? The girl?"

Laurent snorted.

"I don't know. But the mother is in prison."

Maggie turned to him in surprise. She hadn't expected that.

"Whoever the girl is," Laurent said, "she and the mother are two of a kind."

"What is she in prison for?"

"Does it matter?"

He released her and went to the dresser where he brought back two bottles of water. He was perspiring lightly and wiped his forehead with the back of his hand.

Maggie sipped her water and watched him. She felt the

flood of love she had for him swamp her in every corner of her being.

Would he go to prison? Was the evidence against him strong enough to indict him?

Maggie remembered that the button she'd pried out of Esmé's hand was still on their dresser. Her own hand itched to go find it and throw it out the window into the sea.

"You are all right, *chérie*?" Laurent asked, frowning at her.

She nodded, feeling not at all *all right*. In one terrible flash of insight, she had a premonition of her life without him.

What would she do? Where would she go?

Luc and Jemmy were in the States along with her mother and Nicole. Would she have to sell Domaine St-Buvard? Move in with Grace and Danielle? Go back to the States with Mila?

A sour taste developed in her mouth at the thought and she found herself twisting her wedding ring on her finger in agitation. She looked up to watch Laurent as he resituated the candles on the dresser. She studied his profile, serious but calm, and realized that the very idea of a life without him was unimaginable.

## 37

Grace didn't actually sleep. She and Windsor moved to her bedroom where she listened to the pounding of the rain against the roof and he held her in his arms. She reveled in the nearness of him, the very fact of him, feeling his skin against hers, smelling his scent—so familiar—until she could just imagine she would ever get enough of him. It was like the interim years had never happened.

Like she had never lived in Paris and met the wrong man—so many wrong men. Like she had never lost custody of Zouzou or her friendship with Maggie for two long years.

Instead she'd always been wrapped up in the arms of this good man who'd always adored her and had only ever wanted to make her happy.

Her mind continued to reel against the background sounds of his burring snores—so familiar to her although it had been more than a decade since she'd heard them—and the feel of his breath against her cheek.

Finally, when there was a bare glimmer of light

attempting to break through the gray downpour outside, she slipped out of bed and dressed. Turning back to look at him in her bed, she thought how natural it looked—him there. Where he belonged.

When was the last time she'd had an experience like this where she felt satisfied and truly content after a night of passion? Ever?

She turned to go to the kitchen where she put the water on for coffee. Windsor would be fending off the vestiges of his jet lag for several more hours. She glanced at the clock. It was not quite four. Too early for Philippe and possibly even for Danielle.

She would have an hour to herself. An hour with a mug of freshly-brewed coffee staring out the kitchen window into the sodden garden as she watched the dawn evolve into another day, as the softened rays crept over the lawn, touching the dwarf boxwood and the flower beds, and lighting up the gold and crimson leaves on the oak trees that lined the driveway.

Imagine, she thought as she hugged herself. Just imagine never having to go on another date again. Imagine never having to endure another painful introductory litany of personal history from one more man whose background was as long and painfully convoluted as hers. And weren't they all? If they were looking for love at this age?

*This is why people need to fall in love young*, she thought as she poured herself a mug of coffee and stirred a dollop of fresh cream into it.

*Because once you're in your forties you've got too much baggage to unpack—or hide.*

She went to the little sitting alcove and collected the liquor glasses from last night, bringing them to the kitchen before coming back and deciding to start a fire in the room's franklin stove. It was a rainy chilly autumn morning and she could think of few things more exquisite than curling up with a mug of coffee, a small crackling fire in front of her and the heavens pouring down all around her own little garden of Eden.

*Would he move here? Surely he knows I can't leave. What about little Peoria? Dear God, did they really name her that?*

She sipped her coffee and watched the fire and the rain outside the window. She tried to remember the last time she'd felt so content, so satisfied with life.

So happy.

*Does happiness really just come knocking on your door in the middle of a thunderstorm? Is that why I never found it up to now? Was I looking in the wrong direction?*

She heard a shuffling noise but knew immediately it wasn't Windsor or Philippe. She glanced again at the clock. Four-thirty. Danielle didn't typically sleep for long. Grace was glad she'd built the fire. That, and the aroma of the coffee in the French press would draw Danielle into the little sitting room.

The cozy little room had a set of tall French windows that opened onto a stone slab terrace shaded in summer by a pergola draped with wisteria. Grace watched the leaves swirl and dance on the terrace in spite of the drizzle. She could see the black branches of the mimosa trees over the garden shed as they waved in the breeze.

She'd proofed cinnamon rolls the day before so that she could bake them this morning. She'd smiled as she thought of the household waking to the fragrance of caramelizing cinnamon. She wouldn't put the rolls in the oven too soon. She didn't want their enticing scent to wake Windsor before he'd had his rest. But neither did she want him to sleep too late either. And of course Philippe loved warm cinnamon rolls.

"You're up early," Danielle said, moving into the cozy alcove, her coffee in her hand. "And you made coffee."

"Sleep well?" Grace asked.

"Well enough." Danielle took her spot in her armchair near the stove. "The worst of the storm has moved on."

"You'd never know it," Grace said.

She felt as if she were vibrating with her news. Could Danielle tell? Could she tell that the world had changed?

"My bedroom radio said the storm is still stalled on top of Mont St-Michel," Danielle said.

"Ugh, that's awful," Grace said, feeling an odd disconnect with Danielle. Was it normal for them to discuss the weather at such length? Was there a tension between them?

"Maggie and Laurent sure picked a great time to visit," Grace said.

The silence grew between them until Danielle cleared her throat.

"That was a surprise seeing Windsor last night," she said.

"It was," Grace said, wondering why she felt suddenly on edge. "I think he's having some trouble at home."

"Ah." Danielle set her coffee mug down and picked up her knitting from the basket by her feet. "I noticed you didn't put him in the blue guest room."

"No," Grace said. "There didn't seem much point."

Danielle looked up at her.

"Are you sure you know what you're doing, *chérie*?"

Suddenly Grace saw the situation from Danielle's point of view. Of course Danielle wouldn't want Windsor to move in here and change the balance of their living situation. Or, God forbid, maybe she was worried that Grace would pack up and head back to the States! Naturally Danielle would be insecure about the kind of cataclysmic change bringing Windsor into their lives would generate.

Grace bit her lip. How to alleviate Danielle's worries? What words could Grace say to temper the older woman's concern when the fact was, she *didn't* know exactly what she was doing?

She saw that Danielle was watching her. Waiting for an answer.

"You know me, Danielle," Grace said softly, her eyes going back to the sight of the rain-soaked garden. "I'm not all that sure about anything."

"That's *not* what I know about you, *chérie*," Danielle said. "You are a strong woman who has done a difficult thing."

"What? You mean run a Bed and Breakfast?" Grace said with a snort. "Plenty of people do that."

"No, *chérie*, I'm not talking about what you have done at *Dormir*. I'm talking about the long road you have come from where you started. And no, not a lot of people could do that."

Grace gazed at Danielle and then suddenly reached out and took the older woman's hand.

"Thank you, Danielle," she said, her eyes misting with tears. "It's just that sometimes I get so tired, you know?"

"Of course, I do."

"And I'm not ready to be alone."

"I don't wish that for you, *chérie*." Danielle squeezed Grace's hand. "I wish you joy and excitement with a man who loves and thrills you."

Danielle's eyes filled with tears and Grace realized she was talking about Jean-Luc. The two of them had loved each other for nearly a lifetime before they finally got together.

And while their time together was short, oh, how happy they had been for that short time.

Grace smiled sadly and turned back to the rain where she tried to see her future as a strong woman whose children had left the nest and whose heart no longer longed for what she couldn't possibly have.

## 38

The candlelight in the bedroom flickered, creating a stuttering effect around them. Maggie sat on the bed and watched through the small bedroom window as great sheets of rain, propelled by the still-howling wind, hurled against the windowpane. The incessant thunder rattled the glass in the pane over their bed.

"We need to do something, Laurent," Maggie said, feeling an urgency begin to throb tightly behind her sternum. "The cops will be here soon and Antoine is going to throw you under the bus and everybody here is going to help him do it."

"What do you suggest?"

"I suggest we find who killed Esmé and Soeur Thérèse before they come."

"Do you have any guesses?"

"Maybe. Do you remember...did Paul come with Antoine and the others to the dungeon?"

Laurent frowned as if thinking. "No. He arrived first."

"Don't you think that's odd? He and Hadley have been inseparable."

Laurent frowned. She noticed he had a bead of sweat on his forehead.

"Does it matter?" he asked.

"I don't know. It's just that when Paul and Antoine were carrying Soeur Thérèse out, I noticed that Paul's clothes were wet. Why would his clothes be wet?"

"He could have been out in the storm."

"Maybe. Or he could've been in a dungeon half-filled with seawater bashing a woman over the head before leaving her to drown."

"You think Paul killed Soeur Thérèse?"

"Well, think about it. If he killed Esmé—and unlike the others he had plenty of reason to—and if Soeur Thérèse saw him, he'd be motivated to kill her."

"How would she see him?"

"Are you kidding? She was always skulking around. And she knows all the secret passageways."

"Okay," Laurent said, his tone dubious.

"Plus, remember it was Paul who told that terrible story about how prisoners were executed by letting them drown in the high tides coming into the dungeon."

"But why would he tell that story if he intended to do it himself? Surely that would be very stupid."

"Or perhaps he gave the idea to one of the others?" she said. "We still don't know where Alex was during the time Soeur Thérèse was killed."

She knew she sounded as if she didn't have a clue. But that was only because she didn't.

"Do you have any idea where Soeur Thérèse was leading me other than the Black Madonna?" she asked.

He shrugged.

"The Black Madonna is not really near anything," he said. "Except the dungeon."

"Where is the Black Madonna in relation to the church?" she asked.

He frowned.

"It's up another two levels. But," he conceded, "not far from the stairs. Do you think she intended to lead me to the church?"

"Didn't Antoine say all the religious members have their private quarters there?"

"*Oui*. In the refectory."

"So maybe she wanted to lead you to her quarters where she had evidence to show you."

"I suppose we will never know now."

Maggie nodded, her mouth a line of determination. But Laurent knew her well.

"*Chérie, non*," he said firmly. "You are not going to her room."

"Oh, hell, yes, I am. It's not dangerous."

"A second woman was just killed! No. I forbid it."

Maggie grinned. She had to admit she used to always find him fairly adorable when he got all macho, especially since, after twenty years of marriage she couldn't remember a single time when his blustering had ever amounted to her actually obeying him.

She moved over to where he sat in the room's occasional chair. She thought he looked a little flushed.

"I can't believe Hadley accused you of killing Soeur Thérèse," she said.

"She is just afraid."

"Or she has something to hide. The real killer would try to implicate other people in order to cover his or her trail. Honestly, you don't look so great, Laurent."

He was pale and a thin dribble of perspiration had made its way down from his scalp to his chin. Maggie tried to remember the last time she'd seen him looking ill. She put the towels aside and sat on the bed.

"I am fine," he said as he used his sleeve to wipe the sweat from his face.

"Remember how you noticed there was mud on the floor by Esmé's body?" she asked.

"Yes, but it was raining."

"Which would account for it being wet but not muddy. And there's no nearby access to the outdoors from the crime scene."

"You are thinking someone came in from the outside?"

"They could have come through a secret passageway to the spot where Esmé was killed."

"Wouldn't the mud have rubbed off by the time they made it through the passageway?"

"Many of the passageways have a combination of dirt and stone flooring. Those would have stayed muddy."

"Who from the outside would want to kill Esmé?"

"I think a better question," Maggie said, "is *who is now inside the abbey who shouldn't be?* You heard Antoine say this place was a labyrinth of secret passageways and hidden rooms."

Laurent appeared to be struggling to keep his eyes open. His cheeks glistened with perspiration.

"It's just a theory," she said. "I've got nothing really to base it on."

"Except the mud at the crime scene."

They were silent for a moment.

"I keep wondering if I could have gotten to her in time," she said softly. "I heard her moan."

"It was too late, *chérie*."

"Maybe," she said and then reached out to take his hand. It felt warm. Too warm.

"You look terrible, Laurent."

"I don't feel wonderful."

Could Antoine have drugged him again? For what reason? But that was obvious. Nobody in their right mind would be up to the task of approaching Laurent in order to tie him up. And locking him in his room was useless since all the rooms locked from the inside. Plus, in that case, they'd have to lock Maggie up too.

No, drugging him would be a surefire way to keep him safely restrained before the police came.

Maggie stared at Laurent as he drifted off to sleep or unconsciousness, his breathing slowing as he did. Her stomach roiled in dread as she squeezed his hand and watched the fluttering in his eyelids as they slowed the deeper he fell into sleep.

One way or the other, it looked like she was on her own.

## 39

Pellets of ice pinged and rattled against the window faster and faster until they sounded like machine-gun fire. The dull rumble of thunder boomed out across the marsh, obliterating the noise of the hail.

Maggie watched Laurent as he slept in the bedroom chair. He seemed comfortable and his breathing was regular.

It had to be Antoine who was responsible. She needed to find him to see what it was he'd given Laurent. She prayed that the fact that they were nowhere near a medical emergency department didn't end up proving disastrous.

Restlessly rubbing her hands against her sweatpants, she got up and laid a hand on Laurent's forehead. It was damp but not too warm. Deciding that had to be a good sign, she blew out the two candles on the dresser but left one lit by the bed. She didn't want him to awake in the dark and she couldn't leave their only flashlight since she would need it.

After one last look at him, biting her lip in worry and

apprehension, she slipped on her sodden moccasins and stepped out into the hall.

Instantly the cold pierced her. She wore Laurent's heavy Barbour jacket because her own jacket was still too wet. Laurent was a big man and his jacket dwarfed her, but it was better than nothing. She hurried down the narrow stone hall until she came to the first guest room door.

She rapped on the door and hunched inside Laurent's coat against the cold.

The door swung open, but instead of Antoine, Paul stood in the doorway with a frowning Hadley behind him peering at Maggie.

"Yes?" he said coldly.

"I am looking for Antoine," Maggie said, realizing that these two had clearly decided not to bother hiding what they were doing. She wondered again where Alex was.

"Well, Antoine is not here," Paul said as he shot an arm out to close the door in her face.

Maggie jammed her foot in the door.

"Why were you wet?" she asked.

He looked at her, his face a mixture of guilt and indignation.

"What the hell are you talking about?"

"Tonight, when we found Soeur Thérèse your clothes were wet."

"Dear God! Are you still trying to hang this on anyone besides the one who did it?" he said crossing his arms in a clear attempt to intimidate her.

"Oh, tell her, Paul," Hadley said as she moved beside him in the doorway. "She's only trying to help her husband."

Maggie noticed that Hadley had changed her clothes. In spite of the night's catastrophic events, she looked amazing in a black velveteen unitard. Her cloak, still settled around her shoulders, made her look like a heroine straight out of a seventeenth-century romance novel. Something tugged at the base of Maggie's brain as she looked at Hadley's cloak, but she couldn't put her finger on what it was.

"I was *wet*," Paul said dramatically, his voice laced with sarcasm, "if you must know, because I was up in the cloister looking for Hadley and I got caught in the rain."

That sounded plausible. Maggie certainly had no way of proving that what he said wasn't true. She felt her throat constrict in disappointment.

"And *I was* in the cloister," Hadley said, "because I have a disgusting nicotine habit and that's the best place to indulge in it without offending everyone. Happy?"

"Where's Alex?" Maggie asked.

"He's in our room," Hadley said, pursing her lips in impatience. "Asleep."

"Are we done?" Paul said to Maggie, his hand on the door handle.

Maggie couldn't help but think that if this self-important ass *was* the killer—and he had more motive than anyone—she couldn't waste an opportunity to ask him the hard questions. It might be her only chance and she would bet the cops wouldn't bother once they had Laurent in handcuffs.

She didn't expect Paul to break down and tell the truth —certainly not in front of his girlfriend –but she had to at least try.

"Rumor has it that Esmé had a life insurance policy for a million pounds," Maggie said. "The cops will find this out, you know."

Paul's face reddened and he curled his hands into fists by his side.

"It doesn't matter what they find out if there's no physical evidence linking me to her murder," he said coldly.

"What about your prenup?"

"How...how did you hear about that?" Paul said in surprise.

"Alex told me," Maggie said. "It seems he overheard Hadley telling a girlfriend."

Paul turned to face Hadley.

"You *told* people?" he asked, his voice incredulous.

"Was it a secret?" Hadley asked innocently. "I didn't mean anything by it."

"Well, it wasn't for public consumption. Who did you tell?"

"Just a girlfriend. I'm sorry, darling, if I spoke out of turn."

"We'll discuss it later," he said stiffly. Maggie watched Hadley's face whiten at his tone.

"Can I ask where you two were during the time of Esmé's murder?" Maggie asked.

"You can't be serious," Hadley said. "You know we were together."

"The whole time?"

"Yes, the whole time!" Hadley said. "We were only about thirty minutes into the exercise before all the screaming started."

Hadley blushed at her word choice and glanced nervously at Paul. *When all the screaming started* would be the moment when Esmé's bloodied body was discovered. And it was Hadley's husband Alex doing the screaming.

Paul pulled Hadley close to him and kissed her on the forehead before turning to Maggie.

"Do you have to go around upsetting everyone?" he said, his eyes narrowing at her.

"You don't look particularly upset to me, Paul," Maggie said.

"How dare you!" Hadley said, blinking back tears. "He lost his wife!"

"It's all right, darling," Paul said to her, as he patted her shoulder. "She's desperately trying to find someone else to fit the bill for Esmé's killer because she knows the police will be here in a matter of hours to arrest her husband."

Hadley looked at Maggie with what Maggie thought was a glimmer of sympathy in her eyes before she looked at the floor, all the while holding tight to Paul's hand.

"This whole weekend has just been a nightmare," she murmured.

Paul turned to Maggie.

"Which is why I must insist you leave now," he said. "We both have alibis. We were nowhere near where poor Esmé died."

"Yes, but you were both drugged," Maggie said. "So you can't say for sure in a court of law that you were with each other every minute."

"Oh, I think you'll find we can," he said smugly.

"Well, that's perjury," Maggie said. "As I'm sure your lawyer will explain to you."

"If I were you," Paul said, a flash of anger in his eyes, "and you're looking to pin this on someone other than your husband, I'd start with Alex."

Maggie glanced at Hadley who had snapped her head up to look at Paul in surprise.

"Alex denies being with Esmé last night," Maggie said, glancing between Hadley and Paul.

"Have him take a lie detector test," Paul said.

Hadley put a hand on his arm. "Paul, don't."

"What exactly would his motive be for killing *your* wife?" Maggie asked.

"I'm no psychiatrist but perhaps he was angry at her

because he thought she couldn't keep her husband engaged," he said.

Maggie stared at him in disbelief.

"You're suggesting that Alex blamed *Esmé* for you and Hadley getting together? And so he killed her?"

Paul smiled at Hadley and they joined hands, gazing moonily at each other.

Maggie turned and left before she threw up what little dinner she had managed to eat.

## 40

After leaving the canoodling lovebirds, Maggie went to the next door down the hall and knocked. No one answered. It was either the room where Alex was sleeping—too soundly to hear the knocking—or it was Antoine's room who was either not there or was refusing to answer the door.

She stood for a moment in frustration before turning away. When she returned to the door of her own room, she hesitated. It occurred to her that now was as good a time as any to go through Soeur Thérèse's room. Or she might track down the priest to find out where *he* had been during the critical hour.

Her stomach clenched at the thought of questioning Père Jean as a suspect in Soeur Thérèse's death. He'd looked devastated when he found her on the stones outside the dungeon.

On the other hand, she'd had some experience with killers who had no trouble pulling off a bereft and devastated look in order to save their skins.

Plus, Père Jean *had* gotten to the scene of the crime very quickly and had gone straight to Soeur Thérèse.
*Almost as if he already knew she was dead.*

Deciding to check on Laurent before she climbed the four hundred plus steps to the refectory where she assumed Soeur Thérèse's personal quarters were, Maggie let herself back into the room and saw that he was just as she'd left him, sitting slumped in the chair, his head thrown back, his eyes closed.

She went to the bathroom to fill a small bowl with tap water that she brought back a washcloth to where he was sitting.

His breathing was slow and regular which reassured her, but he lay perfectly still, one arm thrown across his forehead, obscuring his eyes.

He stirred and groaned slightly. The heat seemed to come off him in almost visible waves but when Maggie gently pulled his arm away from his face, his skin felt cool.

She held the cool cloth to his forehead and he stirred again, his eye lids fluttering as if attempting to come to consciousness.

As she gently sponged his face, she found herself remembering those days so many years ago when he had first come into her life.

Except for the few threads of silver that shot through his thick brown hair—and the fact that he no longer wore it to his shoulders as he had when he was younger—he looked exactly the same. The strong, proud jaw, the straight Gallic nose and long lashes.

She remembered the exact moment she'd met him twenty-one years ago in Cannes at the *Gray d'Albion* Hotel. She'd gone there in a fluster of gut-wrenching, emotional upheaval to find her sister's child, Nicole, and to bring home Elise's body from France. She remembered the combined agony of guilt and helplessness as she sat at the breakfast table on the terrace of the *Gray d'Albion* working with her contact in France—Roger Bentley—a man hired by her father—and as sly and conniving as any conman working the French Riviera.

Except for possibly Laurent.

She smiled wistfully as she remembered when Laurent appeared that day, looming over her breakfast table—a complete surprise in so many ways. He'd affected not to know much English—a lie, as it turned out—and which had made him all the more mysterious to her.

*Plus, it's hard to question someone you don't think speaks your language.*

Laurent frowned and Maggie put the back of her hand to his forehead and watched his grimace dissolve at her touch. She went to the bathroom where she found the small jar of Tiger Balm she always traveled with. She dipped a finger into the sharply pungent ointment and dabbed it lightly on his temples.

Even in his sleep, he wrinkled his nose at the strong smell. She smiled. He'd never allow her to put it on him if he were conscious.

So strong-willed, taciturn, resolute, and stubborn.

Even in the beginning, which was mired in lies—so many that any normal woman would've run for her life when they all began to be revealed—his eyes had held a truth that she had believed.

*Isn't that why he avoided eye contact with me these last weeks?*

*Because I'd have known in a flash that it wasn't us that was the problem.*

She got up and went to the window and stared out at the night's sky. The rain thrummed against the small window, deep-set into the stone walls.

And when she'd taken that incredible, unpredictable step to believe in him despite everything, their life together had truly begun.

They'd gotten the vineyard and then their precious babies in short order. Their life together in France had taken shape and when it did, it was bigger and more extraordinary than she could ever have imagined.

They'd believed in each other through it all, trusted each other. Through Bentley's constant attempts to lure Laurent back to his old, criminal way of life, through Maggie's father's Alzheimer's and subsequent slow, heartbreaking demise, through the moment when they'd stood shoulder to shoulder and finally told Nicole the truth about who she was—or in her case, who she wasn't.

And through all of it, they'd been, if not exactly of one mind, then at least of a similar enough mind to support and bolster the other.

Through every step of the way it had been Laurent working to take care of them all. To protect them and keep them whole and safe.

Maggie walked back to where he sat in the chair and sat down in the chair opposite him, her hands on his knees.

It was the reason he'd been so frustrated when Jemmy and Mila both rejected the future he'd created for them.

She picked up the washcloth cloth again. And it was also the reason, in the end, why he'd accepted their choices too.

And now he'd discovered that he'd done something a long, long time ago that he was not only being called to task for—but even worse, in his mind—he was being forced to risk all he'd built and all he valued.

Maggie brushed the hair from his eyes, still long, if no longer worn to his shoulders. Those shoulders that had carried so much without complaint.

And now? She looked away from her sleeping husband and felt a burgeoning sense of determination. Now he needed *her* to protect the family.

*I need to get a confession from the killer before the storm allows the police to breach the castle's defenses. Otherwise, I am going to lose Laurent.*

It was as simple as that.

She stood again, suddenly too antsy to remain seated. As tired as she was, she needed to think. She needed to see what she wasn't seeing. She needed to make sense of the clues that were right in front of her. Her eye went to the travel alarm clock on the nightstand. It was four-thirty in the morning. That meant she had less than two hours before it was all over. She rubbed a hand over her face.

*Think! Think!*

Who could it be? Her recent conversation with Paul and Hadley had been worse than useless. Paul—who had all the motive she could wish for—appeared relatively clueless to her. Not that vacuous people aren't capable of murder, of course. But even with the insurance policy taken out in Esmé's name and the prenup, Maggie thought Paul's stunned and then obstreperous vow of innocence felt real. She scolded herself.

*When will I learn to stop going with my intuition?*
*She would not take Paul off the list.*

Or Hadley, for that matter. In fact, Hadley might have the best motive of everyone—get rid of her lover's wife and at the same time enable him, and presumably her, to get rich off the insurance policy.

Was the woman really that cunning? That devious?

"I have seen that look before."

Maggie turned to look at Laurent. His eyes were closed but he had shifted his position in the chair. She sat down in the chair opposite him and put her hand to his cheek.

"How are you feeling? Can you make it to the bed? I think you need to lie down."

"I have been thinking," he said, as he allowed her to slip her shoulder under one of his arms and help him to his feet. After a moment of dangerous swaying with Maggie trying to support part of his weight, he staggered the short distance to the bed where he sagged heavily onto it.

Maggie pulled off his shoes and dropped them on the floor.

"Drink some water. I don't know what that bastard drugged you with, but I'm sure it can't hurt to stay hydrated."

She held a water bottle to his lips and he raised a hand to touch her fingers on the bottle. He opened his eyes briefly, holding her gaze.

"You said Soeur Thérèse and the priest were the only ones who knew the abbey," he said.

Maggie put the water bottle on the nightstand and watched him closely.

How sick was he? Should she attempt to keep him awake? Should she check his pupils? She wasn't sure what that would tell her or what she should do if they were dilated.

"But the author would know the abbey too," he said in a whisper.

She arranged a sheet over him.

"I would agree with you," she said. "Except, from the few things I've learned about Jenny, it seems the only people she *doesn't* hate are women. If she was truly homicidal why would she kill Esmé when you and Alex were right there and both helpless from the effects of the drug?"

He grimaced slightly and didn't answer.

"But I've been thinking about Soeur Thérèse," Maggie said. "Why did she even go near the dungeon? She must have known the water was rising."

"We will never know."

"I don't know *right now*," Maggie said with a frown. "But I will."

Laurent smiled faintly. "Like a terrier with a bone. When will I learn?"

"That is a very good question. You spent the last week driving me crazy thinking you were having an affair or a midlife crisis instead of just *telling* me what the problem was."

"An affair," he murmured and shook his head slightly as if the word itself was a conundrum.

*I know. It sounds crazy to me too. Now.*

"Maybe you should sit up," she said. "I don't know what this drug is that Antoine's given you, but I don't like the idea of the blood rushing away from your head."

Laurent said nothing but shifted his position. Perspiration appeared on his forehead.

"And Laurent?" She patted the sheet that she had just pulled up to his chest as if she didn't know what to do with her hands. "I can't be going to all this trouble to prove your innocence only to have you murder Antoine in front of witnesses as soon as you feel better. So kindly let it go, okay? For now?"

He smiled and his hand reached for hers. His face was

relaxed and peaceful. Except for the niggling worry that he might be slipping into a coma, Maggie felt encouraged. She watched the gentle rise and fall of his chest.

"What about the priest?" he murmured just when she was sure he'd fallen asleep.

Maggie frowned since they'd already discussed the possibility of the priest not two minutes earlier. Had he forgotten?

"It's true he has no alibi for Esmé," Maggie said, "but he also has no motive or evidence implicating him."

"You said he...hated...women?"

Maggie wiped the sweat from his face with the damp cloth. His eyes fluttered as if he was attempting to stay awake.

"No," she said. "I said he got upset at loud women wearing too much makeup and wearing what he considered inappropriate clothing."

Laurent turned his head, looking finally ready to give up the struggle to stay awake.

"Like Hadley," he murmured.

His words vibrated ominously in her brain. She watched him for several long moments until she was satisfied that he had indeed fallen back asleep. She checked his pulse and put a hand to his forehead—still warm. Then she stood up, hearing the ticking of the clock behind her like a waiting bomb.

She pulled on Laurent's coat again. Yes, she needed to talk to the priest and she needed to look through Soeur Thérèse's room. But first she needed to track down that bloody Antoine.

## 41

Maggie walked down the stone hallway, her wavering flashlight beam weakly piercing the darkness before her. All the torches seemed to have burned down or been snuffed out.

She took in a long full breath and let it out. When she did she realized it was the first full breath she'd taken in hours. She felt the tension as it coiled in her shoulders. She shivered as she walked. The cold was always worse in the dark.

Her initial impulse had been to go to Antoine immediately but it occurred to her that talking to him without a shred of evidence to motivate him to tell her the truth was going to be a waste of time.

And she didn't have time to waste.

First she needed to find out what it was that Soeur Thérèse had wanted to tell Laurent. She needed to find where she was leading him. The logical place had to be the nun's quarters off the refectory.

Maggie quickly retraced her steps back up the stone stairs that led to the church on the top floor. She'd taken

Laurent's larger flashlight but it was bulky in her jacket pocket. As she walked, she kept her ears open for any sound of a footfall on the stairs.

She hurried past the floor where the Knights Hall and the breakfast room were located and felt a shudder of amazement that dinner—with Esmé and Soeur Thérèse both alive and well—had been only last evening.

The top of the stairs spilled out onto a huge stone atrium—devoid of any furnishings and also, Maggie noted, any possible spot to hide. To her right was the entrance to the cloister near the Blue Room where they'd all gathered when they'd first arrived. To her left was the refectory which housed the clergy's quarters, and the church itself.

The double doors leading to the refectory and the church were wide open. Maggie assumed this was because Père Jean was inside with Soeur Thérèse's body.

A narrow wooden door was recessed into the paneling by the library with a plaque above it that read *Dortoir*.

*Dormitory.*

*Very helpful*, she thought, as she turned the doorknob which opened onto a cramped hallway revealing a series of doors on both sides.

Maggie remembered Antoine telling them that there were several other people in addition to Père Jean and Soeur Thérèse living at the abbey. She would have to go to every single room, praying the doors were open, or break the locks on those that weren't. She walked to the first door and turned on her flashlight. To the right of the door was a small cubbyhole for mail. Over this was a plaque with a name on it. *Sr Thérèse*.

Taking a careful breath in, she turned the door handle and entered.

The room was not much more than a cell with a single

narrow bed, a nightstand, an armoire and a dresser. There were no pictures on the wall, no windows and only a crucifix above the bed.

Maggie hated going through Soeur Thérèse's personal belongings—what few of them there were. She went to the armoire first. Inside, she found a second habit—this one less severe than what Maggie had seen Soeur Thérèse wear. The hem on the garment was mid-length—the way nuns used to wear their habits in the seventies. Maybe Soeur Thérèse had worn this style when she left the island, Maggie mused, or when she visited family.

She felt a catch in her chest as she thought about Soeur Thérèse's next of kin. They would be told that she had been murdered in the dungeon. Maggie shook the ghoulish thought away and turned to the dresser.

Not surprisingly, Maggie found very few things that indicated that the woman had ever been in the secular world. Only a Bible, and a small, framed photo of a woman which looked like it might have been taken in the late eighteen hundreds. Certainly nothing that looked like a clue to the identity of Esmé's killer.

Maggie looked in every dresser drawer and found only cotton underwear, a wool sweater, thick cotton tights and two heavy flannel night gowns. She looked around the room in mounting discouragement.

What could Soeur Thérèse have wanted to show Laurent?

Maggie didn't even know for sure that Soeur Thérèse was hoping to lead Laurent back here. Did it even make sense that a nun would lead a man to her bedroom? And even if it did, why choose Laurent?

*Would a nun really have felt comfortable bringing Laurent to her dorm room?*

Maggie hesitated as she looked around the room before feeling a heaviness in her chest.

*Wild-goose chase,* she decided dejectedly. *One more dead end.*

She sat on the bed, finding it just as hard as she guessed it would be, and put her hands under the pillow and the wool blanket. She found nothing.

Then, using Laurent's flashlight, she got on her knees and looked under the bed using Laurent's flashlight, but she didn't even find a dust bunny. Finally, she jammed her hands under the thin, hard mattress and jumped when her fingers touched something.

She wrenched the mattress up with one hand while shining the flashlight on the object. It was a folded piece of paper.

She snatched it up and sat on the bed to examine it. It took her all of five seconds to scan the page to realize what it was.

And to confirm to herself that there could be little doubt that this was the evidence that Soeur Thérèse had wanted to show Laurent.

It was a love letter. Written to Hadley from Paul.

Maggie skimmed the letter. It was mildly erotic, evidence only of the sexual relationship between Hadley and Paul.

Why had the nun felt it was damning?

Maggie's brain spun for a moment and then she got up and went over to the nightstand where Soeur Thérèse's Bible was. She picked it up and flipped it open. It was in English.

Soeur Thérèse spoke English?

Maggie stood there holding the Bible and frowned. Because the woman had never spoken, Maggie hadn't questioned her assumption that Soeur Thérèse was French. But why would a French nun have an English-language Bible?

Was Soeur Thérèse English? Or American? Was that significant?

Maggie looked again at the letter. If this was the evidence that Soeur Thérèse had found to implicate either Hadley or Paul in Esmé's murder it was too late and way too little. Everyone knew the two were having an affair, and while a steamy love letter might appear damning in the eyes of a cloistered nun, it wouldn't matter one whit to a jury in the face of—or lack of—DNA evidence.

Maggie frowned. Was Soeur Thérèse killed because the killer thought she had something more concrete than this? She refolded the letter and tucked it into one of Laurent's jacket pockets and when she did she froze.

She heard voices. If she hadn't been so engrossed in the discovery of the letter, she would have realized that she had been hearing them for some minutes now.

She looked around the room, then stood and walked to the door and put her ear against it. But the voices weren't coming from the hallway. She stepped back and frowned. The room she and Laurent were in had an old-fashioned radiator to warm the space but she didn't see anything like that in Soeur Thérèse's room. She stepped over to the armoire and saw that there was a heating vent on the floor beside it.

Maggie had read that there had been some modernizations done to Mont St-Michel in the last twenty years. Apparently a new heating system in the dormitory was one of them. She crouched down and then laid on her stomach in order to put her ear to the vent.

Instantly the voices were as clear and distinct as if she were in the same room with them.

"Forgive me, Father, for I have sinned," a familiar voice said. "It has been two years since my last confession."

Maggie sat up with a jolt.

The voice of the person confessing his sins was Antoine's.

She sat on her heels in shock. The vent in Soeur Thérèse's room gave direct access to the confessional box in the church.

*I can't be listening to this.*

On the other hand, she thought as she resumed her position on the floor by the vent, this was exactly the kind of break she'd been looking for.

"….not really my fault, Father," Antoine said. "She was trying to blackmail me! *She's* the true sinner here."

Maggie's mouth fell open in astonishment.

"But we are only here to discuss your transgressions, my son," Père Jean said.

"Okay, fine. So she said she was going to use some…use an incident against me and announce it publicly at the international conference I'm attending next month. It would have ruined me, Father! I don't have to tell you, my career is built on trust!"

Maggie tried to make sense of what she was hearing. Was he talking about *her*? It was true she'd threatened to go to the conference to complain about his methods but he couldn't have thought she intended to blackmail him!

Or was he talking about someone else?

"I tried to mollify her, Father," Antoine said. "But she wanted something I couldn't give her."

He was definitely not talking about her, Maggie realized. Someone else had threatened him. This had to be the reason why he had reacted so vehemently when Maggie had threatened to go to the International Marital Counseling conference.

*Antoine was being blackmailed.*

But by whom?

"She called me daily," Antoine said. "She was relentless. She was not going to let this go. I was beside myself. And you heard Esmé at the dinner! She was warning me—publicly—that she intended to ruin me! What was I supposed to do, Father?" Antoine said.

There was a pause.

"What *did* you do, my son?"

## 42

Maggie gasped and clapped a hand to her mouth. She'd been so engrossed in processing what she was hearing that she'd forgotten that the vent system probably worked both ways—incoming and outgoing.

"Are...are we alone, Father?" Antoine asked in a panicked voice.

Maggie moved away from the vent, but as she did her knee pressed on a loose board which produced a loud creak.

"Someone's here!" Antoine said, his voice laced with fear. "Where...where does that vent lead?"

Maggie jumped to her feet. This was not the time or the place to confront Antoine about killing Esmé. Fear drove icy fingers up her spine. In fact, this quiet, dark cell was actually a perfect place for him to break her neck and swear he'd found her that way.

Maggie looked frantically round the room.

There was no place to hide.

She heard muffled footsteps from the narrow hallway coming toward Soeur Thérèse's bedroom.

Fighting down a growing panic and with no better idea about what to do, Maggie dropped to her belly and slid under the single bed, clicking off her flashlight at the very second that the room door was flung open.

She felt the blast of cold air from the outer hall as Antoine entered the room. She could see his feet as he stepped to the armoire, nearly ripping it off its hinges as he opened it.

The very air in the room was thick with his fury.

"Dammit!" Antoine shouted. "I know they're here somewhere!"

Any second now he was going to drop to his hands and knees and see her under the bed. Maggie silently cursed herself for picking the most obvious place to hide. But there had been nowhere else.

Suddenly she saw the edge of Soeur Thérèse's bedding go flying off the bed and onto the floor. She squeezed her eyes shut. Just when she knew it was all over, she heard a loud thumping sound followed by a moan from Antoine. There was silence for a few seconds and then she heard movement—unsteady and lumbering—before the distinct sound of the door shutting firmly.

Maggie opened her eyes.

What had happened? Was he trying to trick her? She waited a full minute and couldn't believe that Antoine really had the self-discipline to be quiet for so long. She carefully inched her way out from under the bed and looked around the room.

She was alone.

Still shaking, she sat down gingerly on the bed.

What had happened?

She looked around the room and saw something she hadn't noticed before. It was a shadow on the wall near the window that looked out over the outer western terrace of the cloister.

A shadow in the shape of a woman.

Maggie swallowed and felt the perspiration pop out on her forehead.

How could she not have seen that before? Had it been there? The more she looked at the shadow the more she realized she was looking at the darkened outline of the Black Madonna.

It wavered gently on the wall like heat shimmering above the desert. Like it was breathing.

Telling herself that this had to be some sort of residual effect of the drug Antoine had given them all earlier, Maggie squeezed her eyes shut to clear her vision.

Had Antoine seen the shadow? But that wouldn't account for the sound Maggie had heard. The terrible thump followed by Antoine's cry of fear.

What was going on?

She decided not to stick around to find out. She had the letter. She'd heard Antoine's confession. That was enough for now. She went to the door and eased it open before sticking her head out with the flashlight and verifying that there was nobody in the hall.

It didn't mean that Antoine wasn't waiting for her in the vestibule across from the entrance to the cloister. She hesitated briefly at the thought. But even if he was waiting for her, she couldn't stay here.

She crept down the narrow hallway until she reached the library door. There she saw another door on the other side of that room which was clearly an outside door. It was over one hundred and seventy meters up—virtually the rooftop garden of the abbey in the middle of a torrential storm—but it was better than running into Antoine alone in the vestibule.

Maggie hurried across the room to the door and was relieved to find it unlocked. A stone overhang ran the length of the building all around the cloister.

She stood under the eaves with the rain crashing down around her and lightning blowing up the sky to the east. There were only knee-high stone walls to prevent anyone from tumbling over the edge to the hard stone terrace below. The storm made it impossible to see what would otherwise have been an impressive view of the sweeping marsh that surrounded the island, the village rooftops below, and in the distance like a hazy smudge, the town of Pontorson.

Maggie looked frantically down the covered walkway of the cloister.

Was there a way down to the other levels from here?

As she looked out across the terrace, the rain splashing against her legs, her left arm throbbed at the spot where she'd broken it twenty years before. She had a flash of memory as she recalled kneeling on the floor of that bakery in St-Buvard—Grace, heavily pregnant with Zouzou, unconscious on the floor beside her.

Maggie remembered the moment she raised her arm to ward off the blow from the maniac with a bat who was determined to kill all three of them. She shivered at the memory.

*And yet we survived. We're alive and well and Zouzou is living in Paris with an exciting future ahead of her. A future that could've ended that night before it began.*

As Maggie stood there, unsure about her next move, her mind went to what she had heard tonight. She had overheard a perfect motive for Esmé's murder, making Antoine her best suspect so far since, in addition to his motive, he had been one of the few people on the island not befuddled by drugs last night.

The other thing she'd experienced—seen?—was harder to explain. Where had the shadow of the Black Madonna come from? Was that Soeur Thérèse's doing?

Maggie quickly dismissed the notion. She'd been terrified and on edge. She was in the room of the recently departed and the whole world was blowing up around her with this terrible storm. She could hardly be surprised that she was seeing things. Especially not with the vestiges of the drugs that Antoine had given her still in her system.

*Yes, that's all it was. A bad waking dream under the worst possible conditions.*

She leaned against the wall of the covered walkway and worked to moderate her breathing to settle her nerves before figuring out what to do next. It was at that moment that she felt the resurgence of the annoying little pinging sensation at the back of her brain. She realized it was the same sound she'd felt before.

This time when she felt it, she saw the image in her head of Soeur Thérèse in the swirling waters of the *Cellier*, her black gowns billowing around her.

And then she heard Soeur Thérèse's voice—as melodic yet commanding as the wind and the rain as they beat against the building behind her.

"*You're wrong*," the voice intoned, vibrating into the air.

The wind was picking up now, whipping faster and harder as it came twisting around the building like a phantom's demented scream.

"*You're wrong.*"

Suddenly Maggie didn't even care where the voice came from or if the wind could speak. Suddenly she just knew in her bones what it meant. The ping, that annoying sensation in the back of her mind, erupted into a billboard lit up in her head revealing the truth in giant letters.

All of the clues so far had been trying to tell her this but she hadn't been able to see it!

*What if we're wrong? What if everyone is wrong? Including the killer? What if Esmé's killing was just a terrible accident?*

*What if it was really Hadley who was supposed to die?*

## 43

The more Maggie thought about it the more it made sense.

If Hadley had actually been the intended target and not Esmé, it meant that both Paul, Alex and Antoine were in the clear. Because Alex—unless he was too high—would probably be able to realize he had *Esmé* with him instead of his wife Hadley. And Paul would likewise know he had Hadley and was therefore unlikely to mistakenly kill his own wife Esmé.

And finally, while it was true Antoine had a motive for wanting Esmé dead, there was no other evidence to support him actually having killed her. And he had no motive for killing Hadley.

As these thoughts zipped through Maggie's mind, she noticed a small light moving in the darkness on the far side of the cloister. She squinted into the downpour until she could make out two figures walking on the protected walkway surrounding the large square green space of the cloister. As they walked, she recognized Hadley's sweeping cloak. That meant the other figure must be Paul.

*Safety in numbers*, she thought as she hurried toward them under the canopy. It was much colder this high up—even worse than it had been when she had stepped outside earlier in the evening to go to the Saint-Pierre chapel.

She shivered as she made her way toward the couple, who had stopped walking and were standing together now. The feel of the love letter in her pocket seemed to vibrate through her coat.

Was it enough to implicate them? Soeur Thérèse clearly thought so.

It didn't matter. If what Maggie now believed was true—that *Hadley* had been the intended victim—then love letters and even blackmail were irrelevant.

Keeping her flashlight off, she approached the couple until she was only five yards away where she stopped and stood hidden beside one of the posts supporting the walkway canopy. She was close enough to see the glow of Hadley's cigarette in the darkness, and close enough to hear their voices which were amplified under the covered walkway.

"It will all be over soon, sweetheart," Paul said as he leaned over Hadley, nearly shouting over the sound of the rain.

"I know," she said, her voice reedy and shaky. "It's just that it's all fairly horrible right at the moment."

"Are you really smoking? You know you'll have to give them up when we marry."

"I will, Paul. I promise."

He kissed her and then walked away in the opposite direction where Maggie was standing. Maggie noticed that Hadley waited until she couldn't hear the sounds of his footsteps before she pulled out another cigarette and lit it.

Maggie stepped forward out of the shadows.

"I'm pretty sure Antoine does a whole workshop on dominating men who try to control their women," Maggie said as she came into view.

"Oh my God!" Hadley said, clutching her hand to her throat. "You scared me to death!"

"Did you think I was one of the ghosts from the dungeons?"

Hadley grimaced at her.

"Why are you skulking around in the middle of the night? Wait, don't tell me. You're trying to find someone who'll admit to killing Esmé."

That was surprisingly accurate given what Maggie had just heard Antoine do not twenty minutes ago, but she knew Hadley was being sarcastic.

"Should you be out here on your own?" Maggie asked.

"I'm not on my own. You're here."

"You probably should stay in your room until the police come and sort everything out."

"Like you?"

*I'm not the killer's target.*

"Did I hear that you and Paul are getting married?" Maggie asked.

"We've been talking about it."

"Is that what you want?"

"Of course," Hadley said, shaking her head as if surprised at Maggie's question. "Of course it is."

Hadley's assurance sounded like false bravado to Maggie. Was it possible she'd only wanted a little break from the monotony of marriage and hadn't bargained for a complete regime switch?

"How did you meet him?" Maggie asked.

"Alex and I joined the Paris expat club a few months back."

"You all live in Paris?"

Hadley nodded.

Looking at her the way she appeared now, relaxed and out of the orbit of the two men who would attempt to govern her, Maggie thought Hadley seemed softer somehow.

"I honestly feel terrible about Alex," Hadley said. "We married when we were both too young." She grimaced. "It wasn't until I met Paul that I realized what I was missing."

"How long has it been going on?"

"About three months. Trust me, sneaking around like this has been agony for both of us. But Paul has a son—a teenager and you know that age can be prickly."

"You and Alex don't have kids?"

Hadley shook her head. "I wanted some. But Alex couldn't do it. Paul said it's not too late for us to have one."

"Is that what you want?"

Hadley tossed her cigarette over the parapet, then lit another.

"I guess. Maybe."

She was quiet for a while. Maggie held her breath and gave her time. People often confided in strangers when they were given enough time and space.

"I worry about Alex," Hadley said. "He doesn't make friends easily."

"He's still relatively young."

Hadley laughed. "You'd think so, wouldn't you? But he's got the soul of a sixty-year old, trust me. I mean, he can be very dear if you get to know him." She looked out over the Cloister's famous hedges. "I really hope he lets someone get to know him."

"Well, he's been pretty solidly drunk the whole time he's

been here," Maggie said. "Does he have a drinking problem?"

Hadley frowned.

"Honestly? I would've said no before this weekend. Maybe I wasn't looking closely enough. I admit I've been distracted."

"Is Antoine helping you? I mean, giving you advice about all this?"

Hadley made a face. "Seriously? I think Antoine's been completely useless."

"I'm certainly no expert on marital harmony," Maggie said. "But if I were you—especially if you and Paul intend to go off into the sunset together—I'd give Alex a little attention right now. He knows something's wrong."

Hadley looked at Maggie and then nodded.

"Thanks," she said. "Look, I hope I haven't said anything too unforgivable throughout all this. I think I get caught up in the moment and tend to shoot off my mouth."

"No worries."

Hadley smiled almost shyly, flinging her cigarette onto the pavement, then turned and walked away down the walkway, holding her cloak tightly around her.

As Maggie watched her go, she pulled her own coat more snugly around her. The cold was still invasive but it didn't feel as miserable. It occurred to her that taking a break from her thoughts seemed to have helped her put them in better order somehow.

Only minutes before she'd been sure that Antoine was the one the police should concentrate on when they arrived. However, while it was true that he had the best motive for killing Esmé, if the intended victim really was *Hadley*, well, Hadley wasn't trying to blackmail Antoine.

On the other hand, Père Jean was someone who clearly

had a deep and entrenched pathology for those women he considered loose or disreputable. Then there was Jenny who, while she was a woman who supposedly hated men, would likely make an exception for that special category of women known as "the other woman."

Maggie considered her two prime suspects for wanting to kill Hadley—Père Jean and Jenny. Both had opportunity. Both knew the castle well enough to maneuver around in the dark. Both had motives.

But in Maggie's mind, as much as she liked Jenny, *her* motive trumped Père Jean's since annoyance with women's risqué clothing didn't often prompt cold-blooded murder, while a pathology rooted in the worst betrayal ever done to you just might.

Plus there was the not-so-little matter of Jenny having killed her fiancé—in exactly the same manner that Esmé was killed—with a knife slash across the throat.

Maggie shook her head in impatience. She could debate the various suspects and their motives all night long. But the bottom line was, if the killer *had* gotten it wrong and the intended victim *was* Hadley—it changed everything.

## 44

Maggie kept Hadley in view as she left the cloister. She watched her rejoin Paul who was waiting for her in an alcove between the cloister entrance and the refectory.

Paul frowned when he saw Maggie. He shook his head as if she were a naughty child whose antics did not at all surprise him.

Maggie was glad Paul was there since whoever was trying to kill Hadley likely hadn't given up yet. She was pretty sure that that someone wasn't Paul. Why would he want to kill Hadley? And how could he have mistakenly killed Esmé instead? Plus, he and Hadley had been together during Esmé's murder—regardless of what Maggie had said earlier about their alibis being no good.

That fact did count for something. Even drugged, it would be pretty hard to disappear for ten minutes, go murder someone, and then slip back into someone's embrace without them realizing you'd left.

Paul's presence did tend to lessen Maggie's nervousness

however about running into Antoine in a dark corner of the fortress.

She let Hadley and Paul get several steps ahead of her as they descended the staircase. But she didn't immediately follow them because her attention was snagged by a moving light in the refectory.

She hesitated for a moment remembering the ghostly apparition or whatever it was that she'd seen in Soeur Thérèse's room but in the end decided she had imagined it.

Within a few steps past the library she realized what she was seeing was light coming from dozens of tapers leading the way into the interior of Mont Saint-Michel's crowning glory—the abbey church itself.

As Maggie moved into the church she looked up at the vaults and dramatic arches that pegged it as Romanesque in an otherwise Gothic-styled abbey.

When she looked up at the ceiling of the choir she felt a tingle in her arms and legs. The towering windows were made even more dramatic by the repeated lightning flashes outside. It made her feel small and insignificant.

*Prostrate before the majesty of the Almighty.*

*In fact,* she thought as she stepped deeper into the church, if the island abbey of Mont St-Michel was majestic, its church was downright terrifying.

She saw Père Jean as soon as she entered the church. He was kneeling with his back to her in front of the altar in the choir which was ablaze with candlelight. Maggie walked toward him across the ancient stone floor. The draped body of Soeur Thérèse lay on a table in front of the altar. Maggie shivered at the sight.

Regardless of what Laurent said about the nun's probable time of death, Maggie knew she had been the last person to touch her while the nun was still alive. Maggie felt a visceral connection with Soeur Thérèse.

"She shouldn't be here," Père Jean said, not turning around.

Maggie paused at the pew nearest to him and eased into it, surprised at how suddenly weary she was. She massaged her aching legs, feeling the cut on her palm suddenly activate.

He turned to look at her, his face a portrait of sadness and guilt.

"I should have taken her to the chapel."

Maggie wasn't sure whether he meant the chapel in the lower level—the one by the Black Madonna—or the one outside in the storm. It didn't really matter.

"Why are you wet?" he asked.

"I was in the cloister."

He made a strangling sound in his throat. "Are you all mad?"

*I guess after tonight, that's a fair question.*

"I'm sorry about Soeur Thérèse."

He stood up and walked to Soeur Thérèse's body, holding his hands over her without touching her.

"She was a constant irritant to me," he said.

Maggie didn't speak. She knew he was going into his own private torture chamber of guilt and memories. She wouldn't interrupt that.

"She never gave me a moment to myself," he said, gingerly touching the covering on her foot. "She hounded me at every turn."

"That must have been exhausting," Maggie said softly.

He turned abruptly at her words as if the spell had broken at her words. Maggie watched him as he reran his own words in his head. Then he turned and, after bowing briefly at the altar, hurried down the long aisle under the awe-inspiring vastness of the soaring church ceiling.

Maggie watched him go, the sounds of his footsteps echoing throughout the cavernous space framed by the enormous polygonal pillars holding up the heavy stone arches. She leaned back in her seat. As these things went, being *hounded* by someone who loved you more than was healthy might not be much of a motive for murder—under normal circumstances.

She looked at the body at the front of the altar.

*But killing that person because they saw you commit murder would definitely qualify.*

It was time to go.

She got up and left the church, hurrying down the long hall of stone, hoping she'd chosen the right passageway to connect with the stairs that lead to the guest residences level. The cold temperature engulfed her. And no matter how far she held her arm out with the flashlight, she could see no endpoint to her path, just more darkness.

With every step she took, she found herself imagining she would suddenly come upon another skeleton—this time real and not generated from illicit drugs—grinning at her from a corner on the floor or perhaps hanging in a cage from the ceiling.

She was still mildly concerned about running into Antoine in the dark but comforted herself with the fact that he couldn't know for sure that it was her who had overheard his confession.

Once she reached the stairs, she found herself walking too quickly and had to force herself to slow down lest she slip and fall. She'd been away from Laurent at least twenty minutes and her anxiety had begun to inch upward with every minute that passed.

What if the drug was not benign? What if it was slowly killing him?

She kept one hand on the staircase wall to steady herself, her heart pounding in her throat.

As soon as she touched the bottom tread, she pivoted on the landing to hurry toward her room.

She made it five steps before a dark figure stepped out of the shadows to block her way.

## 45

Maggie gasped as she stopped short of slamming into Jenny in the narrow aisle. She closed her eyes for a moment until she felt her heart restart again.

"You scared the life out of me!" Maggie said angrily.

"I'm sorry. But I knocked on your door and nobody answered. I need to talk to you."

"I'm in a bit of hurry," Maggie said, her annoyance at being frightened trumping her curiosity as to what Jenny might want.

"I know, Maggie, but this is important."

Maggie narrowed her eyes at her. Jenny was wearing what looked pajama bottoms and a heavy winter coat over her top. Maggie tried to remember what Jenny had been wearing when they'd stood around poor Soeur Thérèse's body.

*Is she wearing pajamas because her other clothes are wet?*

"Which is your room?" Maggie asked. "I need to check on something first but I'll be come afterward."

"I'll come with you," Jenny said.

Something about the way she said it made the hairs on the back of Maggie's neck stand up. She already knew that letting anyone know how vulnerable Laurent was at the moment was not a good idea.

"No," Maggie said firmly. "I'll come to your room in five minutes."

She turned and hurried down the hall, not bothering to see how Jenny reacted. She paused at her room door and looked both ways before letting herself in and locking the door behind her.

Laurent was still sleeping peacefully. His breathing seemed regular and not labored. Maggie let out a small moan of relief. He wasn't perspiring any more either. In fact, he looked like he was just sleeping and Maggie prayed that was so. She touched his arm. He wasn't warm to the touch, so no fever. That was good. She glanced at the travel clock and saw that she'd been gone an hour.

Just then she felt cold fingers trace down her spine.

There was still enough time left to do *something,* but with all the conflicting information she now had, she wasn't at all sure what that something was.

She stood up, biting her lip for a moment before deciding that she'd go see what Jenny wanted and then go and find Antoine. At the very least, she needed to confront him about drugging Laurent. And she needed to let him know that she knew his secret about Esmé blackmailing him and see what that shook loose.

She dearly hoped it wasn't all her teeth. She stepped back out into the hall, locked the door, and headed to where she could see Jenny standing outside her room waiting.

"Thank you so much for coming," Jenny said, letting out a huge breath. She held open the door to her room and Maggie hesitated before entering.

Jenny locked the door behind them and motioned for Maggie to take a seat on the bed.

"I know you must think I'm mad," she said. "But I had to talk to you."

"I'm listening."

"Look, I just want to say before anything else that I don't think you had anything to do with Soeur Thérèse's death. I want to make that clear straightaway."

"But you think Laurent did."

Jenny gave a helpless hunch to her shoulders. "I guess I don't really know."

"What was it you wanted to tell me?" Maggie asked. She could already hear the minutes ticking down in her mind before the cops showed up on their doorstep.

"I saw something tonight," Jenny said. "I thought about waiting for the cops to tell them but then I thought that maybe you should know about it first."

"If it has to do with Laurent being Soeur Thérèse's killer, you can save your breath."

"No, it's about Antoine."

Maggie had stood up and was two steps toward the door when Jenny spoke. She turned around. She hadn't forgotten that Jenny had openly accused Laurent of killing Esmé.

"Let's hear it," Maggie said.

Jenny sat down in the desk chair opposite the bed and took in a long breath. She fingered the gold chain around her throat and kept glancing at the door to her room.

"Antoine told me last week that he wished Soeur Thérèse would fall off the western terrace."

Maggie frowned. "I've noticed Antoine doesn't really have any filter or sense of the appropriate."

"I'm telling you he was angry," Jenny said. "He was having a private consultation with one of his clients in the library and I guess they got frisky on the couch and Soeur Thérèse tried to chase them both out with a broom."

Maggie's eyebrows arched. "Really."

"Well, Soeur Thérèse *was* a little nuts," Jenny said. "But she'd been oppressed by the worst of the male-dominated church for her whole—"

Maggie put up a hand.

"Spare me the tirade. Just tell me what he said."

"He said he wished she was dead."

"Why would he tell you that if he intended to commit murder?"

Jenny frowned as if just seeing the illogic in this.

"Well, he didn't mean to tell me! He blurted it out without thinking! And I'm not saying his killing her was planned. It was probably a spur of the moment thing. But the whole time we were all at the dungeon with Soeur Thérèse's body, he kept looking at me guiltily as if *he* knew that *I* knew he'd wanted her dead."

"Not much in the way of evidence," Maggie said. "And if you don't mind my saying so, when it comes to who to believe, you or Antoine, I'm not sure your credibility stands up either."

Jenny's mouth fell open and then she closed it as a veil seemed to drop over her face.

"The bastard told you I killed my fiancé, didn't he?"

"He did, actually," Maggie said. "So while I'd appreciate anything that moves the focus away from Laurent—"

"He's lying," Jenny said, her face a mask of cold enmity. "Do you have any interest in hearing the truth?"

## 46

Maggie stared at Jenny, her own face impassive and unconvinced.

"So you *didn't* kill your fiancé?" she said.

"I did not. That bastard," Jenny said, shaking her head in disgust.

"Well, in any case," Maggie said. "If Antoine lied and you *didn't* do time for first-degree murder, then you would have every reason to hate Antoine for spreading lies about you. Maybe to the point of spreading a few lies of your own. No offense."

Jenny turned to her desk and pulled open a drawer.

"I want you to see something," she said.

Maggie was still standing but her curiosity kept her from leaving. Jenny pulled out an electronic tablet and quickly scrolled through it.

"Don't get excited," Jenny murmured without looking up. "It's not WIFI enabled. It's just an electronic photo album."

She found what she was looking for and handed the tablet to Maggie.

The first thing Maggie saw was a photograph date stamped five years earlier. It was a photo of Jenny—looking younger and happier—in the arms of a young man with a big toothy grin. Maggie noted the engagement ring on Jenny's hand in the picture.

"That's Gilbert," Jenny said with a sigh. "My fiancé."

"Okay," Maggie said with a shrug.

Jenny turned and scrolled to another picture. This photo showed the same man—a few years older—with a smiling blonde woman and a little boy between them. It was date-stamped six months ago.

"This is Gilbert today," Jenny said. "With my sister and my nephew."

Maggie sat down and took the electronic album in her hands. It was definitely the same man.

"They married three years ago," Jenny said with a sigh.

Maggie looked up.

"So he...?"

"Yes, he had an affair with my sister. That part is true. But nobody got killed. I was even invited to the wedding."

Jenny took the picture album back and as she gazed at it, she made a face. "My sister has all the tact of an inflamed hemorrhoid. But she and Gilbert are definitely both alive."

"I'm so sorry," Maggie said. "I believed Antoine when he said..."

"I know. It doesn't matter. I mean, I honestly think Antoine is a pathological liar and after this weekend, maybe worse than that. What he did to you people tonight was criminal, as in a felony."

Maggie watched Jenny as she put her photo album away and realized that she was mentally crossing Jenny off her list of suspects. Not that Jenny ever made sense anyway. Not for Hadley *or* Esmé.

*Which brings me back to Antoine.*

But only, Maggie reminded herself, if the intended victim really was Esmé.

And then there was Père Jean. Like Antoine, he hadn't been drugged last night either. But would he have killed Esmé just for being an annoying loud-mouth?

*Is that really a motive?*

Maggie ran a frustrated hand through her hair, feeling one of her bobby pins bounce free when she did.

"Are you okay?" Jenny asked with a frown.

Maggie shook her head

"I'm really not. I've got less than two hours before the cops come to find out who killed Esmé and Soeur Thérèse, and every time I think I might know who it is, I talk myself out of it."

"Can I help?"

Maggie looked at Jenny's earnest face and realized that with Laurent out for the count, she could really use someone to bounce ideas off.

"Do you know what I do when I get boxed in with a tricky plot point?" Jenny said. "I go back to the beginning with a clean sheet of paper and start over."

Maggie exhaled gratefully.

"Okay," she said. "Let's do that. What if Esmé *wasn't* the intended victim?"

Jenny's mouth fell open.

"Whoa! Seriously?"

"It's just that there are so many motives floating around for killing Hadley but very few for killing Esmé."

Jenny frowned. "Are you suggesting Esmé was accidentally killed?"

"Mistakenly killed. Yes."

"How do you *mistakenly* kill someone?"

"We were all hallucinating on that stupid drug Antoine fed us," Maggie said.

"That man really ought to be arrested. He did it without your consent?"

"He said it was in the fine print of the contract we all signed."

"If the drug is illegal—which I'd bet anything it is—it won't matter what you signed. He'll go to prison."

Maggie felt a wave of mounting frustration. She was happy to imagine Antoine in prison for illegally drugging them but right at the moment she had to clear Laurent.

Right now she had to figure out if it was Hadley who the killer meant to kill? Or Esmé?

"Can I mention two people—besides myself," Jenny said, "who were *not* hallucinating last night? And who therefore couldn't have *mistakenly* killed anyone as different as Esmé and Hadley were?"

Maggie frowned. She was very aware that Jenny had drunk from the same bottle she had in the Knight's Hall. She was either saying she hadn't been drugged that night...

...or she was lying.

"Maggie?"

"Yes, sorry," Maggie said, blushing. "You were saying there were two undrugged suspects last night besides yourself."

"That's right. Père Jean and Antoine," Jenny said.

*She hates Antoine*, Maggie reminded herself. *Can she be trusted to be objective?*

*But what if she's right?*

"Okay, but Père Jean has no motive for killing Esmé," Maggie said. "I mean, beyond her extreme obnoxiousness. It's possible he has a motive for killing Hadley. He ranted to me earlier tonight about how much he detests the way certain women dress and behave."

"Oh, lucky you to be on the receiving end of that little well-worn screed," Jenny said with a grimace. "But the problem with that is, it *wasn't* Hadley who got killed. And unless Père Jean was high on incense, he wouldn't have mistaken Esmé for Hadley."

"Good point," Maggie said.

"Which brings us back to Antoine."

Maggie didn't want to share with Jenny what she'd learned about Antoine being blackmailed by Esmé. But the fact was, if Esmé *was* the intended target, then Antoine had to be the killer. He had the best motive and, as Jenny said, *he* wasn't drugged out of his mind.

"Antoine has no known motive for killing Hadley," Maggie said, hedging.

Jenny's eyebrows shot up as if she'd just read between the lines of Maggie's words.

"The keyword there is *known*," Jenny said tartly. "Never mind. Don't tell me then. Let's assume Hadley *was* the intended victim. Who, besides Père Jean—who we've just ruled out—would want to kill her?"

"Maybe her husband?"

"Alex? For what reason?"

"Well, they were married, so there could have been any number of reasons that we wouldn't be aware of. And of course she was cheating on him."

"But I thought Hadley was with Paul all night, right? So how was Alex supposed to escape Esmé—who at that point was hanging all over him—then find his wife Hadley in the corridors, and do away with her without Paul witnessing it?"

Maggie threw up her hands in frustration.

"Plus," Jenny said, "while it's true Alex was hallucinating

off his head, do you really think he wouldn't be able to tell Esmé apart from his own wife?"

"Argh! You're right. This is so frustrating!" Maggie said, her fists tight with her fingernails biting into her palms. "If I look at this as a case of mistaken identity, *two* people fit the bill for wanting to kill Hadley—but neither could have done it mistakenly."

They sat in silence for a moment.

"So maybe I table that thought for a minute," Maggie said.

"Yes?"

"Well, if Esmé was the intended target, I have to say Père Jean did complain a whole lot about her nonstop talking. She was all over him last night at dinner."

"So he might have a motive for killing Esmé?" Jenny frowned skeptically.

"A weak one," Maggie admitted. "Plus I just saw him upstairs in the church with Soeur Thérèse's body. While it's true he looked upset about her death, I couldn't help but think there was something else in his manner."

"Something else?"

"Guilt."

"Good Lord," Jenny said, throwing up her hands as if in frustration although she was smiling. "Do you think Père Jean might have killed Soeur Thérèse too?"

"Do you?"

Jenny threw her head back and laughed and Maggie joined in.

"I know how that sounds. I want you to know I do resist seeing him as a murderer, I swear!"

Jenny, still laughing, said, "I know how you feel. I mean, after all, if we can't give a *priest* the benefit of the doubt for a double murder, then who can we give it to?"

## 47

By the time Maggie left Jenny's room a few minutes later, she felt better. After working through all the viable options and clues with her, Jenny who—not surprisingly for an author—was very good at objective reasoning and timeline reconstruction, helped give Maggie the confidence she needed about the direction she needed to go.

The fact was, Père Jean *was* a suspect for trying to kill Hadley.

Possibly.

But not Esmé.

And Antoine was a suspect for killing Esmé.

But not Hadley.

Maggie's mind was still spinning as she made her way to the end of the hall heading back to her room. But in spite of that she felt as if she had a much shorter list to work from. Thanks to Jenny, she also had a sort of plan.

She would check on Laurent and then finally confront Antoine. After all, Antoine didn't know for sure *who* had overheard his confession. He only knew that *someone* had.

Maggie reminded herself that she was fully armed with the facts for this battle. It was Antoine who would be on the back foot. Because of what she knew about him—and because Antoine was almost certainly guilty of drugging Laurent a second time—she had the upper hand and she needed not to be afraid to use it.

Even so, she would feel better with someone by her side. She'd suggested it to Jenny, but the author had paled at the thought, arguing that her strengths lay on the page or in the planning stage, not in the actual implementation. Laurent was obviously out of the picture, but Maggie thought that possibly Alex might serve the purpose—if he wasn't too drunk. While he may not be effective in actually protecting her if things got physical with Antoine, he could at least serve as a witness if Antoine attacked her—which might prevent Antoine from actually doing so.

As she walked back to her room, Maggie realized that everything in her world—Laurent's freedom, her children's happiness, even their very futures—was riding on her being able to get the killer's confession tonight before the police showed up in a little more than an hour. If she dropped the ball now, if she failed to get the confession...

She shook the thought from her head.

*No, the plan will work. Killers are not infallible.*

And someone like Antoine—if he was in fact the killer—was particularly ill-equipped for the lies and subterfuge needed on the back end to keep his secret safe. Once Maggie apprised him of the fact that she knew he was being blackmailed by Esmé *and* that she had heard him admit to whatever he'd done as a result, a confession was bound to come swiftly.

She lifted her chin and straightened her shoulders.

At least she fervently hoped so.

When she came back to the room, Laurent was still sleeping.

Looking at his face, so familiar and dear to her, she thought of the agony he must have been feeling these past weeks. She leaned over and kissed his cheek.

"It's a fleabite, darling. In the scheme of things, it's just a fleabite and you and I have weathered plenty of those. We'll weather this."

"You smell like smoke," he said.

She felt a sliver of hope when he opened his eyes. She smoothed his hair from his face.

"Laurent? How do you feel?"

"Tired," he murmured, his eyes still closed. "Need...sleep."

"Yes, that's good," she said, feeling the relief flutter through her.

He did look merely tired. His breathing was normal and there didn't seem to be anything worse happening behind his eyes. The fact that he was conversing with her at all—and lucidly—was the best sign yet.

"Go ahead and sleep," she murmured to him, kissing his cheek again. "When you wake up we'll go home to Domaine St-Buvard. We'll go home to our lives there and Grace and Danielle."

"*Je...t'aime, chérie*," he murmured before letting sleep claim him again.

She felt tears well up in her eyes.

"*Je t'aime* you too," she whispered.

She stood up and walked to the dresser, overcome with emotion, determination and hope. On the dresser she saw the button that Esmé had taken off Laurent's shirt. Picking it up, she slipped it into her pocket and felt a little stronger.

She patted the pockets of her coat for the flashlight. She

clicked it on and off to make sure the battery was still strong. Before leaving she looked around the room, her eyes falling finally on Laurent, a gentle snore coming reassuringly from the bed.

She had a plan and a course of action. Win or lose, she would go forward, leave no stone unturned, no opportunity unexplored. No matter what it cost. She took in a breath and let it out. She looked at the travel clock. Less than sixty minutes until dawn. Instantly she felt her breathing begin to speed up and she took another breath to quell her mounting anxiety.

She was as ready as she would ever be. She had a plan for getting the confession and, even more helpfully, she had a good idea about who to get it from.

Regardless of the pep-talk she'd given herself, Maggie felt a sliver of apprehension run through her as she closed the door behind her.

One thing she'd learned many years ago—and that the hard way—knowing who the killer was, was often only half the battle.

## 48

Stepping once more into the frigid sterility and darkness of the stone abbey corridors, Maggie hesitated just long enough to guarantee that the door to her room was locked.

Antoine and Père Jean both likely had keys to their room. She wasn't sure what Père Jean's motivation would be for entering the room when Laurent was so vulnerable, but she had to hope that Antoine—who'd succeeded in immobilizing Laurent—would find it unnecessary.

A shiver seized her at the thought.

*If the killer has already killed Esmé and Soeur Thérèse, it would take a very little to make it three.*

*I can't let the police take Laurent. I can't face Jemmy and Mila and tell them I let them take their father. And Luc. He'll never get to have the relationship with Laurent he was intended to have. Oh, why did we wait so long to tell Luc the truth? Now it will come too late to matter.*

She stopped walking long enough to force herself to get a grip. Now of all times, she needed to be confident, not full of self doubt!

She said a silent prayer for Laurent's safety and hurried down the corridor to find Alex to serve as her designated wingman. She only hoped he was sober enough for the job.

One thing she knew, if she knew anything, was that if she *wasn't* able to get Antoine to confess before the police came, it wouldn't matter that he killed Esmé and Soeur Thérèse. In Maggie's experience the police rarely did the work necessary to uncover the truth. And they certainly wouldn't bother with an available suspect in the form of Laurent at hand.

*None of that will happen,* she told herself firmly. She would get the confession tonight and everything would be fine.

She took in another long breath to steady her nerves and focused on the flickering torch a few yards ahead of her. Squaring her shoulders, she marched down the corridor to the room she believed to be Alex's. When she heard something from the direction of the stairs, she hesitated.

Someone else was walking about. It didn't sound like Paul and Hadley. Besides, except for Hadley's need to find a place to smoke every few hours, they had no reason to leave the comfort of their room.

Maggie turned slowly toward the corner and felt her heartbeat speed up. She heard the sound again: a shuffling sound like someone standing—or lying in wait—around the corner.

"Hello?" she called, hating to hear the anxiety in her voice.

There was no answer.

She gritted her teeth and pulled the flashlight out of her jacket pocket. She didn't need it at the moment because the hall was illuminated by the torches. But it was the closest thing to a weapon she had. She took in another breath and then stepped around the corner.

Immediately a hand grabbed her by the front of her jacket. Just by the smell of him Maggie knew it was Alex. He pulled his face up close blasting his breath into her face.

The shock at being grabbed quickly turned to fury as Maggie reached out and smacked him smartly on the forehead with her flashlight. Alex looked at her in surprise before jerking the flashlight out of her hand with a curse.

Not waiting to see what his next move was, Maggie put both hands against his chest to stabilize herself and swung her right knee up as hard as she could between his legs.

Alex yelped shrilly and went down like a tree felled in the wood. Maggie stood with her back against the wall, feeling the coldness seep into her shoulder blades, panting from the exertion.

"What...is your problem?!" she sputtered as he curled on the ground cupping his groin and groaning loudly.

"Thought...thought...you...were...her," he gasped, rocking back and forth, his face a richter of pain.

"Who? Hadley?" Maggie asked.

Alex didn't answer but continued to rock from side to side, the malodorous fumes of alcohol hovering over him.

Maggie studied Alex. His pink tie, now askew around his neck, was stained and crusted with vomit. She found herself trying to imagine how he fit into this weekend. He was the cuckold, but as far as she could tell he hadn't even realized that until a few hours ago.

Was it possible he'd wanted to kill Hadley, his cheating wife, but under the influence of drugs—and way too much wine—he'd killed Esmé instead?

Maggie couldn't see it.

It wasn't that someone as basically inept as Alex couldn't have a moment of ruthless brutality in him.

It was the aftermath that clouded the picture for her.

It took a stone-cold killer to engage with people like nothing was wrong after he'd committed murder. Not everybody could do it.

Actually, Maggie thought as she studied Alex moaning and rocking on the floor, only true sociopaths did it easily.

Maybe that's why Alex stayed so steadily drunk. But Maggie didn't think so. Alex had not acted like someone who'd just committed murder.

He just acted pathetic.

"I know she's sleeping with Paul," he moaned. "She set up this whole weekend so she could be with him."

"I'd feel a lot more sympathetic toward you if you would quit attacking me," Maggie said sternly as she poured a glass of water and handed it to him. "This is the second time."

"I don't know what's the matter with me," he said miserably, holding the water but not drinking.

She realized with a sinking feeling that she would have to confront Antoine alone. Alex would be no help at all.

"You can make it up to me by telling me what's going on," she said.

He shook his head and looked at his hands.

"I can't," he said, his voice garbled by tears.

"Do you have something to hide? Because otherwise you have no reason not to tell the truth."

"I do," he said softly, in a whimper.

"You do what?" Maggie said, feeling the strings of impatience begin to twitch inside her.

She didn't have time for this. She needed to get to Antoine and get her confession!

"I do have something to hide," he said.

"Oh, yes? What is that?"

He looked up at her, his face a picture of misery and shame.

"I killed her," he said, his shoulders collapsing as he hung his head to his chest. "I killed Esmé."

## 49

Maggie felt a sudden coldness in her core at his words. She studied him where he sat and wept into his hands. She noted again that his clothing was stained and torn. She bent down and picked up her flashlight and put it back in the pocket of Laurent's jacket.

"Tell me what happened," she said.

"It doesn't matter."

"Yes, it matters, you oaf!" she said, nudging him with her foot and feeling her patience coming to its abrupt end. "You've been letting Laurent carry the blame for murder, so it matters! Tell me what happened."

"What's going on here?"

Maggie turned around just as Paul and Hadley came down the corridor. Hadley pushed past Paul and ran to Alex. She knelt by him.

"We heard voices," Paul said.

"I'm so sorry, Hadley," Alex cried as she put her arms around him. "I'm so sorry."

"It's alright, sweetheart," Hadley said.

"It's not," he said, shaking his head. "It's never going to be alright again."

"If you don't mind," Maggie said, "your husband was just explaining to me how he killed Esmé last night."

"Are you serious?" Paul said with a frown, turning to look at Alex.

"No!" Hadley said, twisting around to glare at Maggie and then back again at Alex. "No, he did not! He couldn't! Alex, hush! You're drunk!"

"It's true, Hadley," he said, his eyes full of tears. "I *was* with her last night." He looked at Maggie over Hadley's shoulder. "Your husband shoved her into my arms. Just like he said."

Maggie felt a deep sense of relief at his words. This had to mean that Laurent was in the clear.

"How did you do it?" Maggie asked.

"For the love of God, stop it!" Hadley shrieked. "You are bullying him! He's not in his right mind! He doesn't know what he's saying!"

"I did it," Alex sobbed, grabbing Hadley's sleeve and looking at her, his eyes filled with guilt and remorse. "I killed her with my bare hands! I grabbed her around the throat and I choked her until that annoying horrible grating voice finally stopped! I'm sorry, Paul! I'm so, terribly sorry." He broke down weeping.

Maggie stared at Alex for a long moment to see if there was anything about what he was saying that could suggest he might be deliberately fabricating what he was saying. Between his crying and his obvious intoxication, it was hard to say for sure. But in the end, she thought he was telling the truth. At least as far as he knew it.

"Look, he didn't mean to do it," Hadley said to Maggie.

"He was drunk and stoned at the time. He's not responsible for what he did!"

"Yes, I am!" Alex said. "I see it in my head all the time! I see it in slow motion! It's like a movie that won't turn off! I killed her."

"No, you didn't," Maggie said with a sigh that actually hurt. For one brief moment she had Laurent off the hot seat. One brief, fleeting moment.

"Yes, I did!" Alex said almost angrily as he looked at Maggie. "I...I had to shut off that incessant noise! Her nonstop talking! I grabbed her by the—"

"Esmé wasn't strangled," Maggie said.

Even as she spoke, she tried to remember if anyone had openly discussed the manner in which Esmé had died, but she couldn't. Either Alex was a whole lot sneakier—and a lot better actor—than she thought, or he was telling the truth about what he remembered.

"What? But I...I killed her," he said less confidently now.

"Nope," Maggie said, "you didn't. You are only guilty of killing her in your mind."

Alex slumped against the wall, his head in his hands. His wife pulled back and sat on her heels, watching him as if she had never seen him before.

"So if he didn't kill Esmé, who did?" Paul asked.

The way he asked it, it seemed to Maggie that he really wanted to know.

"I think I know," Maggie said. "But I need your help to prove it."

"What? No. Why?" he said, taking a step away from her.

"We should all go to our rooms and let the police handle this," Hadley said reaching for Paul's arm.

"This man is your husband," Maggie said pointing at

Alex. "*You* are going to stay here and sit with him while Paul and I go and talk to Antoine."

"You think Antoine killed Esmé?" Hadley asked. "That's ridiculous. Why would he?"

"Just stay here until we get back," Maggie said before turning to Paul. "Alex is in no condition to help me, so it's got to be you. As for why you should do it, how about because Antoine may have killed your wife? Can you think of a better reason?"

Paul looked helplessly at Maggie and then Hadley who finally nodded.

"Go on," Hadley said as she eased herself down onto the cold ground next to Alex. "But please, hurry. It's freezing here."

"Darling?" Alex said to Hadley. "Do you hate me?"

Hadley patted his arm as she pulled out a cigarette and lighted it.

"Of course not, Alex."

Maggie turned to Paul, her jaw set and determined.

"Let's go," she said. "We've got a killer to catch."

## 50

Antoine's room was around the corner at the end of the line of guest rooms. Maggie had already made up her mind that, if he wasn't in his room, she would scour the abbey looking for him—even if it took the rest of the morning until the police came.

One way or the other, Antoine would answer for what he'd done.

She rapped loudly on his door and stood, waiting, aware of Paul, restless and impatient by her side. She tried to keep her mind focused on her questions, on the plan she and Jenny had devised and, most importantly, on the need to pivot and change it all up if necessary.

She reminded herself to keep front and center the key point of Esmé's murder which had gone largely unaddressed until now. It was the point that Jenny had drilled home to Maggie: the fact that Antoine was one of *only three people* in the abbey who had not been drugged. He wouldn't have *mistakenly* killed anyone. He would have known exactly what he was doing when he killed Esmé.

This made perfect sense to Maggie.

*As long as the intended victim wasn't Hadley.*

The door opened and Antoine appeared. He looked first at Maggie and then Paul. Maggie could see his mind debating between acting outraged or reverting back to the affable, jokey host he'd played since she'd first laid eyes on him.

He took a deep breath and his chin dipped to his chest in what Maggie saw as a classic picture of guilt.

She pushed past him into his room which was identical to hers and Laurent's. She noticed he had a suitcase on the bed as if he was packing to leave.

"What is the meaning of this?" Antoine said. "What's going on, Paul? You and Maggie together now?"

"What is *wrong* with you?" Paul said, his eyes bulging in horror. "Is that supposed to be funny?"

"I fear our Dr. Anders has no natural instinct for what is socially appropriate," Maggie said. "Which is probably one of the reasons why his career in marital psychology is going down in flames. That and the whole illegal drugging thing."

"How dare you," Antoine said to her. "That isn't true! I'm very well-respected in the marital therapy community."

"Is that why Esmé was planning on exposing you at your industry conference next month?" Maggie said.

Antoine's jaw dropped and he paled..

"I don't know what you're talking about," he said. "Whatever she told you is a lie."

"Esmé didn't tell me," Maggie said. "You did."

He looked at her, his eyes widening suddenly in realization.

"It was you! That...that is a crime against...against— "

"And while we're on the subject of your professional behavior," Maggie said, "I'm pretty sure Laurent didn't sign any contract allowing you to drug him a second time. That's what the courts call recidivism, Antoine. And trust me, your defense attorney won't thank you for it."

Antoine licked his lips and looked at Paul before pushing a hand nervously through his hair.

"There's no way I'll be liable for that!" Antoine said heatedly. "First, the drug is legal! Second, it was my responsibility to make sure your husband didn't kill again. Hadley and Jenny were both terrified! If anything, I'll get a medal for keeping everyone safe!"

"You're a fool if you really believe that," Maggie said. "Speaking of Jenny, I found out tonight that you lied to me about her. I saw the pictures of her very much alive fiancé and her sister."

Antoine shook his head.

"I don't know what she told you but I won't apologize for telling the truth."

"You accused her of murder!" Maggie said hotly, advancing on him, her fists by her side, her anger threatening to boil over the top. "You told me she *killed* someone!"

"I say, Antoine," Paul said to him, his face a grimace of disgust. "That's a bit much."

"Look," Antoine said, his voice hitching as he addressed Paul who was looking at him as if Antoine had just confessed to eating roadside kill, "I admit I shouldn't have... told Maggie what I did. But at worst what I said was gossip and beneath me as a marital therapy professional—not a lie."

Maggie shook her head in astonishment.

"You're sticking to your story that Jenny did time for killing her fiancé?" she asked incredulously.

"I absolutely am. She told you otherwise? Well, she would, wouldn't she?"

Maggie stared at him. He stood before her, rubbing his

face, his chin quivering and his eyes darting about the room like a wild animal looking for a place to run or hide.

Her instinct was to believe Jenny over Antoine, because it was such an outrageous lie—*if it was a lie.*

*On the other hand*, a niggling voice said in her ear, *Would Antoine tell such a falsehood knowing that with one thirty-second Internet search, he'd be found out?*

Plus there was the little worry that Jenny had told Maggie she hadn't been stoned last night when, if she drank the wine as Maggie had seen her do, she definitely had been.

Which meant that Jenny had lied.

Maggie shook the doubts from her mind. *No. Stop. It doesn't matter. Not at the moment anyway.*

"Let's get back to you drugging us," she said. "Even if the drug cocktail you fed us is technically legal, we'll still sue you for secretly drugging us, signed contract or not."

"I think you'll be busy fighting other battles in court," Antoine said, smugly.

"If you're referring to the murder charge against Laurent I have to say I'm a little less worried about that now that I know Esmé was blackmailing you. That *was* the word you used with Père Jean, wasn't it?"

"How dare you!" Antoine said, but his look was panicked. Sweat was pouring off of him. "You...you can't use anything like that against me. It was said in the sanctity of the confessional."

Maggie actually laughed in his face.

"Hey, *I'm* not a priest, bub. I can testify to anything I hear."

"That's...you're...I can't believe...well, it's your word against mine. I'll deny it."

"Sorry, Antoine," Paul said with a shrug. "Esmé actually

mentioned something about this to me last week. I mean it didn't make sense at the time or maybe I was only half listening. Something about you having slept with one of your clients?"

Antoine whitened at Paul's words.

Paul turned to Maggie. "Are you saying Esmé was blackmailing him over it?"

"I overheard Antoine telling Père Jean that Esmé was threatening to expose him at the upcoming conference."

As soon as Maggie said the words, an uncomfortable thought occurred to her. She realized that she hadn't actually heard in the confessional Antoine admit to killing Esmé.

*And wouldn't he do that if he'd killed her?* He was in the sanctity of the *confessional.*

She reran her memory tapes to what she'd heard him say.

*"I tried to mollify her, Father. But she wanted something I couldn't give her. What was I supposed to do?"*

Maggie groaned internally. Antoine hadn't been asking for forgiveness for having killed Esmé. Now that she thought back on it, it sounded more like he was asking forgiveness for not minding that she was dead.

*Big difference.*

Once more Maggie forced herself to push her doubts aside. There was probably an obvious explanation for why Antoine hadn't actually confessed to killing Esmé.

*Beyond the fact that he hadn't done it.*

Once again, Maggie was left with her whole case hinging on whether or not the killer really meant to kill Esmé. And not Hadley.

"You'd have lost your whole career if it came out,"

Maggie continued. "More than anyone here you had the most to gain by killing her."

"But I didn't kill her! It was horrible and I was...yes, I'm sorry I was glad she was out of the picture. That was hideous, I know, and I feel terrible about it."

"What in the world was she asking for?" Paul asked him, a hand to his forehead in bewilderment. "Money?"

"It's hard to explain," Antoine said, hesitating.

"I'll bet you can if you try," Maggie said.

Antoine threw up his hands in frustration.

"She wanted some one-on-one time with me after the retreat was over."

"She wanted to *sleep* with you?" Paul asked, incredulously.

"She was a very lonely woman, Paul!" Antoine said heatedly. "I can see why you might not have noticed, but she was desperate for attention. Even to the point of blackmail." He turned to Maggie. "But I wouldn't have killed her! I'd have slept with the stupid cow first. No offense, Paul."

Maggie sank onto the bed in a brief moment of discouragement and confusion. She let the effects of the long exhausting night wash over her as she tried to process his words and what her brain—and the little aggravating ping in the back of her mind—was telling her. It was still just Antoine's word that he didn't do it. And except for one other person, he was still her strongest candidate.

"Do you have any other evidence other than your word that you didn't do it?" she said with a sigh.

"Yes, actually, quite a lot, considering how poor Esmé was killed," Antoine said, his face going white.

"What are you talking about?" she asked.

"I have a problem with...the sight of blood."

Maggie flashed back to the moment that Antoine threw

up at the crime scene when Laurent bloodied his nose. As soon as she'd started to construct her theory that Antoine had killed Esmé, Maggie thought that his throwing up had been self-loathing or guilt.

But if he was telling the truth...

Before she could force her exhausted brain to put together the next part of the puzzle, Paul walked over to Antoine and took his arm. Maggie saw the small penknife glint in the candlelight from the tapers set around the room.

"Hey, what do you think you're—?" Antoine said seconds before Paul drew a thin shallow cut down his arm.

Maggie jumped to her feet in astonishment as Paul closed up his knife and turned to her.

"Just thought we should cut to the chase," he said. "I promised Hadley we'd be right back."

Before Maggie could respond, she watched Antoine's eyes roll to the back of his head and collapse to the floor.

"Well, I guess that answers that," Paul said with a sigh, turning to the door.

Maggie's mouth was open with mute stupefaction as she stared at Antoine on the floor.

One down. Literally.

Which could only mean...and she swallowed hard at the realization.

*Paul was Esme's killer.*

## 51

As Maggie helped Antoine to a sitting position on the bed, her mind was racing with what she now knew.

It had to be Paul. There could be no other explanation. The process of elimination had just laid the charge unerringly at his feet.

Maggie helped Antoine put his head between his knees, his face was bone white.

"Where are your Band-aids?" she asked him.

He waved feebly in the direction of the bathroom.

"Paul?" Maggie asked, looking up. Paul had stopped at the door and was regarding her with a strange look on his face. "Can you get him one, please?"

"He won't bleed to death."

"No, but he'll likely continue to faint if we don't cover the wound," Maggie said.

Paul snorted in impatience before striding to the bathroom and noisily began looking for the band aids.

"The cops will be here before long," Maggie said to

Antoine in a low voice. "And I intend to identify the real killer before they get here."

"We all appreciate how tenacious you are in trying to vindicate your husband—" Antoine began, his head still between his knees.

"Shut up, Antoine," she said briskly. "Laurent had nothing to do with any of this. If you want me to believe that *you* didn't either, in spite of the fact that you have the best motive, you'll do what I tell you."

"I fainted!" he said, raising his head to gape at her in indignation. "How much more do I have to do to prove—"

"Stop talking!" she said firmly as Paul came back into the room and handed her a Band-aid. "Just *listen* to me. I believe one of two people in the abbey could be Esmé's killer and Jenny Jamison is one of them."

"Jenny?" Paul said. "You mean the author?"

"She's certainly done it before," Antoine said, taking a deep breath while Maggie applied the bandage to his cut arm. His face was bone white.

There was no way he was faking this, Maggie thought.

"I need you to find her," Maggie said.

"Who, Jenny? She'll be in her room," Antoine said. "She always is."

"Great. If she's there, keep her there. But be careful, Antoine. If she is the killer, she'll be dangerous."

Antoine's eyes bulged as he looked from Maggie to Paul before putting both hands to his head.

"And how exactly am I supposed to keep her there?" he said in a shrill voice.

"For the love of God, stop being so helpless! Sit on her if you have to! Just keep her there until I come. Now, go!"

"What *now*? I barely have the energy to stand up!"

Maggie stood and pulled him to his feet. "Do it, Antoine,

or I swear I'll show up at your conference myself with Esmé's information and my own personal testimony."

"That's blackmail!"

"Clearly it's the only way to get through to you!"

"Children, children!" Paul said with a wry smile.

"I don't have time for this! Go!" Maggie shouted at Antoine, making him start violently and then turn and stumble toward the door.

"But where are you going?" he asked, looking from Maggie to Paul.

"We have to do something," Maggie said. "But we'll be there shortly. Now, go!"

Antoine turned and walked out the door. Paul and Maggie stood for a moment in Antoine's room. The rain tapped insistently against the window. It made Maggie think of the window in her own room. Which made her think of Laurent. Her stomach twisted in anxiety.

"Do you seriously think the author killed Esmé?" Paul asked, with a frown. "Why ever would she?"

*Actually, I'm pretty sure you killed her*, Maggie thought, her lips pinched in a tense line.

"I don't know," she said. "Between her and Père Jean, both of them had motive and opportunity."

"Père Jean?" Paul's eyes widened before he shook his head. "Now I *know* you've lost your mind if you imagine either of them capable of murder. Look, I've done what you asked and now I'd like to return to Hadley. We should all just wait in our rooms for the police to come and sort this all out."

"Yes, we could do that," Maggie said as she began to walk back down the hall in the direction they'd come in. "But in the meantime, who else dies?"

"What are you saying?" he said as he walked behind her. "Why in the world would anyone else die?"

Maggie whirled on him, knowing her fury was fed by her own doubts and indecision. The plan she'd created with Jenny seemed to be dissolving into nothing as the seconds ticked away.

"Don't you get it?" she said. "If *Antoine* didn't kill Esmé, there's no other viable candidate for her murder. That can only mean that she was never the intended victim."

"What? What are you saying? Then who…?"

His face suddenly paled as his brain began to grasp what she was saying.

"Exactly," Maggie said. "And right now Hadley is alone with Alex—who's in no shape to protect her if the killer tries again."

Maggie didn't have time to gauge Paul's expression. He was already tearing past her to where they'd left Alex and Hadley. He twisted around the corner until he came to the spot where they'd left them.

The corridor was empty except for a scrap of something left on the ground. As Maggie hurried to the spot, she shined her flashlight beam on it.

It was Alex's pink hearts tie.

## 52

Maggie stood holding the tie in her hands, her heart beating in double time as she watched Paul react to not finding Hadley where he'd left her. His face was flushed and he was breathing heavily. He twisted his head around as if to look everywhere at once before finally racing down the hall to his room and wrenching open the door. Maggie followed him and saw that the room was empty.

Paul turned and pushed past her to run back down the hall, his footsteps pounding loudly on the stone floor, to Hadley and Alex's room. He hammered on the door.

"Hadley? Are you in there?" he shouted.

By the time Maggie caught up with him, he was going to every door in the hall, pounding on each one in turn.

"They're gone!" he said to her. "Where could they be? It has to be that crazy man-hating bitch author!" Paul said, his eyes wide.

With the whites of his eyes showing, he reminded Maggie of a spooked horse about to run amok. He was the absolute picture of a man pushed beyond his ability to endure.

Of course Hadley and Alex's disappearance was all a part of the plan that Maggie and Jenny had devised. Regardless of the fact that Maggie had faltered in her trust of Jenny after what Antoine told her, everything was still going roughly according to their plan.

The only exception was that, until a few minutes ago, Paul, who had been on Maggie's short list of suspects, was now by the minute about to drop completely off it.

Would someone act like this who *didn't* think Hadley was truly in danger? Maggie felt an ominous sensation trace down her spine as she watched Paul rip his hair out in a frenzy of near hysteria. She immediately realized—if Paul was truly as distraught as he appeared—what this meant for the plan she and Jenny had come up with.

"Why would she want to hurt my beautiful Hadley?" he said, looking around the hall, wild-eyed.

Could he be faking this? For what reason? Why would he bother to try to fool Maggie? If he was the killer, why wouldn't he just...kill her too? She studied him, trying hard to judge whether his reaction was authentic.

"No," Maggie said, still holding Alex's tie in her hands. "It couldn't be Jenny who took them. Remember? I sent Antoine to keep her in her room."

In fact, if Jenny was still going according to the plan, then *nobody* had taken Alex and Hadley. But of course Paul didn't know that and after a moment of hesitation Maggie decided to continue on regardless and attempt to implement the plan as closely as possible.

Even though the cast had changed. Drastically.

"Are you sure?" Paul said, turning to her in a helpless panic.

"Yes, I'm sure. Think about it. Jenny wouldn't have been able to force Hadley and Alex to come with her." She put a hand on his shoulder as if to calm him. His body was vibrating with tension.

*Can he possibly be faking this?*

"If Jenny was the one who wanted Hadley dead," Maggie said reasonably, "she'd have just killed Hadley on the spot."

Her words had an immediate visceral reaction in Paul as he brought both hands to his head in horror.

"I think," Maggie said, watching him closely, "what this means is that the killer has to be Père Jean after all."

"The *priest*?" Paul said, his voice groaning in incredulity. "For what possible reason?"

"For the same reason he tried to kill her the first time and failed," Maggie said, watching Paul's eyes carefully for his reaction. "He sees Hadley as a paragon of debauched womanhood."

But Paul was no longer listening. He walked back to the spot where he'd last seen Hadley and shook his head in disbelief.

"I can't believe this is happening," he said.

"Listen to me, Paul. You need to snap out of it. If we're going to save Hadley, I need you to come with me and do exactly what I tell you to do. Do you understand? Don't try to be a hero. Don't get any wild ideas. Just do what I tell you."

Paul clenched his fists by his side but he wasn't listening to Maggie. Sweat coated his skin and he shook his head as if to eject the demons residing there.

*Showtime*, Maggie thought, licking her lips and hoping she could get him to play along. She needed to get upstairs to the church and pray there were no more deviations from the plan. And then she needed to pray Paul really was just an amazing actor because otherwise the plan had just gone totally to hell and they were officially out of time.

"This is all my fault," he said, shaking his head. "Hadley didn't even want to...I mean, at first, I..."

Maggie grabbed his arm.

"Stop. Not interested. Tell it to Antoine or some other qualified relationship counselor. Later. Right now I need you to come with me and for the love of all that is holy, *stop talking.*"

Then she turned and hurried toward the narrow winding staircase that led up to the church, knowing as she did that there was a very good chance that the man who'd brutally killed his wife along with one troublesome nun was just one half step behind her.

Or at least, she very much hoped so.

## 53

Maggie entered the church and was struck again by the same overpowering impression of grandeur and majesty she had felt before. This time, she forced herself not to look up at the vaulted ceilings and the heavenly soaring arches. Lightning flashed intermittently in the blackened windows of the choir.

Paul walked behind her, his breathing loud and ragged. She could feel the restlessness coming off him in waves.

Soeur Thérèse's body still lay on a table in front of the altar, a sheet draped over her. Père Jean was kneeling at the altar just as he had been earlier.

As Maggie entered, she was aware of the strong scent of incense. The light from six heavy brass altar candlesticks flickered almost menacingly against the stone walls. Maggie forced herself not to glance around. She knew that, if things went bad, at this point there was nobody to help her. Laurent was unconscious, Alex—wherever he was—was drunk. Antoine, with his fear of blood, would be no help. And she'd already determined that Paul was the kind of man who thought first and acted later. If he acted at all.

*And if he isn't the murderer himself, of course.*

Hearing their footsteps, Père Jean turned to watch them enter the choir. When he did, Paul surged past Maggie.

"You bastard!" he shouted at the priest.

"Paul, no!" Maggie said, grabbing his arm.

He turned to face her and when he did, she saw without a doubt that he wasn't acting. He was genuinely terrified that Hadley was in danger. And genuinely determined to beat the truth out of a member of the clergy.

*This is all wrong!*

"He killed Esmé!" Paul said to Maggie, his voice shaking as he pointed at Père Jean. "And now he's got Hadley! Where is she, you bastard?"

"I'm sorry?" Père Jean stood up and began to walk toward them.

Maggie gestured to the priest to stay where he was. He stopped, his face a mask of confusion and irritation.

"He didn't kill Esmé," Maggie said to Paul, her hand still on his arm. "And he doesn't have Hadley."

His face blanched.

"But you said..."

"I said I believed the intended victim was Hadley. But now I know that's not true. The killer aimed for and got the right victim. Esmé."

Paul frowned until his face cleared.

"Wait. Are you saying you think *I* killed Esmé?" he said, his voice bordering on rage.

Was this still going to work? Maggie wondered desperately. She felt a coldness invade her body that made her feet and hands go numb.

"I did," she admitted. "Until about five minutes ago I would've sworn it was you. I mean, you had every reason to want her dead. There was the prenup *and* you have a new girlfriend."

"And exactly how was I supposed to have killed my wife with Hadley by my side the whole time?" he said angrily. "Answer me that! Not to mention, drugged out of my mind?"

It was then—at that moment—when all doubt left for good and Maggie knew the truth for sure. In a way she'd known for much longer, but in the past fifteen minutes that knowledge had coalesced in her brain until there could be no other answer.

"That's a very good question," Maggie said. "And I think I know just the person who can answer it for you."

She turned to the choir and raised her voice.

"Or do you want to tell it in your own words, Hadley?"

Paul emitted a sound like a wounded animal—relief and anguish together—as Hadley appeared from the darkened interior of the choir and began to walk toward them.

"I can't believe you, Paul," she said as she approached him and kissed his cheek.

He pulled her into an embrace, his arms wrapped tightly around her. His relief at seeing her alive was as real as anything Maggie had ever seen.

"Thank God, my darling, I was so worried," he said.

Hadley stared at Maggie over Paul's shoulder. Her eyes were calm, even amused. Maggie thought she saw respect warring with annoyance in her gaze. Hadley shook her head very subtly and then pulled back from Paul's embrace.

"I need you to do a favor for me," she said to him.

"Angel, you have no idea what I've been through!" Paul said. "I thought...well, you're not going to believe what I thought!" He turned to glare at Maggie.

"I know," Hadley said, patting his arm. "It's been a horrid

night for everyone. But I need five minutes alone with her. Okay?"

Paul looked at Maggie, his face flushed with exasperation and confusion. He turned back to Hadley.

"Do you have any idea what I've just been through? She made me believe you were in danger! That you'd been taken by Esmé's killer!"

"I'm sorry she did that, Paul," Hadley said, touching his cheek. "But we talked about this. Remember? She'll do anything to protect her husband. You can't blame her. It's just love. And you and I know a little something about love, don't we?"

Paul turned to Maggie.

"You are despicable," he said angrily. "And frankly I think your husband might prefer prison to living with you."

"I'm literally ten seconds from punching you in the nose," Maggie said.

He took a step back from her, his eyes widening.

"Let me talk to her," Hadley said, gently pushing Paul toward the door. "I'll meet you outside, okay?"

Paul ran his hand down Hadley's arm and gave Maggie a stern look before turning back to Hadley.

"Five minutes. You had me so worried, Hadley!"

"I know," Hadley said with a smile.

As Paul walked away, Maggie turned and saw that the priest had disappeared. Now it was just the two of them.

"Where's Alex?" Maggie asked.

"Don't worry," Hadley said, pulling out a cigarette. "I didn't kill him if that's what you're asking. I'm sure he's passed out somewhere."

She lit the cigarette and tossed the spent match onto the stone flooring. Maggie imagined Hadley probably didn't feel like abiding by any rules at this point.

"Did Jenny tell you to come to the church?" Maggie asked.

"She did. She and Antoine showed up about twenty minutes after you and Paul left. She told us you wanted to set up an ambush for witnesses to hear Père Jean admit he killed Esmé."

Hadley turned to lean against one of the pews and blew out a thin trail of smoke.

"Did you know Jenny is super religious?" Hadley said. "Honestly, the idea that you were hoping to entrap a Catholic priest really didn't sit well with her. It didn't take much to convince her to walk away. She and Antoine are drinking down in Knight's Hall."

"I see."

"Sorry to mess up your grand scheme. You know what they say about mice and men."

"Would you mind filling in the gaps for me? I'm assuming you're not going to try to kill me, too?"

"Oh, darling, you are so funny," Hadley said, squeezing her eyes shut in an approximation of mirth. "No, I don't think that'll be necessary since it'll be your word against mine and absolutely no evidence to support your outlandish claims."

Hadley inhaled deeply on her cigarette. Maggie could tell Hadley was proud of how she'd killed two women and nobody even suspected her. She could see that Hadley couldn't wait to tell her how she'd done it.

"Firstly," Hadley said primly, "unlike the rest of you, I did read the small print in Antoine's contract. Honestly, I'd heard a rumor from a friend who'd done a retreat with Antoine a few years ago so I had a bit of a heads-up. I made sure not to drink a drop of anything that was in a bottle that I hadn't opened myself. And I ate only bread at dinner."

She looked at Maggie as if expecting praise.

"Okay, so you weren't drugged," Maggie said with a shrug.

"No. What I *was*, was sick and tired of waiting for Paul to pull the trigger on his divorce."

"So killing Esmé was premeditated."

"For all the good knowing *that* will do you, darling," Hadley said with a raised eyebrow. "I even brought the knife with me. Granted, I didn't know for sure that I'd get a chance to use it, but I knew that *Paul* wasn't going to make things happen. If it was up to him, we'd just carry on like we were doing until Esmé died of old age."

"Plus there was the insurance policy," Maggie said.

"Mm-mm," she said with a smile. "There certainly was."

"How were you able to do it with Paul right there with you?"

Hadley snorted and then laughed.

"He was so stoned! He became fascinated with some kind of bug on the wall and just stood there gazing at it so long that I simply walked away. I followed the sound of Esmé's honking voice and found her with Alex. He had his back to me—and of course he was drugged himself."

Maggie braced herself to hear what she knew came next.

"Esmé saw me," Hadley said. "But she was doped too. I just walked up to her, slipped behind her so the blood wouldn't get on me, grabbed her hair and bent her head backwards."

She mimed the action of cutting Esmé's throat.

"You wiped the blade on her jacket," Maggie said hoarsely.

"I did!" Hadley said. "Clever you. Then I went back to find Paul, who was still obsessively staring at the bug." She laughed lightly.

"And the knife?"

She shrugged. "The next time I went out for a ciggie, I tossed it in the sea."

Neat and tidy.

"What about Soeur Thérèse?" Maggie asked.

"The wretch was going through my room!" Hadley said, truly offended. "She found the knife before I had a chance to get rid of it. We had words and then later, when I was supposed to be having a smoke on the cloister deck, I saw her leave her quarters so I followed her. She went to your room first where I heard her tell your husband she knew who killed Esmé."

"So you followed her to the Black Madonna?"

"Is that where she was going? I just followed her and gave her a good bash with my flashlight. It was right next to the dungeon, so I pushed her in and locked the door. Spit spot."

Maggie shook her head in revulsion.

"What did you do with the flashlight?" Maggie asked, hoping Hadley was going to say she'd thrown it into the dungeon waters with the nun. If she did, the police could find it and run forensics on it.

Hadley smiled and shook her head.

"Sorry, darling. I wiped it clean. It's not mine anyway. It belongs to Paul."

"Speaking of whom," Maggie said, "what are you going to tell him?"

"I'm going to tell him that you're a desperate woman who is running around blaming everyone in a futile attempt to save your husband."

She ground out her cigarette on the floor with her shoe. "You can accuse me all you want but I'll never admit to anything."

"I think we've heard enough," Antoine said in a loud voice.

Hadley jerked her head around as Antoine, Jenny and Alex emerged from the darkness in the back of the church. Hadley turned on them, her body stiff with rage and indignation.

"You said you were going to the Knight's Hall!" she said hotly.

"We lied," Jenny said.

"Everybody able to hear okay?" Maggie asked.

"We heard it all," Antoine said.

"You bitch!" Hadley snarled at Maggie as she snatched up a heavy four-foot altar candlestick beside her. "I'd rather go to prison for killing *three* women as long as you're one of them!"

Maggie instinctively stepped backward as Hadley swung the candlestick onto her shoulder like a batter in a ballgame, her eyes angry and focused on Maggie.

"I'll say you attacked me!" Hadley said. "And Paul will back me up. Nobody's going to believe anybody else here tonight."

She swung hard and Maggie jerked her head back a split second before the candlestick would have connected. She felt the breeze it made as it sailed past her chin. Then she felt the pew behind her, blocking her escape, and the look in Hadley's eyes when she realized Maggie was trapped.

Panic roiled in Maggie's throat stifling her breath until all she could do was gasp. She couldn't duck, she couldn't get out of the reach of the deadly bludgeon. The smell of incense seemed to pour over her in a sickening wave of noxious gas.

Hadley planted her stance for another swing and Maggie leaned back desperately. She lost her balance and fell onto the stone floor as Hadley moved to stand over her, her eyes glittering with hatred.

Hadley pulled the candlestick back for the final swing.

Suddenly a high-pitched voice screamed out, "*Murderer!*"

It wasn't a voice of this world. It was ethereal and terrifying. The hairs on Maggie's neck prickled and she saw Hadley's eyes dart away from her.

That was all she needed. She turned and scrambled over the pew behind her.

Jenny screamed. "It's Soeur Thérèse! She's here!"

Separated now by the pew, Maggie saw Hadley when she turned back to her, her face furious.

And then charged her, the heavy candlestick swinging in her hands.

## 54

Maggie put her arms up as the only defense she had. Then she watched in shock as Hadley jerked to a stop as if she'd been yanked from behind, her face an almost comical mixture of surprise and disbelief.

The sound of the heavy brass candlestick falling to the stone floor reverberated throughout the ancient church and echoed up into its rounded Romanesque arches.

Maggie raised herself up onto the pew and saw Alex holding Hadley, who was screaming in demented fury, her hands punching the air impotently and her nails scrabbling to reach his face.

"Let me go!" Hadley screamed as she fought to be free of Alex. "Paul! I need you!"

"What you need is a good lawyer!" Jenny called out.

Maggie turned toward the altar in time to see Soeur Thérèse sitting up, her shroud puddled around her, her arms open wide as Père Jean appeared from behind her and eased the nun's body back down again, an expression of grim satisfaction on his face.

"Did he just do what I think he did?" Maggie asked softly in wonder.

Jenny laughed shakily.

"If you mean did he just sit Soeur Thérèse up and make it look like she was bringing down God's holy wrath on all of us from beyond the grave, then yeah, he did."

Alex and Hadley continued to struggle, their curses echoing obscenely in the holy space. Maggie glanced at Antoine, who was gaping in shock at the scene around him.

"Antoine," she called to him.

He turned to look at her with dull, uncomprehending eyes.

"Please don't give me an excuse to slap you, Antoine. It wouldn't be good for my character. I need you to snap out of it and go find something we can use to tie Hadley up with. Do you understand?"

He nodded. "Yes, yes, I understand," he said, and walked away.

"You will not get away with this!" Hadley shrieked at Maggie before turning on Alex. "Let go of me, you buffoon!"

"You made me think I killed her!" Alex snarled at her, pulling her arms hard behind her. "I can't believe you did that!"

Maggie began to fear Alex might accidentally break one of Hadley's arms and hoped Antoine would hurry up with the rope.

"You told me I wasn't in my right mind when I killed her," he said, angrily. "And all the time it was you who did it!"

"Oh, shut up, Alex," Hadley said curling her lip. "And by the way, I'm leaving you."

"Trust me, I know," he said, his body tense with bitterness. "That tends to happen when one of us goes to live in a French prison for the next twenty years."

At that moment, Maggie heard footsteps rushing into the church as Paul appeared, his mouth open in stupefaction as he stared at Alex wrestling with Hadley.

"Hey, there!" he shouted, charging Alex. "Leave her alone!"

Suddenly, Alex's gaze seemed to clear as he stared at Paul. He stopped struggling with Hadley and released her.

"With pleasure!" he said, taking a step toward Paul, his entire body tense with determination.

The golden candlelight continued to waver and shimmy throughout the church where they sat silently on the polished wooden pews. The adrenalin that had pulsed through the room just moments before had dissipated as quickly as it had ignited.

Maggie sat opposite Alex and Paul, both of them with their heads in their hands, blood still dripping from Paul's nose.

She wasn't precisely sure why they'd all decided by mutual unspoken consent not to split up. It was freezing in the church, but nobody wanted to go back to their rooms. Maggie would go check on Laurent in a moment, but there were still some things she needed to clear up first.

Hadley sat by herself, her hands tied in front of her. She had refused to speak ever since Alex punched Paul and then turned on her like he might take a swing at her too.

Maggie had never been so grateful as when Antoine finally showed up with a long coil of tasseled pew rope. And although the blood gushing out of Paul's nose had then dropped him like a rock, Père Jean and Alex had managed to secure Hadley with the rope.

Maggie was still impressed with Père Jean's trick of

seeming to create a briefly levitating nun when he'd propped up Soeur Thérèse's body and mimicked her voice long enough to save her from being brained by the four-foot brass altar candlestick.

Somewhat recovered, Antoine now sat beside Jenny. He still looked shaky but had gotten his color back. Maggie wondered if the night's events had possibly brought the two of them a little closer or at least had created a détente between them. When Jenny saw her looking at her, she walked over.

Maggie knew she still needed to find out the truth about the author once and for all. But not tonight. Jenny sat down next to Maggie.

"We did it," Jenny said. "I guess I thought I'd feel more triumphant."

Maggie nodded. "I know what you mean. It's great to have the guilty party in custody, but..."

"But two women are still dead."

They were silent for a moment, both watching Hadley as she sat with her head held high.

"I didn't even consider Hadley," Jenny said finally.

"I know," Maggie said. "I only did peripherally, and then I dismissed the idea."

"Our plan still worked though."

Maggie smiled at her. "It did. It was a good plan. It kept open the possibility of a drastic rewrite on the spur of the moment."

"Which is always what every good story needs," Jenny said. "I feel bad now for thinking it was Antoine. You're right. It's because I don't like him. I let that color my thinking."

"You're human."

"What made you suspect Hadley?"

"A couple of things," Maggie said, her eyes on Hadley who sat with a flat expression like one of the stone statues in the cloister garden. "She wasn't drinking the wine, for one thing. I noticed it early on and didn't think much of it beyond wondering if she might be pregnant. But then later, when you and I kept talking about who was and wasn't drugged, something tugged at the back of my mind that we might need to add Hadley to the list of people who were unimpeded by mind-altering substances."

"Good. What else?"

"Well, I noticed that Paul was wet when we discovered Soeur Thérèse's body. When I confronted him about that, he said he'd gone outside looking for Hadley and that's how he got wet."

"Ah. So he unwittingly told you that the two of them had been separated."

"Exactly. Combine that with the fact that Hadley was wearing that big cloak of hers after we found Soeur Thérèse's body and could've been soaking wet underneath and nobody would've known."

"Don't forget she always had the best motive for murder, too."

"She did," Maggie agreed. "Except for Paul, who had the best motive of all. But even with that, there was the fact that Hadley mentioned that Paul was dragging his feet on getting the divorce because he didn't want to upset his son."

"Hardly the typical affect of a cold-blooded killer."

Maggie glanced at Paul who was sitting next to the man he'd wronged—Alex—both looking shell-shocked.

"But more than anything," Maggie said, "once I moved away from the distraction of thinking that Hadley was the intended victim, honestly Esmé's killer could only have been Hadley."

They sat quietly for a moment before Maggie stood up.

"I need to check on Laurent," she said, although she knew she would probably find him asleep. "But first, I need to ask how you got separated from Hadley. Did you figure out it was her, too?"

"Not really," Jenny said regretfully. "I mean, except she started acting weird when Antoine and I told her and Alex to go hide in the church. She was resistant, you know?"

"Speaking of Antoine," Maggie said. "Did he give you any trouble when he showed up at your door?"

Jenny laughed. "What had you told him? He came to my door and practically threw me on the bed and sat on me! It took me forever before he'd let me up so I could show him the note you wrote. And even then he didn't believe it for a while."

Maggie smiled. At the time she had needed to make Antoine believe that Jenny was the killer so that Paul wouldn't get suspicious that Maggie was on to him, who, at that time, she had thought might be the killer. She'd written a note for Jenny to give to Antoine—or Paul if it turned out their roles were reversed and Antoine *had* been the killer—telling him to go with Jenny to find Hadley and Paul—since at the time she wrote the note Maggie thought she would have *Alex* with her— to the church and hide in order to hear the killer's confession.

"I definitely had not expected *Antoine* to show up at my door!" Jenny said.

"Well, things got fluid," Maggie said, grinning. "And by that I mean everything went sideways really fast."

"Well, I just went with it," Jenny said. "I figured if you sent me Antoine that must mean you believed he couldn't be the killer—"

"He couldn't be," Maggie said. "He has an incapacitating aversion to blood."

"Oh, okay. Well, when he told me you were with Paul, I knew that meant my mission was to collect Hadley and Alex and get to the church."

"Good pivoting," Maggie said with a smile. "Which brings us back to my question of how you ended up separated from Hadley?"

"When Antoine and I found her and Alex and told them we needed them to go to the church with us to hear the killer's confession, Hadley started acting weird."

"You mentioned that. How so?"

"Well, for one thing, she lied. She told me she knew about the plan—which I couldn't believe you would have told her—and then she asked who you were going to try and get the confession from."

"What did you say?"

"Well, since I didn't know—and neither did you at the time—I said I didn't know."

"So where did the lie come in?"

"Because she told me that you told her that the killer was Père Jean! Who we'd already eliminated. And she said she was amazed I was okay with laying a trap for a priest."

Maggie glanced at Hadley.

"That is some seriously fast thinking on her feet," she said. "But you never suspected *she* was the killer?"

"I honestly didn't. But I knew she lied. So whether she was the killer or Paul was, I knew she was hiding something."

"So you allowed her to believe you were appalled at the thought of my accusing a priest of murder and that you and Antoine would just go off and get drunk?"

"Yep. I told her you and Paul were headed to the

church to confront Père Jean and that Alex and Antoine and I would go to Knight's Hall to drink the rest of the night away. But actually we went up to the church and hid."

Maggie glanced at Alex but before she could ask, Jenny said, "He fell asleep as soon as we got here. The only concern I had was that he might start snoring, but he didn't."

"How did you get here before Hadley?"

"Easy. We had a three-minute head start. Plenty of time to get up here and get hidden before she came."

"Three minutes?"

"That's the time it takes to smoke a cigarette. She was pulling one out of her bag as we parted."

Maggie had sat back down during the telling of Jenny's story and now they sat silently for a moment, lost in their own thoughts, the scent of incense and the soft murmurings from Paul and Antoine the only sounds in the room, until Jenny spoke again.

"I can't believe she killed Soeur Thérèse," she said, her eyes on Hadley.

"I'm sorry, Jenny," Maggie said. "Antoine mentioned you had a friendship with her."

Jenny nodded and wiped a tear away.

"The one thing he hasn't lied about," she snorted.

"I know you drank the drugged wine last night," Maggie said after a moment.

Jenny's eyes went round as if startled and then she relaxed her shoulders.

"Yeah," she said. "It's true. I was as wasted as everyone else."

"But you told me you weren't."

Jenny's cheeks reddened and she looked away.

"I didn't want you to think I might want Hadley dead because she was 'the other woman.'"

"I didn't think that."

*Except at one point I definitely did.*

"I feel bad about lying to you," Jenny said. "It felt great to have a sister again at least for a little bit. I guess I didn't want to spoil it. I'm sorry."

Maggie noticed that Jenny looked tired. The initial jubilation that she'd seen in the woman had faded and now she looked depleted and lost. Maggie leaned over to give her a hug.

"I understand," Maggie said. "You did good work tonight. If not for our plan, and you implementing it, getting the confession wouldn't have mattered. You out-Nancy-Drewed Nancy Drew *and* you helped clear Laurent's name."

"You're not so bad, yourself," Jenny said with a smile. "In fact, if you do decide to go forward writing mysteries, I have a feeling you'll do great."

"Thanks."

"And Maggie? I'm glad Laurent isn't going to be nailed for this. I still don't think much of his sex, but if you like him, I guess he must be different."

Maggie reached for her hand at the same moment she heard the faint sounds of approaching police sirens in the distance. She gave Jenny's hand a squeeze.

"He is," Maggie said, her eyes glittering with surprise tears. "He really is."

Then she turned and hurried out of the church to go check on him. The long train ride back to St-Buvard would take most of the coming day but it didn't matter.

She and Laurent had already completed the hardest part of the trip before they even left the island of Mont St-Michel.

## 55

A platoon of olive and fig trees lined the pebbled path from the terrace at *Dormir* where the luncheon table was set with a view of the undulating grape fields beyond it. Even in October, with its mild temperatures and ever-present sunshine, Maggie could detect the strong scents of rosemary and woodsmoke in the air.

Sundays were special at *Dormir*.

Years ago, Danielle and Grace had convinced Laurent to move the Sunday lunch to *Dormir,* insisting that few things said *Provence* like this particular meal—always somewhat formal and shared with family. When they did, the lunch became an instant memory maker for whatever guests were staying at *Dormir* at the time.

At first Laurent had not relished the thought of allowing strangers to join in this special family ritual, but if the travel review sites were anything to go by it had been a definite benefit in luring new guests to the *gîte*.

This Sunday, a week after Maggie and Laurent had returned from Mont St-Michel, they were preparing to enjoy their afternoon meal without paying guests—a welcome, if rare, occurrence.

As usual the meal prep took most of the morning and all afternoon to see those efforts enjoyed. There had been a time, Maggie mused as she walked around the table set in the garden, when she'd felt that sacrificing a whole day to doing nothing but making and eating a single meal was a luxury they could ill afford.

But over the years she had come to see these Sunday lunches as a necessary time to relax and enjoy the fruits of their weekly labors. A time to reach out to each other and reconnect. Many a Sunday lunch she and Grace had sorted out a child's problem or planned a future project over tapenade toasts, wine from Laurent's vineyard, or Zouzou's famous *gâteau au citron*.

Today as always, the luncheon table was set with Grace's good linen tablecloth and silver. Zouzou had placed dried lavender stalks in faience jars that lined the center of the table along with lanterns that would light the tableau when the meal drifted inevitably into the early part of the evening. Maggie felt her heart squeeze at the sight of the flowers. Setting the Sunday table was usualy Mila's job.

For today's lunch, Laurent was planning oysters, a *Potage Parmentier* that was a favorite of Maggie's, Steak Diane, and a simple green salad followed by a cheese course. Zouzou, who had come home the day before to nurse a broken heart, had put her angst to good use by whipping up a cherry *Gâteau Basque* that would end the meal—along with coffees and Calvados.

Zouzou had been dumped by Anzar a few days after her dinner with Maggie and Laurent and had come home tearful and wounded. Maggie watched her now at the edge of the garden, the girl's shoulders stiff as she tossed a ball with Philippe.

Grace came out of the house carrying a tray stacked with linen napkins, silver salt and pepper shakers, and six shallow china soup bowls. Maggie recognized the bowls as a set she and Grace had found at a flea market in Arles a few years before.

"Is Zouzou going to be okay?" Maggie asked as she took the bowls from the tray to set them out.

"Oh, yes," Grace said, turning to look at her daughter and grandson. "She'll get over it. Somehow I got the feeling that it's for the best. You met him, right?"

Maggie nodded. "Definitely for the best."

They turned back to putting the last touches on the table. Maggie laid out the silver soup spoons.

"Gregor isn't coming today?" she asked.

"Gregor and I are taking a break."

"Really?"

"You don't have to play dumb, Maggie," Grace said with a wry smile. "I know Danielle told you that Windsor was here last week."

"She said he *proposed*," Maggie said, widening her eyes dramatically as if the incredulous tone in her voice wasn't enough to convey her shock.

"I was going to tell you," Grace said.

"Well?"

Grace waved a hand to indicate the gardens of *Dormir*.

"Let's see. I have a plumbing leak in Plum Cottage. A family of six from Iowa showing up tomorrow with more allergies than a science lab. And an aging handyman who's about as handy as a tuba player with oven mitts. Can you imagine how much easier my life would be if Windsor and I got back together?"

"Would it?"

Grace laughed.

"Well, he's got money," she said. "So there's that. Plus, he's my age. *And* he loves the same children I do."

At that moment Maggie heard Philippe's laughter sail over the boxwood hedges followed by a small chuckle from Zouzou.

"That's important," Maggie admitted.

"It is," Grace said, watching the children, her eyes soft. "And on top of all that, the feelings are still there." She looked at Maggie with misty eyes. "On both sides. Believe me, nobody is more surprised than I am that I might be allowed a second chance at happiness."

Maggie reached out to take Grace's hand.

"You know Laurent and I love Windsor," Maggie said. "I was thrilled when Danielle said you guys might give it another go."

"We're going to take it slow for now," Grace said. "And we both know there are a lot of obstacles. I need to stay in Provence. Not just for Danielle and Zouzou's sake but for me too. Windsor understands that." She dabbed her eyes and smiled at Maggie.

"Enough about my fairytale ending," she said. "What about you and Laurent? You never even told me you were having problems."

"I know," Maggie said with a sigh, her eyes going to pick out Laurent in the kitchen. She could see him through the open patio door. He was talking to Danielle. Just the sight of him—so familiar, his movements so graceful and sure—made her a little breathless.

"I didn't tell you because I was trying not to make it bigger than it was," Maggie said.

"Well, you guys look perfectly fine to me."

"We worked some things out."

"Anything you want to share?"

Maggie smiled. "Eventually. But for now, I think he and I will try to get a handle on it first."

"Well, I'm here if you need me, darling."

"I know that."

"In the meantime, he certainly seems back to his old self."

Maggie smiled because it was true. Ever since they'd returned from Mont St-Michel, Laurent had been himself again in every way.

After unmasking Hadley in the church as Esmé's killer —and with the police sirens growing louder and louder as the national police vans roared up the long elevated causeway toward the island—Maggie went back to her room to find Laurent rousing from his drug-induced slumber.

Even now, she remembered the moment clearly.

∾

On her way down from the abbey church, Maggie passed Père Jean on the stairs on his way to admit the police. She'd already thanked him for startling Hadley long enough for her to escape being bludgeoned by the church candlestick.

However, for reasons she couldn't put her finger on, she felt like apologizing too.

"*Mon père*," she said as she stopped at her floor, forcing him to stop and face her. "I wanted to say I'm sorry for everything."

He gave that classic Gallic shrug that Maggie was so familiar with from Laurent—the one that was normally so tricky to interpret. But this time she seemed to understand what it meant. No wonder the French are so philosophical, she thought, as he gave her a sad smile and continued his way to the registration and gift shop level to let the police in.

Maggie turned to her room, fumbling with the key card in her excitement. She couldn't wait to tell Laurent that they were in the clear. She was also anxious to confirm that he was recovering from his drugged slumber. She entered the room at the same time the overhead light flickered and came on.

The electricity was back.

Laurent was yawning when she entered. He was sitting up in bed and rubbing his face, his hair disheveled and his denim shirt open at the neck. She switched the lights back off, locked the door behind her, and quickly pulled off her clothes before slipping into bed with him.

Instantly his arms were around her, pulling her close to where she fit perfectly beside him, her cheek against his chest.

"You're feeling better," she murmured.

He kissed her and she felt the heat of his body infuse her with a strength and ease she hadn't felt in so long.

"There's about to be a whole lot of activity here in a few minutes," she said. "The police have finally arrived."

"Ah," he said with a shrug.

"I think we're going to be okay, Laurent."

"With the police, you mean?"

"That." She kissed him. "And the other thing."

He cupped her face in his large hand and kissed her. Then he brushed an errant tendril of hair from her face and smiled.

"I think so too, *chérie*," he said.

## 56

The lanterns on the dinner table reflected off the china and crystal glasses that were scattered among the wine bottles and coffee cups. The remains of Zouzou's delicious cherry tart were now scraped clean from the dessert dishes.

With a thick shawl around her shoulders and Laurent beside her, Maggie felt absolutely tranquil thanks only in part to the glass of Calvados she held. Danielle and Zouzou were in the house putting Philippe to bed.

On Maggie's other side, Grace sat, a glass of sparkling water in her hand, her shoulders relaxed. Maggie thought she detected a contented smile on her friend's face. Grace had mentioned earlier that Windsor would return in another couple of weeks.

Everything was working out, Maggie thought. Even with the kids so far away across the ocean. Somehow they didn't feel so far away tonight. Somehow she could easily imagine Luc coming out of the house with a beer in his hand, or Jemmy or Mila's voice coming to her from the house.

They would be back.

She glanced over at Laurent who was staring off into the inky darkness where the garden was no longer visible. The lines in his face were relaxed. Aware that she was looking at him, he turned to her and smiled.

Yes, it was good to be back on track.

"I can't believe those horrid people wanted to pin the murder on Laurent," Grace said, shaking her head. "Unbelievable."

"I know," Maggie said. "They all did. Even Jenny, who became a friend by the time the whole thing was over."

Maggie would be forever grateful for Jenny's help. She honestly didn't think she could have gotten Hadley's confession without her. But in the end Jenny *had* played fast and loose with the truth and Maggie wasn't a hundred per cent sure how to feel about that.

She hadn't even waited to get home before she was on her phone on the train ride to Aix, searching the Internet for the truth about Jenny and her fiancé. What she found out was discomfiting, to the say the least.

As it turned out, Antoine had been telling the truth. At least up to a point. Jenny *had* killed a man and she had done time for it. It wasn't her fiancé though.

The man she killed was someone who raped her the week before. The police said they didn't have enough evidence to hold him, so Jenny followed him to his car and stabbed him to death. Because of the time lag between the two crimes—and the rape only alleged—her attorney couldn't get a verdict of self-defense. She spent eighteen months in a low-security detention facility in the South of France for manslaughter.

Maggie was still trying to sort out how she felt about that, but in the meantime she told Jenny she'd write to her.

Now that they were home, Laurent was back to long days

in the fields ploughing under vines, weeding, pruning, and planning the next year's harvest.

As for Antoine, he had been correct that, technically, the drugs his chemist had created were not yet illegal. It generally took governments a long time to regulate the so-called designer drugs whipped up in basement chemistry laboratories. Maggie had intended to show up at Antoine's conference as she'd threatened to but discovered he had decided against going himself.

In the end, Laurent filed a civil suit against Antoine for second degree assault for the separate drugging incident. Antoine's lawyers were trying to argue that the contract Laurent had signed covered all surreptitious drugging for the entire weekend, and that Antoine was protected under a clause that allowed lawful drugging for therapeutic treatment.

The case would take forever to settle and even if they won wouldn't result in much of a financial settlement but Maggie saw it as a more civilized way of achieving satisfaction than breaking Antoine's nose, which had been Laurent's first choice.

"So how did you figure it all out?" Grace asked Maggie.

Maggie had only processed what had happened on the island in very loose strokes even with Laurent since coming home. She wasn't sure she'd even told *him* in detail how she'd arrived at her answers.

"It was a miracle I discovered who did it," Maggie said, shaking her head as she held her Calvados glass to her nose and inhaled the sweet apple brandy scent.

"I got momentarily derailed when I went down a wrong path thinking the killer might have intended to kill Hadley, not Esmé."

"You thought Esmé was killed by mistake?"

"For a while I did. That's what slowed me down so long and muddied the issue. But it was never a case of mistaken identity. Esmé was always the one targeted to die. As was Soeur Thérèse."

Maggie had thought long and hard about how she'd ended up going down this dead-end—one that had cost her valuable time and energy.

It was true that Laurent had twice suggested that Hadley was more likely as the target. But the turning point for Maggie had been the moment in Soeur Thérèse's room when she saw what she thought was an apparition of the Black Madonna or maybe even Soeur Thérèse herself and then heard on the wind what sounded like someone saying, "You're wrong."

She'd been in a frame of mind to readily accept the possibility that Soeur Thérèse was speaking to her from beyond the grave, although she realized later it was likely just the roar of the wind combined with her overwrought imagination. In any case, both had sent her reeling down a path that led nowhere.

"So when did you realize Esmé was the intended victim all along?"

Maggie sighed.

"Only after I'd exhausted every possible person on the island with a motive and opportunity. I mean, every *drugged* person there had a reason to kill Hadley. But of the *undrugged* people, only Père Jean had a motive for wanting Hadley dead—and then only if he really did have a pathology about loose women——but not Esmé."

"And he couldn't have killed Esmé when he'd intended to kill Hadley," Laurent added.

"Right. Because *he* wasn't hallucinating off his head. So he had to be innocent."

"You did this by process of elimination?" Grace asked.

"Jenny and I did, yeah. Once we established that Esmé had to be the real target, the field narrowed considerably. There were just very few motives for killing her. Yes, she was annoying, but when you looked at the only people in the abbey that night who were not drugged and who could've done it, you were left with only Père Jean and Antoine."

"It wasn't a murder that could have been committed under the influence?"

"Oh, yes, it absolutely could have been. The killing itself, sure. But nobody seeing it? Not getting blood on you in the process? Or leaving incriminating footprints leading all the way back to your room? No. The murderer could not have pulled that off stoned."

"So you eliminated Jenny and the priest."

"I did. I ascertained that only Antoine had motive *and* opportunity for killing Esmé. And of course he wasn't drugged. Then Jenny and I created a plan for getting a confession out of him—and arranged for there to be witnesses to the confession."

"Sounds good."

Maggie laughed ruefully. "Except it turned out that Antoine couldn't have done it because he faints at the sight of blood."

"Are you sure he wasn't faking it?"

"Yes, we did a test. He wasn't faking."

"Well, that left who?"

"You know that line from Conan Doyle that says if you rule out the impossible you need to consider what's left no matter how improbable?" Maggie said. "I now had to consider if any of the *drugged* people could have done the murder. When I went there, I settled on Paul as having the best motive for killing his wife."

"Why not Hadley's husband? What's his name?"

"Alex. I didn't think it was Alex because he'd already confessed to the murder."

"He did?" said Laurent, his eyes widening in surprise.

"But he got the details wrong," Maggie said. "He talked about strangling Esmé but she had her throat cut."

"Why in the world would he confess if he didn't do it?" Grace asked.

"This I also would like to hear," Laurent said.

"I think Esmé was so annoying that when Alex was stoned, he fantasized about strangling her," Maggie said.

"Not very nice," Grace said with an arched eyebrow, but Laurent only laughed, making Maggie think that he understood Alex's perspective.

"Anyway, so after Antoine fell off my suspects list, the only obvious one left was Paul. So he and I headed to the church where I could wring a confession out of him that would be witnessed by the others."

"Only that didn't happen?" Grace asked eagerly.

Maggie appreciated Grace's fascination for all the details. She'd been with Maggie on many a case in the past. In fact, when Maggie suffered her broken arm before Zouzou was born, Grace had suffered one too from the same incident.

"No, because when I told Paul that, I thought Hadley was the intended victim—"

"Why did you tell him that?" Laurent asked.

"Yeah, didn't you just say you no longer believed that?" Grace asked.

"Yes, yes," Maggie said impatiently. "I told him that in order to give him a false sense of security. But I wasn't prepared for his reaction. He became unhinged and frantic to rescue her. There was no doubt he was convinced her life was in danger. That's when I knew it couldn't be him who killed Esmé. He was desperate to find the killer himself *before the killer found Hadley*."

"And of course the only *other* person who had a motive for killing Esmé..." Maggie paused dramatically.

"...was Hadley," Laurent said.

"*Exactement*," Maggie said.

"When did you know that for sure?" Grace asked.

"Honestly? Not until Paul and I were headed to the church and he was in the process of flipping out."

"Talk about cutting it close," Grace said.

Maggie laughed. "You're telling me."

She looked at Laurent and he smiled and lifted a hand in her direction. Their fingers touched.

"So how did Hadley manage to kill Esmé while stoned out of her skull?" Grace asked.

"Turns out she was smarter than the rest of us," Maggie said. "*She wasn't* stoned because she'd read the fine print in Antoine's contract."

Grace gave a very unladylike snort.

"For all the good that will do her in prison," she said, reaching for the brandy bottle. "Top up, you two?"

## 57

Later that night as they drove home to Domaine St-Buvard, Maggie felt contentedly dozy from the late hour and the wine. She glanced at Laurent to ensure he was fine to drive—although he always was. She tried to think if she had ever seen Laurent drunk and knew she never had.

*My always-in-control husband*, she thought with a smile.

He pulled out his phone and handed it to her.

"Shall we call them?" he said.

Maggie knew immediately who he was talking about. While it was two in the morning in France, it was only eight in the evening in Atlanta. She put the call through and felt a rush of delight pulse through her when Mila answered.

"Hey, Mom, what are you doing up so late?"

"Your dad and I are just coming back from Sunday lunch at *Dormir*. How are things there in the Big Peach?"

"Nobody calls it that anymore, Mom," Mila said.

Maggie could practically see her daughter roll her eyes, but her voice was light and playful. This was no longer the glowering cantankerous teenager of last year.

"Are Jem and Luc there?" Maggie asked, darting a glance at Laurent.

"They went to a movie with Nikki," Mila said. "I'm here watching a Hallmark movie with Grandma."

"Oh, that's nice," Maggie said. She formed a picture in her mind of her daughter with her mother and smiled.

"Yeah, but Grandma fell asleep in the middle of it," Mila said.

"Oh, well. That happens," Maggie said with a laugh.

"Can I talk to Dad for a sec?"

"Of course. Hold on."

Maggie handed the phone to Laurent.

"Hello, *chérie*," he said, his voice suddenly soft and full of love. A feeling of warmth flooded Maggie's chest to hear this big, no-nonsense man open up like a flower at the sound of his daughter's voice.

He listened for a few minutes without responding and Maggie wondered what Mila was telling him.

"Yes, they have that here too," he said finally. "Oh, you did, eh?"

He turned to glance at Maggie and the edges of his lips lifted in a smile. Whatever Mila was saying was pleasing him very much.

When they got home, Laurent let the dogs out, then locked up the house for the night. Maggie turned off the lights in the living room and put a bowl of cream and buttermilk out on the counter. In the morning it would have turned into a thick pudding of crème fraîche, a delicious divinity that they used on everything from salads and soups to toppings for pizza and quiches.

By the time she and Laurent met up in their bedroom, the dogs had settled into their beds on the floor and Laurent had opened the heavy sash window to allow the coolness of the night air into the room. Maggie took a quick shower—she always slept better when she took the time, even at two thirty in the morning—and pulled on her favorite flannel nightgown before slipping into bed with Laurent.

He had a book with him as he always did and she smiled at the sight of him with his reading glasses. That was new and reminded her that he wasn't superman—as much as he might like to present himself that way. She snuggled up against him and felt his arm come around to hold her close.

"That was nice hearing Mila's voice tonight," Maggie said as Laurent snapped off the lamp on the night table. "What was she asking you about?"

"She found a beginner's *sommelier* course online and wanted to know if there was an in-person class in Aix or Marseille. I told her I thought there was."

"She's really come full circle, hasn't she?" Maggie said, marveling, knowing how much Mila's sudden interest in wine delighted Laurent. "Does it help?"

Laurent didn't speak for a moment.

"I kept thinking that I'd built all of this for my children," he said finally, nodding his head in the direction of the vineyards outside their bedroom window. "But none of them seemed to want it. I had to ask myself why I'd done it at all."

"It wasn't enough to do it just for yourself? Or for us?"

He looked at her ruefully. "I am as surprised as you."

"But then Mila did her turnaround. And now she wants to be a part of the family business."

He shrugged.

"Trying not to get your hopes up?"

"She is allowed to change her mind," he said. "She is young."

"Is it possible that your disappointment with the kids dovetailed with...the other thing?"

"Perhaps."

"I think that's partly why I reacted the way I did when I found out about Élodie," Maggie said. "I felt like my emotions were a toboggan going down a steep hill, picking up speed so that even when you explained how it all happened, I was already careening out of control."

"Toboggan?"

"I don't know the French word for it. Basically, things were going bad so when something positive happened it didn't help."

He nodded. "For me it is a matter of character. Or lack thereof."

"I don't believe that," Maggie said firmly. "It just means you're human. Welcome to the club."

He smiled at her.

"One thing I do know," he said, turning to her in bed, "I made it worse by not talking to you."

Maggie was gratified to hear him say it. He'd said other things in the past week that had hinted at this, but tonight it felt like a vow to her. Knowing Laurent, that's the way he meant it.

"I'm sorry about that crack about divorce," she said. "I shouldn't have said it."

"*Non*. But I needed...what is it you say? a slap upside the head?"

Maggie pressed her cheek against his chest, hearing his heartbeat in her ear.

"I'm sorry we didn't talk to the boys tonight," she said.

"I talked to Luc earlier today."

"You did?"

"He's coming home for a visit."

"Really?"

"Just for a visit."

She was quiet for a moment. "Does it change anything?"

He thought for a moment.

"I don't think so. He needs to do what he needs to do."

"Very mature of you to recognize that."

He grinned. He'd had a couple conversations with Luc since they'd returned from Mont St-Michel. Each time he'd come just short of telling him the truth of how Luc was related to the family. But each time he'd stopped. That was a conversation that needed to happen face-to-face.

"I think with Jemmy living in Atlanta next year it will be good to have Luc in the same country," Laurent said. "Especially since your mother will no longer be there."

Maggie didn't bother pointing out that Jemmy would still have Nikki in Atlanta. But if it made Laurent feel better about Luc's decision to stay in California, that was all that mattered.

As for her mother and her decision to move to France to live with them, from what Maggie and Laurent had been able to piece together from things Jemmy and Mila had told them—as well as Nikki who'd been there for the showdown—it was a shock but not an unwelcome one.

It seemed that Elspeth had taken a boyfriend at the assisted living center where she lived—a boyfriend in his mid-seventies to whom Luc had taken an instant dislike.

Even Nikki sounded embarrassed that she hadn't been more protective of her grandmother, saying she was just so busy she didn't realize that maybe grandma's boyfriend wasn't a great guy. He never picked up the tab and worse, was always asking her grandmother for loans.

But Luc had seen it. And he'd put an end to it. After three days of witnessing the man's boorish treatment of Elspeth, Luc handed the man his hat and told him he was done and would no longer be pestering his grandmother.

"He was a beast!" Mila told Maggie and Laurent when she related her version of the tale earlier in the week. "I wish you could've heard Luc with his thick French accent tell him off! 'Uncle Bertie' just stood there like he'd been thumped on the head. He looked at Grandma like he was thinking she should back him up and Grandma said, 'You heard my grandson.' It was awesome."

It appeared that Luc had put a firm end to whatever the man's intentions were, good or bad, and somehow managed to do it without upsetting Elspeth.

"I still can't believe all that happened," Maggie said, feeling the first evidence of the day's weariness begin to descend upon her. "I mean I didn't even know Mom was dating!"

"*Le bâtard* probably told her not to bother you with it. But Luc handled it."

It was too dark in the room to see his face, but Maggie knew the pride Laurent felt was written there.

She was very pleased to realize that Luc knew, blood or not, that family took care of each other. And very soon now he was about to discover that he was, in fact, blood, too.

"He takes after you," she said and watched a faint hint of a smile form on Laurent's lips.

"And so," he said gruffly as if embarrassed, "just when we finally get everyone out of the house, your mother moves in? *Incroyable*."

But Maggie knew he was only teasing. If it were up to him, everyone would still be living under his roof, including Grace and Danielle, Zouzou, Luc, Nikki, and of course Mila and Jemmy.

Maggie kissed her husband and felt his arms tighten around her. She sighed with pleasure and relaxed deeper into his embrace. It was late and they were both tired—for once the kind of weariness that didn't involve a buzzing brain that wouldn't let an aching body rest.

Just as she began to sink into sleep, Maggie's mind went to that other place. It went to thoughts of Élodie. She forced herself to push the idea of the girl away and snuggled deeper into Laurent's arms, feeling his breath on her cheek.

There was plenty of time to sort all that out, she thought. Plenty of time to meet Élodie, to forgive her, and see if there was room for her in the family.

Or not.

Maggie felt sleep pull her then in an agonizingly exquisite drift downward, with only the scent and feel of Laurent next to her to keep her moored.

Time would just have to tell.

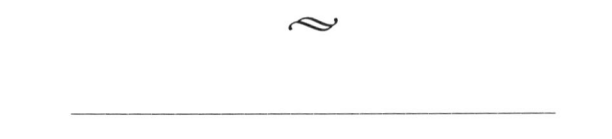

~

---

To follow more of Maggie's sleuthing and adventures, watch for the release of *Murder in the Village, Book 20 of the Maggie Newberry Mysteries!*

# AUTHOR'S NOTE

The Abbey of Mont St-Michel is a stunning paragon of both Romanesque and Gothic-style architecture—believed to date to 708 when Aubert, Bishop of Avranches, built a sanctuary on Mont-Tombe to honor the Archangel Michael. The island soon became a major pilgrimage site and later, when the Benedictines settled in the abbey in the tenth century, a village grew up around it.

With its impressive ramparts and fortifications, Mont St-Michel also served as an impregnable stronghold during the Hundred Years War with England and is considered a brilliant example of military architecture. After resisting all English attempts at siege and full-scale attack of its shores, the abbey became a symbol of national identity in France.

In 1979 Mont Saint-Michel was listed as a World Heritage Site by UNESCO and is the second most popular tourist destination in France.

∽

## Author's Note

For anyone familiar with the layout of Mont St-Michel, I apologize for the few tweaks I felt I needed to make to the abbey's layout to better fit Maggie's story. Both the Blue Room and the library, for example, do not exist in reality. Suffice to say, if you ever visit Mont St-Michel—and you really should if you haven't yet—please do not use the map I've drawn for this book as a way to navigate around the abbey. You will very likely end up in the *Cellier* with all those tortured souls who still haunt the place—plus no cell phone signal.

## RECIPE FOR OMELETTE DE LA MÈRE POULARD

This famous omelette has been described as the *plus célèbre omelette* in the world and is the gastronomic emblem of Mont Saint-Michel. When Annette Poulard and her husband opened their inn on the island in 1888, she began making the omelette for pilgrims and other visitors to the holy site. By 1932 the omelette was on the menu of every restaurant in the village. Annette Poulard was given the title "Mère Poulard" in recognition of her achievement as a great female chef along with Mère Brazier of Lyon, the mother of modern French cooking.

At *La Mère Poulard* the omelette is prepared over an open fire with a long-handled copper skillet, and the recipe has been kept a well-guarded secret for over 130 years. The kitchen at Maggie and Laurent's *mas* has no open fire, but here is the recipe Laurent uses to make one large omelette that comes close to what you will eat if you are fortunate enough to visit *La Mère Poulard*.

You'll need:
    4 eggs

3-½ TB butter
Salt and pepper

1. Crack open 4 eggs into a large bowl.

2. Whisk the eggs for at least 5 minutes until light and foamy —almost like a mousse. Add salt and pepper.

4. Melt butter over medium heat in a frying pan and pour mixture into the hot pan.

5. Cook slowly until the bottom is brown, but the surface is still loose and slightly liquid.

6. Fold in half and serve immediately with a green salad or with sautéed vegetables, lardons and mushrooms on the side.

# ABOUT THE AUTHOR

*USA TODAY* Bestselling Author Susan Kiernan-Lewis is the author of *The Maggie Newberry Mysteries,* the post-apocalyptic thriller series *The Irish End Games, The Mia Kazmaroff Mysteries, The Stranded in Provence Mysteries,* and *An American in Paris Mysteries.* If you enjoyed *Murder in Mont St-Michel,* please leave a review on your purchase site.

Visit her website at www.susankicrnanlewis.com or follow her at Author Susan Kiernan-Lewis on Facebook.

*About the Author*

**Books by Susan Kiernan-Lewis**
**The Maggie Newberry Mysteries**
Murder in the South of France
Murder à la Carte
Murder in Provence
Murder in Paris
Murder in Aix
Murder in Nice
Murder in the Latin Quarter
Murder in the Abbey
Murder in the Bistro
Murder in Cannes
Murder in Grenoble
Murder in the Vineyard
Murder in Arles
Murder in Marseille
Murder in St-Rémy
Murder à la Mode
Murder in Avignon
Murder in the Lavender
Murder in Mont St-Michel
Murder in the Village
A Provençal Christmas: A Short Story
A Thanksgiving in Provence
Laurent's Kitchen

**An American in Paris Mysteries**
Déjà Dead
Death by Cliché
Dying to be French
Ménage à Murder
Killing it in Paris
Deadly Faux Pas

*About the Author*

Murder Flambé

**The Stranded in Provence Mysteries**
Parlez-Vous Murder?
Crime and Croissants
Accent on Murder
A Bad Éclair Day
Croak, Monsieur!
Death du Jour
Murder Très Gauche
Wined and Died
A French Country Christmas

**The Irish End Games**
Free Falling
Going Gone
Heading Home
Blind Sided
Rising Tides
Cold Comfort
Never Never
Wit's End
Dead On
White Out
Black Out
End Game

**The Mia Kazmaroff Mysteries**
Reckless
Shameless
Breathless
Heartless
Clueless

Ruthless

**Ella Out of Time**
Swept Away
Carried Away
Stolen Away

**The French Women's Diet**

Printed in Great Britain
by Amazon